WIND CHIME BEACH

KAY CORRELL

ZURA LU PUBLISHING, LLC

Published by Zura Lu Publishing LLC

This book is dedicated to my family. To the crazy, boisterous times, the endless laughter, and the quiet moments together. I could never do this without all of you. You bring me such joy.

KAY'S BOOKS

Find more information on all my books at
kaycorrell.com

COMFORT CROSSING ~ THE SERIES

The Shop on Main - Book One
The Memory Box - Book Two
The Christmas Cottage - A Holiday Novella
(Book 2.5)
The Letter - Book Three
The Christmas Scarf - A Holiday Novella
(Book 3.5)
The Magnolia Cafe - Book Four
The Unexpected Wedding - Book Five

The Wedding in the Grove - (a crossover short

story between series - with Josephine and Paul from The Letter.)

LIGHTHOUSE POINT ~ THE SERIES
Wish Upon a Shell - Book One
Wedding on the Beach - Book Two
Love at the Lighthouse - Book Three
Cottage near the Point - Book Four
Return to the Island - Book Five
Bungalow by the Bay - Book Six

CHARMING INN ~ Return to Lighthouse Point
One Simple Wish - Book One
Two of a Kind - Book Two
Three Little Things - Book Three
Four Short Weeks - Book Four
Five Years or So - Book Five
Six Hours Away - Book Six
Charming Christmas - Book Seven

SWEET RIVER ~ THE SERIES
A Dream to Believe in - Book One
A Memory to Cherish - Book Two
A Song to Remember - Book Three
A Time to Forgive - Book Four
A Summer of Secrets - Book Five

A Moment in the Moonlight - Book Six

MOONBEAM BAY ~ THE SERIES
The Parker Women - Book One
The Parker Cafe - Book Two
A Heather Parker Original - Book Three
The Parker Family Secret - Book Four
Grace Parker's Peach Pie - Book Five
The Perks of Being a Parker - Book Six

BLUE HERON COTTAGES ~ THE SERIES
A six-book series coming in 2022.

WIND CHIME BEACH ~ A stand-alone novel

INDIGO BAY ~ A multi-author sweet romance series

Sweet Days by the Bay - Kay's Complete Collection of stories in the Indigo Bay series

Sign up for my newsletter at my website *kaycorrell.com* to make sure you don't miss any new releases or sales.

ABOUT THIS BOOK

Sometimes life forces us to make impossible choices.

Lizzie saved Rachel's life when they were young girls and that one moment cemented a lifelong friendship. But twenty-five years later life has dealt them some rough blows.

Lizzie is recently divorced, has a son in college who barely speaks to her, and she's positive her appliances are having a rebellion while demanding the rest of her meager savings. Not to mention, after years of taking care of her husband and son, she has no idea what skills she has to get a job and move on with her life.

Rachel has the perfect life and perfect husband. The only thing she doesn't have is the child she's longed for. She's sure getting pregnant will make her life complete.

Rachel's mother, Sara Jane, has problems of her own. Like her cheating husband who keeps insisting that's all in the past. Until… it isn't.

This book is a celebration of friendship, family, and the strength of three women when pushed to their limits. Try this heartwarming story from USA Today Bestselling author, Kay Correll.

PROLOGUE

The cold, dark water closed around Lizzie. Her chest burned as she shoved off the mucky riverbed and pushed to the surface, grabbing a gulp of air and blessed light. She screamed for help before jackknifing to the bottom yet again. Over and over. Unable to see in the murky water, but reaching out with her hands, trying desperately to find Rachel Benoit. She'd seen her struggle and go down right about this very spot. But after ten dives to the bottom, she still couldn't find her. The uncharitable question popped into her mind about why she was trying so hard to save this girl who had caused her so much grief and pain.

One more launch back to the surface. The sunlight showered through the water above her, breaking through the shadowy darkness and beckoning her to the surface. Her lungs ached. Her muscles screamed. Her mind taunted her with fleeting thoughts of failure. She gulped in three deep breaths and dove back down, reaching blindly in the darkness until finally, finally, she felt Rachel's arm. She grabbed on, tugged, and circled an arm around Rachel's chest. Pushing off the bottom, she struggled to haul them both to the surface.

Air.

Sunshine.

Finally.

With a perfect cross-chest carry she'd learned in lifeguard class, she aimed for the shoreline with constant, exhausted scissor kicks.

As soon as her feet could touch the bottom, she pushed Rachel to the shoreline, still half in the water, and checked for any signs of breathing or pulse. A thready pulse, but no sign of breathing. She started mouth-to-mouth resuscitation, thankful for the life-saving course she'd completed last year. She struggled to remember the drill. Her mind ached from lack of oxygen and the strain of remembering. Her thoughts taunted her. *Too late. Too late.*

She paused her efforts at resuscitation for a

brief moment. "Help!" she screamed as loud as she could. In reality, it sounded more like a croak. She sucked in a deep breath and tried again. "Help me!"

Then Rachel miraculously sputtered and coughed up a stream of dirty river water, God bless her. Lizzie tugged her farther up onto the rocky shore. Rachel opened her eyes, coughing and crying.

"I thought... I—" Rachel coughed again. "I would die."

"You're going to be fine." Lizzie hoped she wasn't lying. "Sh! Don't talk." She pushed the plastered mass of reddish-brown curls, now covered in sand and dirt, away from Rachel's face.

Just then a man came running toward them. Help was here. Tears streamed down Lizzie's face and mingled with the lake water dripping from her hair. She dropped, exhausted, to the sandy shoreline beside Rachel.

Sara Jane Benoit watched her daughter, Rachel, head out the door. It was so hard to watch her leave these days. Ever since Rachel had almost drowned, Sara Jane had an overwhelming urge to keep her daughter wrapped up safely at home. Thank goodness for Lizzie Timmons. What would have happened if Lizzie hadn't arrived at the lake when she did? And why in the world had her daughter decided it was okay to swim at the river alone after her other friends left? She knew the kids hung out there sometimes, but what about the alligators? She shuddered. She herself would never dream of swimming in the river.

And Rachel knew the rules. What other rules did her daughter break that Sara Jane didn't know about? She wasn't sure she wanted that answer. Rachel had almost paid the ultimate price for flouting this one.

Sara Jane grabbed the silver tray she was polishing and rubbed it vigorously with the cloth. Honestly, her silver had never looked better than in the six weeks since Rachel's near death. Sara Jane had ridden wave after wave of nervous energy. Scrubbed and rearranged her kitchen cabinets. Eliminated every speck of dust in her obsessively organized house. Cleaned out the inside of her car and painted the laundry room. And then she'd gone out to the edge of the lake, dropped to her knees, and given thanks that Rachel's life had been spared.

Now a vague sense of unease had settled over her. She was so thankful Rachel was alive. But life seemed short and fragile now, like she should be grabbing every single moment, really living it. But instead, she cleaned and hovered around her daughter, driving her nuts.

And somehow this whole thing was her fault according to her husband.

Steven had yelled at her at the hospital, in front of everyone, while they waited for the doctors to check on Rachel after the incident. She hadn't watched over Rachel well enough. She was too easy on her. Hadn't set limits. Let Rachel get out of control. On and on and on. The nurse had thrown her an apologetic look, but no one ever interfered with Benoit business.

Her husband was an enigma to her. A good old boy from a family that had been right here in Wind Chime Beach, Florida, for years. His mama lived up the way in the family home—a mansion, really. Though originally from Louisiana, the Benoits had been here, active in the town, for over seventy years. She'd considered herself so lucky when Steven—*Bubba*

—had asked her to marry him. She'd be part of that whole enchanting world.

If she only knew then what she knew now. But didn't everyone say that about their life at some point? Still, she couldn't quite understand why it was her fault Rachel had almost. . . died. There, she said it. Died. Where would her life be without Rachel? She'd have nothing. A fancy house and a husband who thought she was a clueless twit and still insisted on her calling him by his nickname. And really, what kind of grown man still went by the name Bubba?

Over the past six weeks, he'd been cold and distant. Not that he'd ever been that warm to her. Well, he had in their courting days, but once they were married—no, if she were being honest, before that even—he seemed to lose interest in charming her. She was a fixer-up project to him. He'd fixed her up and created a pretty, charming wife to show off.

She picked up the silver teapot and stared at her distorted reflection as she slowly rubbed back and forth. Would it be too much to ask for a genie to pop out and grant her three wishes? What would those three wishes be? She guessed she'd already been given one. Rachel was alive. She didn't even dare to let herself imagine what the other two wishes might be. Sometimes it was better not to dream about what-ifs and maybes.

She'd better hurry up and clean up this mess in the kitchen and get the rest of dinner made. It was a Monday, which meant red beans and rice. Because Steven's mama had always made red beans and rice on Mondays, as well as his grandmother, and probably his great-grandmother and who knew how many generations before that.

So, of course, Sara Jane had to make it too. Every Monday. Without fail. Repeating the day over and over like a bad rendition of Groundhog Day. Though Steven was quick to tell her that her red beans and rice weren't as good as his mama's. A part of her had always wanted to tell him to just go up the way to his mama's house and eat her darn red beans and rice. But one, she could never talk to him like that, and, two, she didn't swear, and darn was almost a da... well, you know.

Steven stalked through the door at six-thirty, dropping his briefcase on the table and a stack of papers on the counter. Which, of course, Sara Jane would pick up as soon as he went upstairs to change. The routine never changed. She was expected to pick up whatever he dropped off and move it to his study in the back of the house. He couldn't be bothered to do it himself.

"Sara. I need to make some calls before dinner. Hold dinner for me."

Sara. He always called her just Sara. Not Sara Jane. He said that the double name was just too trashy, low class. He wouldn't call her by her proper name but insisted she call him some ridiculous nickname? But Sara Jane loved her two-part name and always thought of herself as Sara Jane. But to pacify him, she went by Sara to him, his family, and his business associates.

He disappeared down the hallway. She turned down the heat on the beans and rice and put the cornbread in the oven on low to keep it warm. Then she dumped the ice out of the glasses she had waiting on the table. When he actually decided it was time for them to eat, she'd put in fresh ice for the sweet tea.

Her thoughts drifted to magic genies, and she glanced over at the silver teapot. She'd wish a different life for herself. One where Steven came home, kissed her, shared stories about his day. They'd laugh and talk over dinner. Share a glass of wine on the porch afterward, and maybe, just maybe, take a walk in the twilight hours on the nearby beach.

She shook her head. You get what you get in life, her grandma had always said. It's what you make of it that counts.

1

It had been twenty-five years since Lizzie saved Rachel's life. That year she turned sixteen, learned to drive, saved Rachel's life, and fell in love with David Duncan, the most popular boy in school. It was the best summer of her life.

Lizzie had reveled in her rise from obscurity to celebrity and all the attention she received as the local girl who saved the prom queen's life. Really, how often did stuff like that happen in real life? Lizzie went from being one of those girls who most people didn't even notice as they walked by, to one of the popular kids. Invitations to parties, movies, sleepovers, and bonfires at the lake were a daily occurrence. Rachel had taken Lizzie under her wing, and the world opened up in a Cinderella kind of way.

Rachel. What would she do without her? Lizzie divided her life into two sections. Before Rachel and After Rachel. All those years ago, Rachel had swept her up like she did with everything in her wake. She introduced her to David.

David Duncan—star football player—who chose to date her that magical summer and eventually married her.

David had been so charming back then. His teasing smile, thick brown hair, and dark eyelashes that she truly wished were her own. They framed his eyes and made him look intelligent and all-knowing. She'd coveted those eyelashes.

Lizzie wasn't certain how she got from the apex of her sixteenth summer to the depths of this spring, twenty-five years later. She still lived in a beautiful house that David had bought her, though exactly half the furniture was gone. Half of the china, half of the crystal. Did David really use it in his new fancy house with #HesHerProblemNow, as Rachel called David's new wife, complete with the hashtag?

That one chance moment of being at the

river and seeing Rachel go underwater. Saving her. That moment somehow led her to where she was now.

Alone. With a garbage disposal that refused to work.

How had she managed to get from that summit of perfection to this point in her life? Alone in her kitchen, battling a garbage disposal that had backed up and no amount of plumbing cleaner seemed to free the clog. She was sure the chemicals she was dumping into the sink were caustic to her health and the environment, yet they were too wimpy to take out whatever disgusting stuff was down there.

Lizzie wasn't sure what about her current plumbing problem had brought back the memories of twenty-five years ago. Maybe it was the total loss of control she had over her life right now compared to a time when everything had neatly dropped into place.

She stabbed the button that was supposed to reverse the blades on the garbage disposal. It didn't do a thing. Kind of like how she couldn't manage to reverse the downhill spiral of her life. She shoved the handle of a broom down the garbage disposal and jiggled it around, trying to reverse the blades. She flicked the switch and finally the disposal ground to life, and slowly the backed-up sink full of garbage and water began to slip down the drain.

It really was getting to be more than she could take. It wasn't so much the big things... and there were certainly big things, like the divorce. But it was the constant patter of little things that was starting to bring her down.

Like her son, Eric, who as near as she could figure was getting ready to flunk out of college if his last semester grades were any indication. She knew something was up but couldn't figure out what. He'd always been a good student. Until he wasn't.

Then there were the bills. Lots of them. A constant deluge of them. She had to figure out some way to earn money. She'd only worked part-time jobs over the last years, devoting all her time to taking care of David and Eric. She'd never gotten a college degree. She didn't even know what would interest her, what she could do. She couldn't bear to think of going to work at a job that she hated just to make ends meet. Though she knew a vast majority of people did that. Day after day. The thought of it depressed her even more.

The phone rang as she put the broom back

in the broom closet where it belonged. She snatched the phone off the counter. "Hello?"

She realized she could hear nothing over the rumble of the garbage disposal and crossed the kitchen to flip the switch, almost afraid to turn it off. What if it wouldn't start up again? She didn't need another repair bill now.

"Hey, Lizzie."

"Rachel." How did her best friend know just when she needed her?

"What was all that racket?"

"The rebellion of the garbage disposal."

"Liz, I swear, your appliances are having a mutiny this year."

"No kidding." Lizzie grabbed some paper towels to start cleaning up the mess around the sink. First the dryer, then the microwave, now the disposal. "It would have been nice for them to die *last* year." Last year, when David was here to deal with it. When money was no object.

"Want to go out tonight? I'm lonely." Rachel popped past Lizzie's problems.

"I do, and I don't. I don't really have the money for it. But I'd really like a break from reality. But I better say no."

"Oh, come on. You know you want to. Hey, my treat."

Rachel knew things were tight these days. Rachel was basically rolling in money, but Lizzie didn't like her friend to pay her way. She had to get a job. Had to. Soon.

"Come on. Ronnie is out tonight, and I don't feel like staying home alone."

"I really shouldn't."

"Guess I'll have to go it alone then. You were more fun when you were married and had money to burn."

Ouch. But Rachel never really thought before she said stuff. That was just how she was. And she was just cute and bubbly enough to get away with it. It's not like Rachel was deliberately mean. She was just kind of clueless about responsibilities and the real world. Lizzie still adored her, though. Over the years she'd learned to just accept Rachel at face value, and she loved her dearly.

"I'm tired tonight, Rachel."

"I know, I know. I'm just wanting some company."

"You're welcome to come over here." Lizzie was always such a soft touch when it came to Rachel.

"Thanks, but I feel like going out. I think I'll

shop, then maybe stop in at Happy's for a drink."

"You have fun. I'll call you tomorrow and maybe we can do something."

"Yeah, okay. See ya, Lizzie." Rachel's voice was full of disappointment. She usually got her way. Everything in her life always fell neatly into place. The only thing she'd never gotten that she really wanted was a child. She and Ronnie hadn't been able to conceive, and it really tore at Rachel's heart.

Lizzie set the phone down and looked at the mess that was her kitchen. She *was* tired. She was always tired these days. Probably more from the emotional stress than anything else. David had left her and immediately remarried not a week after the ink was dry on the divorce papers. To a gorgeous, energetic woman. Probably fifteen years younger than Lizzie. #HesHerProblemNow—okay, really Kiera—was a gourmet cook according to her son. Eric managed to go on and on about how wonderful his new stepmom was. She baked cookies, loved to go camping and watch horror movies. Really, what more could a kid want out of a stepmother?

Not to mention David had bought Eric a

brand new car when he left for college. And said son had gotten two speeding tickets so far.

Anyway, there was no way she could compete with all David could give Eric now. At least not the material things. She leaned against the counter debating on cleaning it up or grabbing a glass of wine.

Rachel wished she could have talked Lizzie into going out tonight. She didn't feel like sitting home and waiting for Ronnie to come home. Her husband was always out at some business meeting or other. But he eventually came home to her with a smile and a hug and an "I've missed you, babe."

She was lucky in the marriage department. Lizzie's marriage had fallen apart, but then David was an egotistical jerk. She wasn't sure what Lizzie had ever seen in him. Well, maybe she did. Back when they were all in high school, David was *the* boy to date. But he'd never really outgrown the whole football star persona.

Rachel was pretty sure her own mom was miserable being married to her dad too. Honestly, her dad was kind of a jerk. All these rules and worries about who thought what about whomever. Geez, he drove her insane growing up with his ever-growing list of *things forbidden*.

But with her husband, Ronnie, that was a different marriage altogether. Even their names sounded good together. Rachel and Ronnie. She was the first to admit she lived a charmed life. Her parents had money and lavished her with gifts. She was smart and didn't have to work very hard in school, breezing through college with a minimum of effort to receive her teaching degree. She'd found a teaching job right out of college in her hometown, at the high school she herself had gone to. Just two years later she met and married Ronnie, who adored her. She was very secure in that knowledge. She'd quit her teaching job, which was fine by her, because there were so many rules she had to follow there, too. Besides, Ronnie made good money and told her she didn't need to work. So she didn't.

But that brought her back to what she should do tonight. She sighed. Lizzie hadn't sounded very sure of herself when she invited her over. But Rachel didn't feel like being alone.

Fifteen minutes later she was standing at

Lizzie's door with a chilled bottle of pinot grigio in her hands.

"Hey, Rach." Lizzie looked like she'd been half expecting her to show up as she opened the door wide.

"Wine?" Rachel raised the bottle as she crossed into the house.

"Sounds good."

In the kitchen, Lizzie reached up into the cabinet and got "their" glasses down. Two expensive wine glasses that Rachel had bought for Lizzie after David left to replace the ones with their married initials. One with an R etched into it, one with an L. They had packed up the old monogrammed wine glasses that night and stored them in the attic, never to be seen again. Well, half of them had probably gone to David's house.

"Thought you were going out." Lizzie set the glasses on the counter and dug around in a drawer until she found the wine opener.

"I was. But I didn't feel like going out alone." Rachel took the opener, twisted it in, and pulled the cork out with a satisfying pop. "So I thought I'd bring the party to you."

"Glad you did." Lizzie poured two generous glasses of wine and led the way out to her front porch. A nice breeze fluttered the leaves of an old live oak, stirring the oppressive humidity of the day.

Rachel settled down on the Adirondack chair next to Lizzie. "So what's new with you? Found a job yet?"

"Nothing so far. If I just knew what I really wanted to do. They don't have a lot of positions for stay-at-home mom listed in the paper."

"Have you thought about going back to school? You were always a good student."

"I don't know. I feel like I'm past the stage of my life where I can listen to someone pass out narrowly defined assignments and judge me based on their whims. And going to school with all those baby-faced kids. And honestly, it would feel weird to start college at almost the same time as Eric." Lizzie sipped her wine and looked out across the yard. "I do like to learn new things. I'm just not sure academia is where I want to learn them."

Rachel felt sorry for her friend, which she was sure would drive Lizzie crazy if she knew it. But to go out in the world now, after staying home for all those years with Eric? No, thanks. Lizzie had taken a few part-time jobs over the years, but nothing that would support her. It must be tough.

"What would you like to learn or do?"

"Dream job? Don't I wish I knew."

"Are you going to have to sell the house?"

"Probably. I got the house in the divorce, but it's expensive to keep it up. Plus the insurance and taxes. I wanted to keep it so Eric wouldn't have to adjust to too many changes at once. But honestly, when he does come home from college, he usually stays at David's new house." Lizzie let out a long sigh. "But I really do need to find a job and move to somewhere less expensive. I have some money from the divorce settlement, but it won't last forever."

"I'm sure you'll figure it out."

"Look, it must be nine o'clock." Lizzie waved to her neighbor out walking her dog. "Every night like clockwork. Rain or shine. Nine o'clock. Mrs. Muckerman and Tucker."

Rachel glanced at her watch. Nine o'clock on the dot. She probably shouldn't stay long. Lizzie looked beat. "You tired?"

"I'm okay. It's such a nice night out. Cooler than it's been the last week." Lizzie stared into her wine as she gave it a little swirl, then took a sip. "Your mom asked me to her party next week."

"Oh, good. She loves having you there. You're like the daughter she always wanted. The one who doesn't sass her." Rachel grinned.

"Very funny. But I do adore your mother. And I'm looking forward to the party."

"Ronnie and I will be there. I think she just wants some friendly faces in the sea of Daddy's business associates."

"Not to mention you seem to be able to charm your father when he gets into one of his moods. Anyway, I told her I'll be there."

"Oh, look, there's Ronnie. I texted him I was coming over here." Ronnie pulled into the drive, then slid out of his shiny new BMW. He was such a car connoisseur. Loved his shiny toys. She didn't begrudge him, though, any more than he begrudged her the designer purse obsession, expensive shoes, or the cabinet of jewelry she had. We all had our weaknesses.

"Hi, babe." He bounded up the front stairs and leaned over to press a kiss to her forehead. "Hey, Lizzie, how are you?"

"Doing fine."

He perched on the porch railing, the glow

from a streetlight highlighting his blond hair. "What have you two been up to tonight?"

"You're looking at it." Rachel held up her wine glass. Ronnie smiled at her then. His Rachel smile. The one he only used for her.

Geez, she was the luckiest woman on the planet to have found him.

She tilted her wine glass to her lips and finished up the last sip. "We should probably head on out and let Lizzie get some sleep."

"Rachel hasn't corrupted you to her late-night ways yet?"

"Not yet." Lizzie shook her head. "Though, she's been trying for like twenty-five years."

Rachel admitted she loved the late-night hours when the house was still. She loved to stay up late and read. Or putter around the house. Lizzie, on the other hand, was an early to bed, early to rise person. The early to rise was the hardest part of that to understand…

She stood and took Ronnie's hand. "Mind if I leave my car here? I think I'll ride home with Ronnie."

"Not a problem." Lizzie stood and picked up the empty wine glasses. "You two have a good night."

She clasped her husband's hand in hers and

walked through the moonlight to his car. He opened the door for her and gave her a quick kiss. "Love ya."

"Love you, too." She slipped into the car, totally content with the way her evening had turned out.

2

Sara Jane put the finishing touches on the salad and set it in the refrigerator to stay cool. She looked around the kitchen. All the dishes she'd used to make dinner were washed and neatly put away. She'd set the table in the gazebo beside the pool. The drinks were iced down in a cooler with a towel neatly draped over the handle for anyone to dry their hands on after digging down in the cold ice for their beverage of choice.

She'd placed citronella torches around the pool to chase off the mosquitos and strung clear Christmas lights along the fence around the pool for ambience. She just had to remember to flip them on at dusk.

Everything looked nice, special. Hopefully

Steven would be in a good mood tonight. When he was, he was the most charming host, bragging about his wonderful, efficient wife. When he wasn't? Well… if he wasn't in a good mood it would be a very long night.

They were hosting a party for twenty-five tonight. She'd asked Rachel and Ronnie to come. She'd also included Lizzie. She worried about her these days. It seemed like a lot of Lizzie and David's friends had chosen to keep David in their circle and discarded Lizzie. Not fair, but just the way things happened after a divorce sometimes. Besides, she missed Lizzie. She hadn't seen her in quite a while. Though Sara Jane would be busy tonight, she hoped to have some time to chat with Lizzie and see how she was doing.

She untied the apron strings and hung the apron on the back of the door to the large walk-in pantry. She closed the door and looked around one more time. Everything was perfect. Wasn't it?

"Mom?" Rachel burst through the back door. For a brief moment, Sara Jane was thrust back in time to when Rachel would always barge through the door to tell of her great adventures of the day. Her daughter hadn't changed her style much over the years.

She smiled at Rachel. "What is it?"

"I thought I'd come over early and help. But I see you have the backyard all set up. It looks beautiful. As usual."

"Thanks, honey. I'm glad they took the rain out of the forecast." She'd made backup plans on how the party could be moved inside, but it would be cramped and warm and Steven would certainly be upset and somehow blame her for the weather.

Rachel was smartly dressed in black pants, sparkly flip flops, and a bright pink tank top. Always put together. Her shoulder-length hair was swept back with one silver clip on the side. Rachel's hair was the same shade reddish-brown that her own hair was. Well, had been. Now she paid her hairdresser to replicate the color and cover any grays she might have. Not that she even knew how much gray hair she had. It had been carefully covered since Steven had made a disparaging remark on her first one.

Rachel crossed over to the fridge. "Then if you have things under control, let's sit down and have a glass of wine. Get you off of your feet for a minute. I bet you've been running around all day."

Sara Jane was tired. Which wasn't the best way to start off a party, but it always took so long to get everything just right. Steven was proud that they were known for throwing fabulous parties. He often gave her only a few days' notice that he'd invited people over for a get-together. Or sometimes, like this party, she had a month to send out invitations and prepare.

"A glass of wine sounds nice." She sank into a kitchen chair. Just for a moment, that was all.

Rachel pulled down a couple of wine glasses and poured them both some pinot grigio. That was Rachel's new favorite wine, and Sara Jane tried to be sure she had some chilling in the fridge at all times.

"Where's Ronnie?"

"He's coming a bit later. He was running late at work and wanted to go home and change too. He'll be here soon."

A brief knock sounded at the kitchen door before it swung open. "Hi there." Lizzie peeked in. "I thought I'd come a bit early and help."

Rachel laughed her bubbly, infectious laugh. "Like Mom wouldn't have every detail finished before everyone got here. I thought I'd help too. We're both too late."

Lizzie crossed over and gave Sara Jane a quick hug. "Thanks so much for inviting me."

"I love having you here any time. You know you're always welcome."

Rachel fished another wine glass out of the cabinet and held it up. "Join us?"

"Sounds great." Lizzie sank onto the chair beside Sara Jane.

Rachel brought over the glasses and claimed the kitchen chair that had been hers since she was a little girl. She lifted her glass. "To another perfect party by Mom."

Sara Jane felt her face heat up. "Rachel…"

"She's right, Sara Jane. You do throw the best parties."

"Oh, you girls are prejudiced."

"Oh my gosh, do you remember the one she threw for our high school graduation?" Rachel gushed.

"Of course I do. Half the town is still talking about it. The whole Hawaiian theme. The roasted pig." Lizzie turned to her. "And that sand you brought to make that small beach? How fun was that?"

31

"Yeah, Dad was so p—" Rachel glanced at her. "I mean, he was so ticked off."

Sara Jane smiled indulgently at Rachel. Her child had the face of an angel and the mouth of a trucker. She usually tried to keep it in check in front of her though.

"I had such fun throwing that party for you girls and your friends."

"What are you doing?" Steven's stern voice smashed through their conversation.

Sara Jane jumped up. "I didn't hear you come in."

"Obviously," Steven said in a dry, mocking tone that she didn't miss.

"Don't you have things to do for the party?"

"I made her sit down and relax for a few minutes before everyone shows up." Rachel sprung to her mother's defense.

"Maybe you could help her instead of just sitting there."

"Daddy, I *am* helping. I'm making Mom take a break," she said with a wheedling tone and a grin.

Steven relaxed and melted under Rachel's charms. She'd always been able to wrap her father around her little finger. Always being the peacemaker. Smoothing things over, joking him into a good mood. Tonight was no exception. Sara Jane took a deep breath, thankful Rachel had averted a confrontation with Steven. She wasn't sure she had the energy to pacify him tonight. Truth be told, she was completely tired of pacifying him. But it's what she did to keep the peace.

"Okay, then. Far be it from me to interfere with you women. I'm going upstairs to shower and change. I'll be back down before the first guests arrive."

Sara Jane watched as her husband walked out of the kitchen toward the stairs. She wished she could handle him as well as her daughter did. And for one fleeting second, she wished she didn't have to handle him at all.

An hour later Lizzie was busy helping Sara Jane serve cocktails and appetizers to the guests. Sara Jane was everywhere. The ultimate hostess. Making sure people had cold drinks, introducing the new partner in Mr. Benoit's law firm to everyone.

Mr. Benoit. It still struck her as odd that she thought of Rachel's parents as Mr. Benoit and

Sara Jane. She wasn't sure when she started calling Sara Jane by her first name. Sometime that first summer after she and Rachel became friends.

"Lost in thought?"

Lizzie looked up and saw Ronnie standing next to her. She smiled up at him. Ronnie had the face of a teddy bear and the charisma of a beloved pastor. He was one of those people that everyone liked the minute they met him. He adored his wife and let everyone know it. Rachel was one lucky woman to find him.

The conversations swarmed around them and Ronnie leaned in closer. "I've got the best birthday present picked out for Rachel." His voice held a conspiratorial tone.

"What is it?" Lizzie leaned forward and placed her hand on his arm. He always put so much thought into the gifts he got for Rachel.

"Hey, what are you two up to? You look like you're up to no good." Rachel walked up to them with a cold beer in her hand. She handed it to Ronnie.

Lizzie laughed when she saw Ronnie's guilty face. He looked like a little kid caught swiping an extra cookie.

"You are so busted, Ronnie." Rachel gave him a quick kiss on the cheek. "What's up?"

"Nothing, dear," he deadpanned.

"You might as well tell me. You know I'll drag it out of you anyway."

"I can't remember what we were talking about. Can you, Lizzie?"

"Not a clue. Sorry, Rachel." She put on her best innocent face, and Rachel rolled her eyes.

"Fine then. You two just keep your secrets. See if I care." She swiped a sip of Ronnie's beer while she searched the crowd. "Have you seen Mom?"

"She was over by the food buffet when I last saw her."

"I just wanted to check on her. Dad is a bit, um, touchy tonight. I'm hoping he won't get in one of his moods."

Moods. That was one thing to call the way Mr. Benoit acted. The man was a jerk. He bullied his wife. Never had a kind word for her. But enjoyed wearing her on his sleeve like some prized possession. Lizzie had accidentally overheard a conversation between Sara Jane and Mr. Benoit many years ago. Right when she'd first become friends with Rachel. He'd called Sara Jane stupid and low class. And she'd seen the tears Sara Jane tried to hide after Mr. Benoit left. Lizzie hadn't liked the man one bit from that day forward.

"We better go see if we can find your dad. If he's on a roll tonight, I'll see if I can deflect some of his. . . *mood*." Ronnie winked. "And I want to see if your mom needs any help." He and Rachel slipped away in the crowd, hand in hand.

Lizzie stood there wondering what it was that Ronnie had gotten for Rachel's birthday. He'd never said.

She looked over in the opposite direction of where Ronnie and Rachel had headed and spied Mr. Benoit talking to some young blonde woman. The woman hung onto his every word, placing her hand on his arm and flirting in a way that no one could mistake. Mr. Benoit was eating it up. Covering the blonde's hand with his own, a self-satisfied look on his face.

Lizzie wasn't sure why Sara Jane put up with the pompous jerk. But she did. Year after year. Affair after affair. She guessed Sara Jane was raised with the *stick by your man no matter what* mantra drilled into her head. Didn't make it right.

Lizzie caught Sara Jane watching her

husband closely from across the yard, a hurt expression on her face that she tried valiantly to hide. Lizzie was just about fed up enough with men—all men—to do something about this. She strode over to where Mr. Benoit and the Obvious Blonde were talking.

"Oh, hi, Mr. Benoit." Lizzie pasted on a smile.

"Elizabeth." His voice held only a tinge of welcome. Fake welcome.

Mr. Benoit was the only person on the planet who called her Elizabeth. He refused to call her Lizzie. She just caught herself before she rolled her eyes at him. "I'm sorry, I don't believe we've met." Lizzie extended her hand to Blondie.

"I'm Andrea Moore. I work with Steven."

"Really, how nice. What do you do?"

"I'm an executive assistant."

So that's what they were calling it these days. More impressive than... tramp.

"Have you worked there long?"

"I moved here about a month ago."

Lizzie could tell that both Obvious Blonde —Andrea—and Mr. Benoit were getting tired of her chitchat. Good. She hid a smile. "Do you like it there?" She carried on even though she couldn't care less if the woman liked her job.

"I love my job."

She just bet she did.

Just then Rachel walked up. "Hey, Daddy. Judge Falon is looking for you." She motioned over toward the bar area.

"If you ladies will excuse me." Mr. Benoit nodded his head at the three of them and walked off in the direction Rachel had pointed.

"Hi, Andrea. Nice to see you again."

Lizzie had to bite back a laugh. Rachel's tone held no warmth, and her fake smile was anything but welcoming.

"Good to see you too, Rachel. Nice party your father is throwing."

"Actually my mother throws the parties. It's an excellent one though, isn't it?"

"I must find out the name of her caterer. The food is delicious."

Rachel laughed. "The *caterer* is Mom. She's a great cook too, don't you think?" She nodded toward the plate of food Andrea was holding.

Andrea looked at her plate and paused. "Yes, I guess she is. I just assumed she had it catered."

"Nope. Mom has many hidden talents. Do you cook?"

"Me? No. I can't cook a thing that doesn't pop in the microwave." Andrea looked pleased with herself.

"Really? That's too bad." Rachel paused. "Dad really loves a big home-cooked meal. Guess he's lucky to have Mom."

Silence fell between them, and Andrea fidgeted back and forth on her incredibly high, spiked heels. "Ah, uh, I've been meaning to ask. Why Wind Chime Beach? Isn't that an unusual name for a town?"

"Have you been to the beach?" Rachel asked, and Lizzie could tell she was trying not to roll her eyes.

"I'm not much of a beach person."

"Interesting choice, moving to a beach town, then," Rachel said dryly.

Lizzie stepped in. "Town lore has it that one of the first settlers to the area made a few wind chimes out of jingle shells and hung them on trees near the beach. Jingle shells are these delicate shells in lots of colors, and when the wind blows through them, well, they make a jingle noise."

"Now you still see some hung along our

beaches and in the gazebo in the park," Rachel explained.

"Oh, how interesting," Andrea said without a bit of interest in her voice. "Well, I should circulate some. Check in on some of our clients."

"Oh, don't let us keep you," Lizzie said, trying to hide her sarcasm.

Andrea slipped away into the crowd.

"What a b—" Rachel glanced around her.

"Don't worry, your mom's too far away to hear you swear." Lizzie laughed out loud. "You were pretty good with that conversation, though. Impressive."

"The little tramp. Right here in Mom's house. Could she be more blatant? She has her sights set on Dad."

Lizzie didn't point out that Obvious Blonde had probably already snagged the man.

"Let's go find that husband of yours and buy him a drink." Lizzie took Rachel's arm, and they headed off in the direction of Ronnie's laugh.

Rachel stood in the kitchen after the last guests left. Ronnie was outside with big green trash bags picking up trash. Lizzie pushed through the kitchen door with a tray of glasses. That was one thing Sara Jane always insisted on at her parties. Real glassware. None of this plastic stuff for her.

Her mom looked up from wrapping up leftovers. "Just set that on the counter. I've got a load in the dishwasher, but I think I'll just finish up by hand washing the rest of them."

"Let me do that for you," Lizzie said as she set the tray on the counter.

"You don't have to do that."

"But I want to."

That was just like Lizzie. Always helping. Always seeming to instinctively know what a person needs. Sometimes before they know themselves.

Her mom did look tired. She'd probably been up since five this morning, making sure everything was ready.

"I'll help Lizzie." Rachel started filling the sink with hot soapy water. "It won't take long."

"Thanks, girls."

Just then her dad slipped through the

41

kitchen door. Without bringing in any glasses. Or trash. Or anything else for that matter.

"I've got to run out for a bit. Forgot something at the office. I'll be back soon."

Her mom paused in wrapping up a tray of leftover food and looked at her dad with an expression that betrayed little of her feelings. "Okay."

"Don't wait up."

Her mom just nodded.

Lizzie dunked some glasses in the sink. Rachel could tell by the set of her shoulders that she wasn't buying it either. Rachel loved her dad —mostly because he was her dad—but he really was a philandering fool.

Rachel and her mom had talked about it only one time. Rachel had been in her late twenties. Newly married and totally smitten with Ronnie. She couldn't understand her parents' marriage at all compared to her perfect one and had asked her mom why she stayed with her dad. Her mom said because it was the life she'd chosen. It wasn't a bad life. It was just how things were. Then she'd dismissed the whole conversation and moved on.

Rachel wondered if her mom still felt that

way. Not that she'd ever had the nerve to bring up the subject again.

Once again she was so thankful for having found Ronnie. As if on cue, her husband pushed into the kitchen, his arms full of half-empty wine bottles.

"Sara Jane, I put the trash bags in the garage."

"Thanks, Ronnie."

"I need to make a couple more trips to bring in a few more things, then I think you're about set."

Rachel unloaded the armful of bottles from him and set them on the counter. He brushed a kiss on her forehead and headed back outside.

Lizzie looked up from the sink. "You got yourself a keeper there, Rachel."

Rachel smiled. No kidding. She planned to keep him forever.

3

Gabe Smith glanced over at his mother dozing in the passenger seat. The last month had taken its toll on her. Packing up her condo. Getting things ready to move back to Wind Chime Beach.

She had insisted it was too much for him to give up his life in St. Louis and move back with her. But he'd been just as insistent. More so, he guessed, because here he was not ten miles out of Wind Chime Beach, a town he thought he'd put completely behind him years ago.

He couldn't picture his mother moving back here at her age and rattling around that big old house by herself. But she wanted to move back to the town she'd grown up in and had lived in until the year Gabe turned seventeen and they'd abruptly moved away.

His mom stirred and opened her eyes. "Where are we?"

"A few minutes out of Wind Chime."

He watched while thoughts chased across her face. Memories? Regrets? Then she turned and smiled at him. "Good. I'm getting hungry, aren't you?"

"I am. Want to stop at the Seaside Cafe?" Not that he knew if it was even open anymore. It had been a lot of years. "We can eat there, then I'll get us checked into the motel." They were spending a few nights at the motel while he arranged help to move the furniture back into their home.

He still wasn't certain why his mother had kept the family home, renting it out all these years. And as far as he knew, she'd never come back to visit. But when she decided she wanted to move back, she'd called the property company who managed the place and arranged for what she said were a few minor improvements and repairs. The house had been empty for over a year.

Gabe pulled the car into a parking space near the front door of the cafe. He slid out of the car and stretched after the long drive. "Mom, need some help?" He rounded the front of the car and helped her swing the car door open. He watched as she slowly got out of the car.

When had the woman who had always taken care of him become the person he needed to take care of? Not that she really needed to be taken care of… he just couldn't bear to think of her moving back here alone. And he'd grown tired of his apartment in St. Louis with noisy neighbors and a two-year road construction project nearby that never seemed to end. Besides, he moved every few years or so, never putting down roots. He certainly could come back here and live with his mom for a bit while she adjusted to everything. He took her arm and led her into the cafe. They took a seat in the corner and a bubbly waitress crossed over, menus in hand.

"Can I get you something to drink?"

"Mom? What would you like?"

"Some sweet tea would be nice. They don't know how to make tea up north."

"Okay, one tea, coming up." The waitress— Patsy, according to her well-worn name tag— looked expectantly at him.

"How about a cold beer."

"Bud, Bud Light, Mich, Yuengling, Corona," she recited.

"Yuengling is fine." They didn't have that one in St. Louis.

"I'll be right back with your drinks. Then I'll give you a minute to look over the menu." She sashayed away, stopping briefly to flirt with a man in a John Deere hat at a table near the door. She laughed out loud at something the man said and smiled all the way to the glass front fridge behind the counter. She pulled out a cold beer, popped the cap off while almost at the same time pouring a tall glass of tea. She'd obviously been at her job for quite some time.

Gabe returned his attention to his mother as she read through the menu. She was unusually quiet tonight. The trip seemed to have taken a lot out of her. For the hundredth time, he questioned his decision. Was it right to move her back here? It's what she wanted. She kept saying she wanted to go home. But it had been so long since they'd lived here. Lots of things would be different. Change wasn't something she handled very well these days. Or maybe it was something he didn't handle well.

He grabbed a small notebook from his shirt

pocket and scribbled a few notes to himself. He used to use the notebook for ideas for his novels, to make sure the random ideas didn't get lost in the shuffle of everyday life. But these days his trusty notebook was more of a glorified to-do list. He was going to have to hit the writing hard after he got them both settled in. He scribbled another note. *High-speed internet?*

He was thankful he had a job where he could pick up and move and still earn a living. He'd been incredibly lucky—though he firmly believed people made their own luck—when he sold his first mystery novel ten years ago. He'd been writing them ever since. Two years ago he quit his job as a CPA—a job that bored him to tears—to write full time.

"You going to get the fried chicken, Mom?"

"That sounds really good. I'll do that." She placed her menu down at the corner of the table.

Sounded like as good a choice as anything else. "I'll have it too."

Patsy came back by and they ordered their meals. He took a big swig of the ice-cold beer. A welcome reward for his long day. They'd eat and check into the adjoining rooms he'd gotten at the motel. Tomorrow they'd go out and look around the old house. He had such memories of living there with his mom. He wondered what the house would look like now. He only had until tomorrow to find out.

Gabe didn't really know what he expected when they went out to see their old house. He pulled into the tree-lined gravel driveway. They wound their way up the drive, around the curve, and there it was. Just like it had stood for so many days in his youth.

"Oh, my." His mother broke into a smile. "We're home."

"Yes, Mom, we are." It all seemed worth it to see the look on her face.

He popped out of the car and came around to help her out. "I've got it, son. I'm not some doddering old fool."

He smiled. There was some of her old spunk. He stepped back and let her make her own way.

The live oak trees shaded the front porch. He'd have to get some new porch furniture. She loved to sit outside. The veranda wound around the side of the house. The side porch had been enclosed with glass windows since they'd lived here. That was a nice addition. Was that one of her "minor repairs?"

He dug out the key as they climbed up the front steps. After jiggling with the lock, he twisted the doorknob and stepped into the cool interior.

"Oh. It's so good to be home." His mother dropped her purse by the door and started toward the back of the house. To the kitchen, he was sure. She loved that kitchen with its numerous cabinets and the big counter where they'd eaten so many of their meals. It also had a perfect little breakfast nook at the far end.

"Gabe, come look. All nice stainless appliances. They look so nice in here."

He crossed the worn wooden floor and into the kitchen. The sun shone through the windows. The kitchen had always been the brightest, cheeriest place in the house.

"Did you order all those?"

"I did. The manager said the dishwasher wasn't working. The fridge was fifteen years old. The sink had a leak. So I decided to replace all of them. Except for my stove, of course." She walked over and rested her hand on the old gas stove as if greeting a welcome friend.

He flipped on a switch and the kitchen light came on. Good, the electricity had been turned on. The walls looked freshly painted in a light, sunny yellow. He picked up the phone and heard a dial tone. His mother still insisted on a landline. So far, so good. He went to the thermostat and turned on the air conditioner. It clicked on. So far things were working in their favor.

"When can we move in? I can't wait." His mother's eyes sparkled with excitement.

"The movers will be here tomorrow. I should be able to have you sleeping under this roof by tomorrow night if all goes well."

"I'd like that." She was checking out the fridge and adjusting the temperature in there. "We need to go get some groceries. We could do that today."

"That'd be fine." He smiled at her enthusiasm. It all seemed worth it. It warmed his heart to see her so happy. After all his wavering about the move, he was beginning to think he'd made the right decision.

He needed to get them settled in. Then he had to get to work. He had a deadline to meet on his next book, and he was starting to feel the pressure of being behind. This whole move had taken more time than he thought it would. He didn't want to ask for an extension on this book. He wanted it finished. His next book was already taunting him with ideas and the siren call of *come start me. I'm better. I'm more fun.*

"What are you doing?" he asked as his mom headed back toward the front door.

"I'm making a to-do list and a grocery list. Need some paper from my purse."

"I'm going to go check out the rest of the house." Gabe walked through the kitchen and out to the family room. French doors now led from the family room to the new sunroom. He opened the doors and stepped out. It was a good-sized sunroom with a built-in twin bed with drawers underneath it against the far wall. That was a great idea. A nice place to lounge and look out into the so-called orchard. He looked at the trees. He remembered planting them when he was young. Orange trees, lemon trees, and lime trees, all full-grown mature trees now. His mother would love having the fresh fruit from them.

The inside of the sunroom was painted with a whitewash. Even the floor. Definitely an inviting room. It would be a nice spot to bring his laptop and do some of his writing.

Back inside, he checked out the bedrooms. They looked the same. The master bedroom had an attached bathroom that had been updated somewhere along the line. He walked into his old room, and a sense of rightness settled over him. He'd been so happy here. Until they'd had to leave. He just hoped it was okay that they were back now. Surely enough years had passed. But he wasn't going to think about that now.

The house was actually way too large for just the two of them. Six bedrooms, five and a half bathrooms.

One of the bedrooms would become his office. He needed to get some internet set up. He could go to the library and tie into their wireless—he'd checked into that. But he wasn't sure how much he wanted to leave his mom alone until she got all settled in and adjusted. She'd been a bit forgetful the past year. Probably just a normal part of aging, but he still worried about her.

He turned to go find her. The sooner he could get her settled in, the sooner he could get back to writing.

4

Two days after the party at Sara Jane's, Lizzie's garbage disposal finally died. A not-so-nice present for the birthday she was trying to forget she was having today.

After checking on YouTube, she was convinced she could replace it herself. She just hoped she wasn't fooling herself. The hardware store in town didn't have what she wanted, so she'd driven to a big hardware store in Sarasota to pick up the garbage disposal, but now she was running late. She was due at a meeting for the school's big annual fair. She and David were co-coordinators for the event last year when Eric was a senior. Back when they were married. It was expected that the following year the coordinators would help out again. And if it was expected of her… she did it.

The normal route she took from Sarasota was blocked due to construction. She took a quick right on Elm Avenue and cut over to Magnolia Street.

Just that morning she had vowed to change her life. Why she chose that particular day, she wasn't sure. Or maybe she did. A birthday was a reminder that the years were slipping by. A good time to make a change. And she wanted a change. There had to be some meaning to her life now. She wanted to be more than the person who had saved Rachel's life. More than Eric's mother. More than David's wife…well, ex-wife. She craved being more than PTO president, soccer mom, volunteer for about anything that anyone asked her to do. She wanted to be someone whose identity was not connected with anyone else. Her own person.

Only she had no idea who that person was…

So when she found herself taking the back way home, following the detour signs through a cute area being redeveloped to suit the new influx of young people into their small seaside town, she did something she hadn't done since that day she ran into the river to save Rachel—she listened to the small inner voice that was truly her own, not the voice of other people's expectations, and stopped in front of a run-down Victorian house with a for-sale sign in the window.

Old houses in the area were being divided into condos and restaurants dotted the corners of the streets with an eclectic assortment of shops and businesses springing up in between. Electric lights fashioned to look like gaslights festooned the brick roadways. They'd managed to save the old oaks lining the parkway between the lanes. The whole street was just charming.

Here on the corner of Magnolia Street and Rosebud Lane, she pulled her car into a parking space in front of the house, and an idea bubbled through her. It was a bit crazy, but then... maybe crazy was just what she needed right now. She scribbled down the info on the for-sale sign.

With one last long look at the house, she pulled out of the parking space and followed the detour signs away from the area now dubbed The Village. She chewed her bottom lip, knowing she was going to be so late to the meeting. But that one detour made her even more determined to change the road her life had been on, too.

When she arrived at the school, she hurried into the auditorium and slipped into a seat in the back row. All that worrying about being late and they hadn't even started yet. The new chairperson of the fair called the meeting to order, and Lizzie tried to concentrate, but right now all she wanted was to get on the internet and do some research. Look up the price of that house for sale. For the first time in a long time, a glimmer of an idea of what she could do with her life sprang into a glorious full-color photograph in her mind.

She could buy the house. Open a shop there. She knew how to do one thing really well. And that was to decorate. She could put things together in ways that people wouldn't normally think of. She knew she had an eye for color and proportion. People in town were always asking her advice for decor. And she loved to haunt antique malls and flea markets and see what she could find. Could she somehow turn that into a viable business?

She dug out a scrap of paper from her purse and, even more amazing, actually found a pen that wrote. She started to scribble down a few notes.

Lizzie was so engrossed in her thoughts that she didn't notice David slip into the seat beside her until he spoke. "You look lost in thought."

"What? Oh, hi." She crumbled the paper and dropped it back into her purse.

"Having a rough birthday?" He eyed her closely, and she forced herself not to fidget under his gaze.

Leave it to David to still pick up on stuff like that. And remember her birthday. The only person who had remembered it so far today. Not Rachel, not Eric. "No, actually it's going pretty good, thanks."

He looked a bit surprised. Well, why not? He thought her life was falling apart these days. He might even feel a bit guilty over it. Maybe. He probably thought that her birthday would just be another reminder of how old she was and what she'd lost.

Which might have been exactly how she would have been feeling just this moment if not for that detour. She was itching to pull out her phone and start researching, but not with David sitting right beside her.

"Listen, I think Eric is coming home this

weekend. He's staying at my place. Just wanted to let you know. Kiera is having a big barbecue for some of her family and our friends, and Eric wanted to come."

Perfect. Just peachy great.

"Okay. Tell him to drop by and see me."

"Sure, if he has time."

Right… if he had time to visit his mother. The mother who still gave him spending money when he ran low and helped pay his car insurance. It almost felt like Eric had moved out of her life and moved on, just like David.

"You should be sitting up front. The new chairperson might need to ask questions. Does she even know you're here?"

Well, he'd moved on except that he still kept trying to tell her what to do. That was his problem, because today, for the very first time, she truly believed she was ready to move on too.

She turned and smiled at David. "I'm perfectly fine here. You go ahead and move up front if you want."

He looked at her closely, shook his head, and moved to the front, shaking hands with a few people as he went. The new chairwoman gave him a dazzling smile. "Oh, there you are. So glad you're here, David."

She settled back on her folding chair. Everything had been so different last year. She'd been married to David and going to Eric's soccer games. He was a fairly good soccer player. He ran like the wind with his long legs shredding the distance like the field was no longer than their lawn. She loved to watch him run. Watch him bob and weave through the players on the other team. Raise his arms in elation when he made a goal. Shake his head and swear under his breath when he missed a shot. And now he was away at college. He had *just* been a young boy grasping her hand, like yesterday it seemed, flashing his impish grin to get himself out of whatever trouble he'd gotten into.

She only wished he could still get out of trouble with a grin. He was at that age where every teen firmly believed it—whatever *it* was—would never happen to them. They won't be thrown out of college if they flunk their courses. They won't be caught underage drinking, or speeding, or God forbid, drinking and driving.

She'd talked herself blue in the face with her view on drinking and driving. The quickest way to be grounded for the rest of his life, the car taken away, and life as he knew it coming to an end. But she still worried.

And something was wrong now. In the last year, he'd been the boy who broke curfew, copped an attitude, and lived perilously near the edge of believing the world owed him his happiness.

She'd learned all too well that the world didn't owe you anything. There was no guarantee of happiness for any of them. But Lizzie was ready to make some magic. Throw it out there into the universe and get some good mojo going in her life. Maybe this birthday would turn out to be the best one ever.

5

Lizzie entered the Seaside Cafe, glad to escape the harsh sunshine and midday heat. She gave her eyes a moment to adjust to the lighting and scanned the cafe for Rachel. She'd been busting to talk to Rachel but hadn't wanted to interrupt her vacation. Rachel and Ronnie didn't get a lot of time alone together with Ronnie's long work hours and frequent business trips. But now Rachel was home and Lizzie couldn't wait to tell her the news.

"Hey, Lizzie. You here alone?" Patsy grabbed a couple of menus. Patsy was the cafe's waitress slash hostess slash bus person. She'd been here for years. Oh, they had other people come and go. But Patsy was always a fixture.

Pitching in on all the jobs. Making sure things ran smoothly.

"Hi. No, I'm meeting Rachel."

"She's not here yet. Let's get you a booth by the window and I'll let her know you're here when she comes in."

Lizzie followed Patsy past the chrome-and-Formica tables. The red vinyl chairs had been replaced recently with replicas of the original, worn vinyl chairs. They were shiny and new, but she missed the old boomerang pattern of the old chairs. She figured the old chairs were from the fifties though. Not surprising that they'd decided to replace them. At least they'd kept the ambience of the old cafe. If they'd asked her for advice, though, she would have told them to keep trying to find the old boomerang pattern. There were specialty places that still made the vintage patterns.

She slipped into the booth, the vinyl-covered seat catching stickily to the back of her knees. Patsy placed two menus on the table, not that they really needed them. They'd been coming here since high school days. They knew everything on the menu.

"Want some tea while you wait?"

"That'd be great, thanks."

Lizzie watched out the cafe window. The heat shimmered off the hoods of the cars parked along the street. This area of town abutted The Village, the new area that she'd driven past on her birthday a few weeks ago. Things were starting to boom again here on Main Street, too. Gone were the closed-up storefronts. The cafe owners had updated the entryway and spruced up the inside. In addition to the new chairs, they'd put down new linoleum on the floors, still in the original black and white pattern.

She was so glad their small town wasn't one of the many small towns in the U.S. that were turning into ghost towns. It didn't hurt that it was on the gulf. Not a popular touristy town, but quaint in its own way. For some reason, not a lot of hotels had been built as the town developed. They were just north of the beautiful beaches on Belle Island and near the river that flowed into Moonbeam Bay. They were also close enough to Sarasota that people who worked in the city were moving out here to Wind Chime Beach for the lower cost of living to raise their families. Their school ranked in the top schools in the state. All in all, a nice little town.

Rachel pulled into a parking space near the front. When she'd called and asked her to join her here, Rachel had detected the excitement in her voice. But as much as Rachel tried to weasel out of her what was up, she'd just said to meet her here.

Rachel slipped into the seat across from Lizzie and dropped her purse onto the seat. "Okay, spill it."

Lizzie set down her glass of sweet tea, anxious to tell her news. "I'm opening up a business. Interior design business and a home decor shop. In The Village area."

"You're what?" Rachel's mouth dropped open.

"I've started the paperwork. Been to the bank. I'm buying an old house I found there. It's wonderful. It has old wooden floors, this great wrap-around porch. It's two floors and an attic." The place had charmed her the moment she stepped through the door with the Realtor.

"When did you decide this?" Rachel looked at her like she was crazy. Maybe she was. But this was something she longed to do. It was a force that had taken over her soul. She longed to do this, make a success of it. Have something that was hers, and hers alone.

"I saw the place a couple of weeks ago." She omitted the detail that it was on her birthday, the one Rachel forgot all about. "Took a wrong turn on a detour in that area. Or a right turn, depending on how you look at it. I'm going to do a small shop there. Part decorating, part furniture and antiques. I'll decorate the different rooms. Do a theme in each one."

Rachel reached over and grabbed Lizzie's hand. "You go. I think this is a fabulous idea."

"Wait, there's more." She'd expected Rachel's support with opening the store. Now she had to tell her the next part of her news. "And I'm selling the house."

"No way."

"I have some money from the divorce, but I'll need the capital to invest in the business. Buying the store was a stretch, let alone opening the business. So I decided to sell the house. Already talked to the Realtor. She said it should sell immediately. Not enough big housing available for the demand these days. The listing goes up tomorrow."

"I'm glad you told me before I heard about it from someone else." Rachel looked a tiny bit upset that she was just hearing the news. "Where will you live?"

She frowned. Wasn't that the million-dollar question? She hadn't a clue. "I'm not sure. Something small and cheap. I've been looking."

"Can you live at the shop? Is there room for an apartment?"

"No, it's zoned commercial there." Wouldn't that have been convenient?

"What did David say?"

"Haven't told him. Besides, it's my house now. I got it in the divorce settlement. He doesn't have a say over what I do with it."

"Have you told Eric yet?"

"No, not yet." She let out a long sigh. "He was home a couple of weekends ago and stayed at David's. He didn't even stop by to see me. Just texted and said he was sorry as he headed out of town. Said he just got caught up with things and got busy. I'm not thinking he'll care much if I sell the house."

"Well, da— sorry I really am trying to quit cussing—I meant for Pete's sake." Rachel grinned. "I leave town for a measly two-week vacation, and look what happens. You turn your entire life upside down."

It was scary *and* exciting to think about all she'd done in the last few weeks. On her own. Well, her cousin at the bank had helped her with the business plan and figuring out the financing. "I guess you better keep your trips shorter from now on." Lizzie laughed as a smile spread across her face.

"I predict David is going to pitch a fit. He didn't want to be married to you anymore, but he's not going to like you selling the house or opening the store. It's that whole control thing he has going."

"He'll just have to deal with it. I mean really, what can he do about it?"

"Cause a fuss? Tell you what you should be doing? You know, his usual crap." Rachel scowled. She had been just as enamored with David in high school as every other girl at school. But when David showed an interest in Lizzie, Rachel had backed off. Then, over the years, when David the high school football star became David the self-centered jerk, Rachel stood firmly by Lizzie's side.

"Let him. I'm just really happy with all this."

"I think I'm almost jealous."

Lizzie laughed. "Jealous? Whatever for?"

"You're trying something new. Moving, opening a store. Oh, I love my life, but it just sounds so exciting to be doing something all new."

It was exciting. She got up every morning with her head full of ideas. She carried a notebook with her everywhere. She'd researched like businesses, and one lady in Colorado who she'd met on an internet forum had been incredibly kind and given her a ton of information. She felt younger, more alive than she had in a long time. In a weird twist of energy, she'd started walking every morning. Early morning, before most people were up. When the sky was a pinkish-blue color and the heat of the day was just a future thought.

"You make me feel like a slug. Are you going to still have time for me?"

Lizzie detected a hint of honesty in the teasing way Rachel asked the question. "Of course I am." She was relieved to see Rachel smile.

"I think it's a perfect choice for you. My house would be a mess if you hadn't helped me decorate it. And by helped, I mean you picked out everything, and yet you made it feel exactly like I wanted it. Like it's perfect for Ronnie and me. And, you know, everyone is always asking your advice. I could really see this working."

Lizzie chewed her lip, overwhelmed by the enormity of the changes in her life. "What if it doesn't work out?" Even through all her excitement, the fear was real.

"You won't fail. Dam… darn it, Lizzie, you are good at this stuff. You know how to put all this decorating stuff together. You always find the most incredible pieces when you go antiquing. This is going to work."

Patsy came up to the table. "You girls ready to order?"

"We'll start with two double devil's chocolate cake slices, extra fudge sauce on top. Then we'll go from there. We're celebrating." Rachel handed the menus to Patsy.

Lizzie grinned. Only Rachel would insist on dessert to celebrate and forgo a real lunch.

"Two double devils coming up."

Rachel broke into a wide grin and waved her spoon. "And I'm going to help you. I mean, I can't help you do the design stuff, but I can help you open the shop. It will be great fun. I need a project. Ronnie is just out of town way too much these days. This is going to be fabulous."

"You want to help me open the shop?" Lizzie couldn't really imagine Rachel helping with the deep clean the place needed or the painting, but her friend had her heart in the

71

right place. And she had seemed fairly lost lately with Ronnie gone so much.

"I do. I'll be a big help. You'll see." Rachel bobbed her head, and her red hair danced across her shoulders.

"I've got a lot to do, and I need to find a new place to live." She was suddenly overwhelmed with everything that needed to be done.

"This is the most exciting thing that's happened to us in a long time." Rachel's amber eyes sparkled with delight.

She really felt like it was happening to *her*... not to *them*, not to Rachel... but she certainly didn't fault her friend's enthusiasm. And who knows, maybe Rachel would actually help her. Or at least she would mean to.

6

Gabe pushed through the door to the general store. What kind of town still had a general store? Well, Wind Chime Beach did. Over time it had turned into mostly a hardware store. The big Piggly Wiggly grocery store had seized the food market. The chain department stores had stolen the clothes market. But the general store still claimed a hold on the basic odds and ends of the hardware market. At least until the new discount hardware store they were building out on the interstate opened.

The cool air washed over him along with the smells of leather and oil. He'd loved this place as a kid. Back then, Old Man Henderson had an old-fashioned soda machine in the corner that had the coldest, almost icy sodas. He and his friends would pop in here after sports practice and grab a soda, then cross the street to the city park and sit under the live oak tree and talk. Tell stories, really. Stories got bigger and taller as the years went on. Tales of their sexual conquests, mostly based on a tiny bit of fact and a whole lot of fiction.

He wandered the store and grabbed a new ceiling fixture for his mother's closet. The old pull chain light in her closet wouldn't stay on. She had to keep holding the chain for the light to work. He needed some paint for the bedroom he was staying in. Someone somewhere along the line had decided that a shocking turquoise blue was a good color for a bedroom. He didn't think so. He chose a pale neutral color.

There was a woman at the end of the paint aisle carefully poring over a color card, her face a mask of concentration. Her brown hair scraped across her shoulders as she looked up and held the cards where there was better light and pursed her lips covered in a pale pink shade of lipstick. He shouldn't stare, but her intensity drew him in.

She looked over at him. Had she felt his gaze?

"I can't decide." She gave a rueful smile and a tiny shrug of her shoulders.

He covered the few steps between them. "What are you painting?"

"My store. I'm opening a store. An interior design and home decor shop. I'm thinking I need a neutral so it won't clash with what I do with each room of the store. Or maybe I need to paint the rooms different colors, but colors that go well together." She chewed her lips.

He held up his paint can. "I went with neutral. Not very adventurous, I'm afraid. Plus I have no idea what colors go together. But I am planning on covering up some hideous turquoise." He reached out his hand. "Gabe Smith, by the way."

"Lizzie Duncan. Nice to meet you."

"If you're looking for my vote, I'd say to go with the colors if you have an eye for what blends together. I don't. I just know I can't wake up to a turquoise room day after day."

"Did you just move here?"

"Yep, just moved back a bit ago."

"Where are you living?"

"Back at our old house. We used to live here. It's out off of Three Bend Road."

"One of those farms backing up to Willow Creek?"

"That's the one."

"So you used to live here?"

"Lots of years ago. Moved away when I was in high school."

She scanned his face, but there was no flicker of recognition. Good. He glanced at her hand and saw she wasn't wearing a wedding ring but had a smooth silver bracelet on one slender wrist, and a man's Tag Heuer watch on the other. Somehow the man's style watch seemed to fit her perfectly.

He didn't really recognize her, either. Though he vaguely thought she might have been a handful of years behind him in school. Like maybe a freshman when he was a senior. Maybe. He was a horrible judge of women's ages, so he wasn't even going to guess.

"Well, welcome back."

"Thanks." He picked up his paint cans. "Good luck with that decision."

He picked up a few more supplies and headed up to the cash register. The old jangling register had been replaced with a slick computerized model. Too bad. A lot of things had changed here in Wind Chime.

"That be it for you?" The young boy behind the counter started to ring up the sale.

"That's it."

He paid for his items and turned to leave.

"Hey, Johnny, when you have a minute, will you mix up these paint colors for me?" Lizzie stood at the end of the paint aisle.

"Sure thing, Miz Duncan."

"I decided on going with some colors. The heck with neutrals. I'm going bold."

Gabe smiled at her. Somehow he knew she'd go with colors. He bet she'd pull it off too.

"Where's your shop?"

"It's over one Magnolia Street. Have you seen that area? Magnolia Street from about First Street to Third. It's all been rehabbed and it's full of shops, offices, cafes. My place is on the corner of Magnolia and Rosebud Lane."

"Haven't been by there. I'll have to check it out, thanks."

"Stop by my shop in about a month. I should have it up and running by then."

"I'll do that. What's it called?"

Lizzie laughed a contagious siren of laughter. "If only I knew... a bit stuck on that."

"I'll stop by."

He was rewarded with another of her

warm, friendly smiles. Which was great. But she might not be so friendly if she ever found out why they'd left town in the first place.

7

Sara Jane snagged a pair of her husband's pants from the back of the chair in their bedroom. Why the man couldn't hang up a pair of pants when he took them off was beyond her. She crossed the room, carefully straightening the pants to align the crease in each leg. She went into the walk-in closet and grabbed a wooden hanger from the clothes rod. As she hung up the pants, a scrap of paper fell to the floor. Steven never remembered to empty his pants pockets either. She sighed as she fished around on the floor by his shoes to retrieve the paper.

The pink slip of paper mocked her with its faint print. New Haven Hotel, Sea Point, Florida. The date was last Tuesday. When Steven was supposed to be in Atlanta, not fifty miles down the road. Which meant he had found yet another playmate, this one closer to home. She let his pants slip to the floor in a discarded heap.

Her heart skipped a beat, then the anger welled up in her. The anger that she'd spent so long keeping tucked tightly beneath the surface because it wasn't allowed. It boiled over, popping and scorching. She swiped at the tears that slipped down her cheeks. A half moan, half scream escaped. She grabbed at Steven's clothes, jerking them off hangers, dropping them on the floor. She dumped out his neatly folded sweaters and swept his ties from the tie rack.

She looked around, out of control now, but she didn't care. She walked out of the closet and slashed her arm across the top of his dresser, crashing all his things to the floor. A Rolex watch—one of three he had—his box of cufflinks, a stack of his work papers. She walked over to the table by the window, grabbed a vase of white roses—not the colorful, cheerful daisies she preferred—and threw it against the wall. Smashed glass and pieces of rose petals scattered across the carpet.

Looking around at the havoc she'd created, she was surprisingly soothed by it.

She walked back into the closet and sank to the floor, sitting among the shoes and clothes, and stared at the pink slip of paper. She wasn't sure how long she sat there and didn't really care.

Then she finally got to her knees, crawled to the far end of the closet, and grabbed a way-too-expensive suitcase. This playmate of Steven's was one too many. The numerous times he'd been caught, he'd halfway sworn he was through to placate her. Not that she'd believed him, of course. And now, he'd proven her right. Again.

And it was just too cliche to catch him this time with a receipt in his pocket because last time had been lipstick on his collar. The man wasn't very good at hiding his indiscretions. She'd suggested counseling after finding out about his first affair, but he'd yelled at her and said he'd never talk to some ridiculous shrink.

She carefully picked her way through the tossed clothes, broken glass, and chaos that was now the room she'd shared with Steven for so many years. She walked over to the bed, smoothed out the wrinkled pink receipt, and placed it precisely on Steven's pillow.

Two large suitcases and a carry-on later, she walked out the front door. She stopped at the bank, took out a chunk of money, drove across to a bank on Belle Island, and opened a new account in her name only. She paused to call her lawyer, but then she realized that her lawyer was really Steven's lawyer. She'd need to find someone new. She snapped her finger. Yes, that sharp young lady she'd met at a fundraiser for the library. She used her phone to find the number online, then left a message for Michelle Willings, attorney-at-law, to call her.

Then she had absolutely no idea where to go.

She sat in her car, drumming her fingers on the steering wheel before finally deciding to head to the town of Moonbeam. She hadn't been there in years. The town was filled with small shops and a delightful wharf that extended out into Moonbeam Bay. She'd actually asked Steven if they could go there for a long weekend and stay at The Cabot, a recently restored hotel on the bay. But he just laughed at her and said old hotels in small towns weren't his thing, then suggested a trip to

Chicago and a stay on Michigan Avenue. But that trip had never happened. He'd probably gone there with one of his… his… What did she call his numerous flings?

She grabbed her phone again to search for places to stay in Moonbeam. Steven would never think to look for her there. There was still The Cabot to consider, but she wanted something less grand. Quieter. She found the website of a small resort. Blue Heron Cottages. Its brightly painted cottages called to her, and it was directly on the beach. She was in luck. They had a room. It was only a little over an hour away from Wind Chime Beach, but far enough that she shouldn't run into anyone she knew.

But the drive gave her time to think way too much. Think about her marriage. Think about Steven's many affairs. With each mile that rolled beneath her, she felt the tiniest bit freer. By the time she got to Moonbeam, she could finally breathe again.

When she arrived at The Blue Heron Cottages, the owner, Violet, checked her in but discreetly asked no questions when Sara Jane said she wasn't sure how long she was staying.

Sara Jane lugged her suitcase up the front steps to the peach cottage and entered. The front room was flooded with light from the late afternoon sunshine. She crossed to the bedroom and flopped onto the high double bed, staring up at the lacy canopy. She'd always wanted a canopied bed. But there had been no convincing Steven of that. Anyway, if she had convinced him, he'd have wanted some dark depressing canopy anyway. Nothing like this light, airy room. A small cherry writing desk and caned chair sat under one of the windows. Her curiosity got the better of her, and she slid off the bed and crossed to the bathroom.

She actually sighed when she looked in the bathroom. A big, clawfoot bathtub slumbered under the window, with fluffy white towels draped over the edge and gleaming chrome fixtures. The sunlight fractured and splintered through the frosted window, tossing smatterings of light across the tiled black and white floor.

Sara Jane returned to the front room and sank onto the rocking chair in the corner. She started rocking gently. Back and forth. A slow, steady rhythm. Anything to soothe her jangled nerves and calm her anger.

Her carry-on bag rested by her feet, full of jewelry she'd been given as gifts through the years. If the money ran out before she figured out what she was going to do, she'd just sell off the jewelry. It didn't mean much to her anyway. It was always garish and overdone. Always in gold instead of the silver she preferred. Steven was generous with his gifts of jewelry. Only, it was like he was giving the pieces to himself. Baubles for his wife to wear to show how important he was.

Sara Jane fingered the simple silver necklace her grandmother had given her for high school graduation. She hadn't worn it in years. But this morning, after finding the pink hotel receipt, she had plopped the gold necklace with the diamond drop into her jewelry bag and put on the simple silver one.

Back and forth. Back and forth. The chair creaked ever so softly as she rocked.

Now what was she supposed to do? Her days were carefully planned around Steven's schedule. When he wanted dinner, what he wanted for dinner. What errands he wanted her to run. The late afternoon stretched out in front of her like a delicious dessert tray of chocolates too tempting to choose just one. A slow smile spread across her face as she relaxed.

Really relaxed for the first time in she didn't know how long. Her muscles softened and she dragged in an intoxicating breath of air that tasted like freedom.

Boy was Steven going to be ticked off when he got home tonight, expecting her to have everything set for the three couples he'd invited over for dinner. Some new partner in his company, some politician he was thick as thieves with, and the man he hoped would be the next mayor of Wind Chime. And their wives, of course. Though the men would retreat to the den and leave her to entertain the women. Three total strangers to her.

But tonight…

Tonight Steven would have to figure that all out on his own.

The satisfaction of that thought brought a smile to her lips.

8

Sara Jane opened her eyes and squinted against the bright light streaming into the room. Something was wrong. Steven always insisted the curtains be drawn shut and the bedroom kept dark. She rolled over to look at the clock.

That was not her clock.

She rolled back again and stared up at the canopy over the bed. She was alone. Blissfully, totally alone. She stretched and sat up, reaching over to snag her glasses. The room was so lovely. Nothing overly masculine like the rooms she'd spent the last forty-ish years of her life in. It had the perfect beachy feel to it.

She started a pot of coffee in the small kitchenette in the front room and then unpacked some clothes. When the coffee was finished, she grabbed a large mug of it and sat doing absolutely nothing but enjoying the delicious brew.

She glanced at her phone. The one she'd turned off after Steven had called and texted a dozen times last evening. She'd ignored all of the messages and texts. He'd probably exploded with anger at the insult of her not taking his call. Not to mention the bedroom she'd left in shambles. Steven detested any kind of disorder. Ha. That wasn't her problem now, was it?

She ignored the phone, still, and headed to the bathroom for a long, decadent bath. The room soon filled with steam and the faint scent of lavender from the bubble bath she dumped liberally into the tub. She slipped into the warm water and let it lap around her, soothe her, relax her. No surprise, her muscles felt like they'd been strung as tight as a rubber band. They were always that way when she dealt with Steven. But yesterday in the rocking chair, and now in her luxurious bath... she could finally relax. Just... enjoy.

She knew she had a lot to face. Steven would find her eventually. She needed to talk to Rachel but didn't want to put her in the position of standing in between her parents. She needed to figure out a place to live. This would do for a bit, but she would need something more permanent while she figured out what she wanted to do. She couldn't just move away from her daughter, but she didn't want to live anywhere near Steven. She'd have to sort that all out. Later. She'd sort it out later.

Steven would first be furious, then eventually, if true to form, he'd apologize and swear he'd never do it again. His mother would imply that Sara Jane was lucky to have him. And if by some chance his mother found out about the affair, she'd also imply that was Sara Jane's fault. It was all so tiring, and she just didn't want to do that dance again any more than she wanted to go through a divorce.

She really did need to contact her daughter, but she wasn't quite ready to face the music. Rachel would be upset. She might be a grown woman, but she wouldn't want her parents to divorce. Honestly, Rachel didn't like any upheaval in her life. She'd been given everything and things had always come easily to her. Anything and everything she wanted. She'd even cheated death when Lizzie saved her that day at the river. Maybe she'd just text her that she was out of town for a few days but not explain everything yet. Give herself a few days' peace.

Sara Jane sank down into the tub and slipped under the water. The warmth covered her but didn't keep out the fears and doubts racing through her mind. She popped out of the water when she could no longer hold her breath.

Okay, here was her plan. She was going to have some more of the good, strong coffee and hopefully find some decadent sweet pastry. Try the lawyer again. See if it was possible to stay here at Blue Heron Cottages for a week. And she needed to find a store to pick up a few things she'd forgotten to pack. Better go get them now before Steven canceled their credit cards. Could she even get a credit card in her own name? She'd never had one.

Okay, more coffee first, then a pad of paper and a list of things to do. She worked best from lists. She grabbed the fluffy towel and wrapped up in it, tucking it securely above her breasts. A quick swipe at the mirror to clear the steam, and she could see herself standing there. Wet hair hanging on her shoulders, skin bright from the heat. She just stood there staring, then broke into a big grin.

The whole day ahead was hers. All hers. To do with what she wanted, when she wanted. First thing was to avoid Steven for as long as possible.

She was sure it was so wrong to feel this good about wanting to divorce her husband. But she'd tried for so many years. Did what he wanted, listened to him berate her every move. And she'd turned her back on his affairs. Even when he swore it wouldn't happen again. But it did. It always happened again.

But the realization that she didn't have to put up with any of that was exciting, thrilling— a very heady feeling. Although she felt guilty about feeling that way.

She slipped on her favorite black skirt— made of two layers of t-shirt type material. It just went to say that Steven hated it. She reached into the suitcase and pulled out a simple white blouse. She was going shopping today too. For some exquisitely bright turquoise top. It would go great with her silver jewelry.

She walked out of the cottage and saw Violet across the way, sweeping a porch on the yellow cottage. "Hey, Sara Jane. Did you sleep okay?" Violet came over to greet her.

"Wonderfully, thank you. My room is just

gorgeous. Light. Airy. I love the antiques you have in there."

"I want to do all the rooms in antiques and comfortable furnishings. I'm just slowly getting around to it. I've only replaced the furniture in some of the cottages, but I still have some more to redo. They did all get updated mattresses and new chairs. The old ones were…" Violet shuddered. "Not fit to keep."

"Well, my cottage is lovely, and I was wondering if I could stay for a week."

"Of course." Still the model of discretion, Violet didn't ask a question about why Sara Jane was staying here. "I picked up some fresh cinnamon rolls from Sea Glass Cafe this morning. Would you like one?"

"That sounds great."

"I'll get it for you and you can have it out on the porch of your cottage if you'd like."

"Thanks, Violet. I think I'll do that."

She took the offered fresh baked cinnamon roll with too many calories to count and went back to her cottage for more coffee. She walked out onto the porch and sank down into a white wicker chair with deliciously plump cushions. She'd always wanted furniture just like this. Casual. Comfortable.

A light breeze stirred the leaves on the gardenia bushes flanking the porch. The sweet fragrance of the gardenias mingled with the sharp aroma of the coffee. The sun was just warm enough, but not too hot. Sara Jane took a deep breath. It was one of those moments she'd like to wrap up and keep to look at later when everything went to hell.

Look, she'd said a swear word. Well, *thought* one. "Went to hell." Sara Jane said the words out loud and grinned.

"Hell," she repeated, totally enjoying herself.

9

Lizzie looked up from where she was painting the front room of the shop. *Her shop.*

All the paperwork had gone through and it was all hers. She was painting a nice soft buttercream yellow that would blend in with the light mint green she'd painted in the next room and the muted teal in the next. The colors would provide a backdrop to the items she put on display in each room. Upstairs she was leaving the walls a neutral color to allow her to play more and change up things in those rooms.

She'd already started a Pinterest board for her decorating ideas, pinning rooms and furniture and decor that she thought went well together. As soon as she took pictures of the design work she'd done for Rachel and Ronnie, those would go on Pinterest, too. But Rachel had insisted the cleaning lady had to come before Lizzie took pictures, so they'd scheduled it for this afternoon after Rachel's regular weekly cleaning.

She glanced at the time, then down at her paint-splattered shirt. She really should run home and get cleaned up and over to Rachel's. She wanted to open the window treatments in the back of Rachel's house to let in the warm afternoon sun for her photos.

It had been a crazy busy week of getting her house all clean and ready for showings. She didn't have the luxury of a cleaning lady like Rachel did, so she'd scrubbed it all herself until it was bright and sparkly. Hopefully with a lot of her things packed away and the house staged to show better, she would get her full asking price. She needed every penny.

A shadow fell across the flooring from the open front door. Lizzie glanced up. Gabe Smith stood in the doorway, smiling. "Hi there. Hope you don't mind. I was driving past and saw the door open. Thought I'd just pop in and say hi."

She balanced her paintbrush on the edge of the paint can and wiped her hand on a rag she had partially tucked in her pocket to catch drips.

"Gabe, hi. Come in. How did you know this was my shop?"

He laughed. "Lizzie's Interior Design and Decor Shop."

"Oh, right. I just got the sign hung over the front window."

He stepped inside and slowly looked around the room. "This looks nice. The light yellow really makes the room bright and cheery."

"That's what I'm hoping for." She nodded in pleasure at his praise. "Say, did you get your turquoise walls covered?"

"I did." He shook his head and scowled. "Took three coats of paint to cover that sucker up. But it looks good now."

"Those bright colors can be hard to cover with a light color."

"I persevered and won. Gabe one. Turquoise walls zero." His brown eyes twinkled with amusement.

"Always nice to conquer the wall, isn't it?"

"It was. Now I'm in need of a desk. And I don't want it to be just any desk. It needs... character. All wood. Don't care if it's scuffed up or anything." He shrugged. "It's a writer thing for me. I ended up not moving my old desk because I'd held it together with glue and clamps one time too many. Figured it wouldn't survive the move."

"You're an author?" She eyed him, digesting this new piece of information.

"Yes, mystery books."

"Ah, I'm more of a romance book reader, though I do enjoy the occasional legal thriller. Though, I have read some nice cozy mysteries. One had this cat as an actual main character and it was so funny."

He laughed. "Mine are a bit grittier than that. But you gotta love a good cozy mystery. Great escapism. Anyway, I was hoping you might already have some furniture. Even a desk. Guess I'm still too early."

"I'm actually going shopping the day after tomorrow. I got a rental van and I'm hitting some antique malls for items for the shop. Want me to keep an eye out for you?"

He chewed his lip. "Think maybe I could tag along? I kind of know what I like when I see it. I just don't know where to shop around here. But I've got a good strong back. I could help you load up things. Or would I just get in your way?"

His offer surprised her, but she certainly wasn't opposed to any help she could get. "No, that sounds great. We'll see if we can find you a desk and I'll blatantly use you for your strong back." The heat of a blush crept over her cheeks. Would he think she was flirting with him?

"That sounds perfect. I'll meet you here?"

Okay, good. He showed no reaction to her remark. She was just overreacting and second-guessing herself. She cleared her throat. "I want to get an early start. Is eight okay with you?"

"Sure is. And I appreciate this."

"I think I'm getting the better end of the deal."

"Maybe, but I keep thinking if I find the perfect desk, the words will come to me and I can get back to my writing."

"Writer's block?"

"Something like that. The thing is, I have two different characters in this book that I still haven't decided which one actually did the crime."

She eyed him in surprise. "Really? You don't know everything before you sit down to write the book?"

"Don't I wish I were that type of writer, but no. It doesn't work that way for me. I have to kind of feel my way through the story.

Sometimes the bad guy is someone I never saw coming." He grinned at her. "So I have high hopes this desk will help my plot problems. I hope it will actually reveal *whodunnit.*"

"Hope it works that way." She wasn't exactly sure how a desk could help that, but then she wasn't a writer. Who was she to argue if she was getting a helper out of the deal?

"I should let you get back to work with your painting. I'm just heading to pick up some things for Mom. It appears she's on a baking spree. She's never happier than puttering in the kitchen and poring over recipe books. I'm pretty certain her kitchen is her favorite place on Earth."

With a little smile—*he had dimples*—he turned and slipped out the door. She stood there, looking at the empty doorway. He seemed like a nice guy. Certainly willing to help out his mother with her move back here. His name sounded kind of familiar, but maybe she'd seen one of his books.

She shrugged and grabbed the paintbrush to clean it. Better hurry if she didn't want to miss the afternoon light at Rachel's.

Lizzie took dozens and dozens of photographs at Rachel's. Some photos of entire rooms and some closeups of items she'd picked out for Rachel to place on end tables or shelving units. She wasn't quite sure what all she'd need, but she wanted to make sure she had a lot to choose from. She'd been lucky to get there right when the sun was pouring through the family room windows. Perfect warm light filtered in, but not too bright.

Rachel followed her from room to room, padding around barefoot and kind of getting in the way, not that Lizzie complained. "You've folded that afghan three times," Rachel accused, obviously getting bored with the whole photo-taking thing.

"I know. But I'm not sure which way will look the best in the photo." She set the throw down one last time... over the arm of the couch and draping loosely over the edge. A bit of sunlight spilled across it. Yes, that was perfect. Hopefully.

While she did think she had a knack for design, she'd be competing against people who had gone to school and gotten fancy degrees in design. Could she match up to designers like that? Was she crazy to even think she could do this? That thought made her adjust the afghan one more time as the nagging doubts swirled through her. She placed the blanket just so, letting it spill over the back of the couch then added an off-white textured throw pillow resting beside it.

"You done yet? 'Cause I have a bottle of pinot grigio chilling in the fridge calling our names. Can you stay and have a drink? Ronnie's out of town. Again." Rachel's face held a hint of a pout.

She glanced around the room. She probably did have enough photos, and she didn't have the heart to refuse Rachel after she'd let her come and take all these pictures. She'd hoped to hurry home and sort through the photos and maybe even get some uploaded to Pinterest. But Rachel's eyes pleaded with her. "Sure, I'll have a glass. Then I really should go."

"Perfect. Let's have it out on the patio." Rachel grabbed two glasses of wine and led the way outside. The patio was shaded by large trees and had comfortable come-sit-on-me furniture. Lizzie had picked out that furniture for Rachel, too. They sank onto two side-by-side chairs.

She took a sip of the wine, savoring the

taste. Rachel could afford the best wines, and this one did not disappoint.

"So, I got this weird text from Mom." Rachel kicked off her shoes and put her feet up on an ottoman. "She's out of town. I think Daddy did something to tick her off. She just said she needed to get away for a few days. That doesn't really sound like her, does it?"

Lizzie thought back on all the years she'd known Sara Jane. "No, I can't remember your mother ever going away without your father."

"I wonder if they had a fight or something. Daddy can be so clueless. Though, Mom seems to just accept him as he is. I tried calling her but she didn't pick up."

She didn't know how Sara Jane put up with all of Mr. Benoit's transgressions… and they were many. Critical. Judgmental. Not to mention he cheated on his wife. Maybe Sara Jane had gotten her fill of it. If so, good for her. "Maybe she just needs some time to sort things out. Or maybe she just needed a little break."

"I guess. It's kind of strange though. And Daddy hasn't said a word."

"I don't know, Rach." It did seem unusual.

Rachel lifted her hair up off her neck, letting the breeze cool her, then let her curls drop back down around her shoulders. "So, how's the shop coming along? I keep meaning to get over there and help you paint."

And she knew her friend meant it. Rachel probably *had* planned on coming to help. But somehow just never really made it into the shop. She always had the best of intentions, though. "It's coming along great. I'm actually almost finished painting. I've scrubbed everything. Floors, windows. And an electrician got the old chandeliers working. They're beautiful. I pulled down the old drapes... they were in terrible shape. I'll find some material and make new window treatments."

"See... you can say things like you'll *make* windows treatments. I can't even buy them without your help." Rachel rolled her eyes at herself, then grinned. "I'm super lucky to have such a talented friend."

Rachel's compliment was probably her way of apologizing for not actually coming by and helping.

"Oh, and this guy that I met at the hardware store dropped in when he saw my door open. Gabe Smith. He's a writer. Mystery writer, he said."

"Gabe Smith... I feel like I know that name.

But I can't place it. Smith is really common though. Maybe I saw one of his books." Rachel shrugged.

"Anyway, he wants a desk. He's going to go antiquing with me this week."

"Really?" Rachel's eyebrow rose, and she sent a knowing look. "Interesting."

"Why is that interesting?"

"Because... some guy is spending the day with you."

"He just wants help finding a desk. I told him I was opening a design and decor shop when I ran into him at the hardware store. Anyway, I'm going to use his brawn to help load up furniture I find for the shop. I'm not doing all antiques, as much as I love them. But I know some people aren't into them. I'm going to get a simple white, overstuffed couch for one of the display rooms. And one room I'm going to do with a more modern vibe. I want to be able to showcase all kinds of decor. Then I'll have items for sale, too. Or they can hire me to decorate a room... or a house." She grinned. "I'd love to get some big clients. Like someone who just moved into a new house. I need some influx of cash."

"I'm sure you'll be a smashing success. Don't

worry, I'll brag about you to everyone I see." Rachel swatted away a fly buzzing around her in lazy circles.

"Gabe said he used to live here. They moved back into his childhood home. He and his mother. Said he's staying with her for a bit while she gets adjusted to the move."

"He sounds like a nice guy. A good son." Rachel sighed. "If I ever have a son, I hope I get one just like him who will take care of me when I'm old."

She wanted to encourage Rachel and say it would happen. But she knew that Rachel and Ronnie had been trying for years to get pregnant and no luck. In the last year Rachel had gotten more and more depressed every month when she'd found out, once again, she wasn't pregnant. She gave Rachel a look that she hoped was a cross between sympathy and encouragement.

She finished her wine and stood. "I really should go."

"Oh, come on. Stay and have another glass."

"Rachel, I really need to go. I've got a showing for the house tomorrow and I want to make sure it's all looking good. Plus, I'm beat. I can barely raise my arms after all that painting."

"Okay." Rachel stood, and that pout she got when she didn't get her way settled on her face. "I bet you really are going to get too busy to hang out with me."

She hugged her friend. "That will never happen. You just need to give me some time to get things settled."

"Did you find a place to live yet? I hope it's close by. I saw a for sale sign on Wisteria Street. That's only a couple blocks away."

A couple of blocks away and way too expensive for her. "No, I haven't found a place yet. I've already put some things in storage. And, of course, David took a lot of things when he left. So I could really do just a small apartment for a bit." But she really, really needed to find a place. Or she'd be living out at the chain motel on the interstate, something she did not want to do.

10

Sara Jane thoroughly enjoyed herself over the next few days. She went shopping at a lovely boutique in town called Barbara's... owned by Margaret. She laughed when Margaret told her that Barbara hadn't owned it for years, but the name never changed, owner to owner.

It was a new experience, picking out clothes that she loved and not taking into account anyone's opinion but her own. She picked out a multicolored skirt that swirled around her knees. A selection of brightly colored tops. A pair of capris. Steven hated pants that length. Said they were silly. So after remembering his remarks, she went and picked out a second pair. And comfortable flats. No more wearing heels all the time because Steven insisted. Even for her backyard parties, she'd worn heels.

One day she went to the wharf and browsed the shops. There she found a lovely silver bracelet and a print by a local artist named Heather Parker. It was a serene scene of a woman walking on the beach. Not that she had a house to put it in now. But she loved it and bought it. Steven would hate it, but that didn't matter anymore.

She found a bright wrap and draped it around her shoulders in a bohemian style that thrilled her. Everything she picked out just spoke to her. No more dressing to please someone else. She dressed to please herself, a strange and heady feeling.

Her grandmother had always had a shawl wrapped around her shoulders, and this made her feel strangely connected to the woman again. She'd been raised by her grandmother and missed her terribly, even all these years later. Her grandmother had told her not to marry Steven. That he wasn't a good match for her. Her grandmother was a wise, wise woman…

She finally called Rachel and told her she just needed some time alone without telling her what had happened. She could tell from

Rachel's voice that she probably had figured it out, though. It wasn't like Steven's affairs were much of a secret.

Rachel said that Steven had finally contacted her, asking where Sara Jane was, then yelled at her for not telling him. But Rachel could honestly tell him she had no idea, and they both agreed that was for the best, though worry laced her daughter's voice. She'd done her best to assure her that everything was fine and she'd be back to Wind Chime soon.

Ronnie was out of town this week, and Rachel would often come by their house when her husband was gone. Sara Jane figured Rachel wasn't going over to hang out with just Steven. She didn't mean to worry anyone. And she was certain Steven wasn't worried. He was *furious*. But she wasn't ready to go back. She'd have to soon, to figure out what she was going to do. But not yet.

Thank goodness she'd inherited some stock when her grandmother passed away. Although they'd had hardly any money when she was growing up, her grandfather had still invested in a small company. Her grandmother—never a fan of Steven's—had put the stock in a trust so he couldn't touch it. It was worth a nice sum of money now. Not like the ridiculous amount of money Steven's family had, but enough that she should be able to find a small place to live and take her time figuring out her life from there.

Steven's family's money. It had never felt like any of that money was hers. Even when she helped him climb the ladder at work. Even with the countless business dinners she hosted. Even with everything she did to make his home life easy. She took care of the house, handled calling people for repairs, took his clothes to the dry cleaners. Her whole life had revolved around making him a success and making sure everything was just perfect for him at home. Not that he'd ever thought what she did amounted to much. She'd called the wrong repair company, according to Steven. She'd let the dry cleaner over-starch his business shirts. She hadn't shined the pair of shoes he wanted to wear. The towels weren't hung perfectly straight. It went on and on.

When Rachel started grade school, Sara Jane wanted to get a part-time job, but Steven had absolutely forbidden it. *Why had she let him do that?*

He gave her a grocery allowance. An *allowance*. And she had to run every purchase past him. It was all so tiring, but somewhere along the way, she'd just accepted it as her life. She'd chosen to marry him. She just hadn't realized the man he really was. While they dated, he was charming, and she said yes to marrying him without any reservations. But it didn't take long for the real Steven to appear.

She was often the recipient of snide remarks at those business dinners that she worked so hard to host for him. Sometimes she'd see pity in the eyes of the guests. Sometimes they just laughed along with him.

How had she let that go on so long? Why had she? Where was her backbone? How had she slipped into a shadow of the person she'd been when she was younger? And for that, she chided herself. She'd let it happen.

But all that was over now. She'd been in contact with her lawyer and she was determined to start the process of the divorce when she got back to Wind Chime. When she could talk herself into returning. She wasn't ready for that yet. Though each day she kept expecting Steven to show up and start shouting at her. She wouldn't be surprised if he hired a private detective to track her down. Rachel said he was beyond furious with her.

He could just be angry. She didn't care. She was no longer going to dance to the tune he wanted her to follow.

She carried her packages from yet another shopping expedition into her cottage. She hung up the clothes—a few simple blouses. And she was proud of how little she'd spent on her new clothes. Not the designer clothing she wore before. Just nicely made, simple clothes. Comfortable outfits. She slipped on her new bracelet and grabbed the new book she'd picked up. A mystery by Gabe Smith, a new author to her. She rarely found time to read with all the demands that Steven made on her time… plus he rolled his eyes at her if he saw her reading fiction. He still read the paper… in print. And he read some investment magazines. He considered reading fiction a waste of time.

She went outside to the porch, and Violet waved and walked over. "So, did you have a nice time?"

"I did. I bought a few more outfits. And this bracelet I found at a cute little shop on Main Street." She held out her arm. "They said it was made by a designer named Whitney Layton in Indigo Bay, South Carolina. Isn't it pretty?"

"Oh, it is. Silver with sea glass chips. What

nice workmanship." Violet admired the jewelry. "I'm glad you had a good time. I was just going to take a break and have some tea out on the porch of my cottage. Would you like to join me?"

"That would be wonderful."

"Come on over and I'll get it and be out in a minute."

She crossed to the owner's cottage and sank onto one of the wonderful chairs on the porch, vowing to get some chairs just like these when she finally got a place of her own.

Violet brought a tray with a pitcher of tea and two glasses. She sat down and poured their iced tea. "It sure is getting warm, isn't it?"

"It is. Pretty muggy today. But your ceiling fan out here on the porch stirs it around a bit at least."

"One of the first things I did when I got this place."

"How long have you owned it?" She took a sip of the tea. Just the right amount of sweetness.

"Not long. I just recently opened. It used to be called Murphy's, and it was pretty run down when I got it. Which was lucky, because prices have gone up and I'd never have been able to afford it now. I put in central air-conditioning in each cottage. Repainted. Redid plumbing. Fixed roofs. I feel like I'm slowly making progress. I got it to the point where I thought I could open. But there's still more I want to do."

"Well, it's lovely."

"It's getting there." Violet stretched out her tanned legs.

Sara Jane envied so much about the woman. Her self-assuredness. The fact she owned her own business. "I admire your talent with finding this place and making it so lovely. I saw it on a travel blog when I was looking for a place to stay."

"Ah, so that's how you found me."

"I've wanted to come to Moonbeam and stay at The Cabot. I suggested it to my husband once, but his idea of a vacation was a high-rise hotel on Michigan Avenue in Chicago."

"Ah, to each their own. Not everyone likes staying at an old remodeled hotel."

"But then I saw your website with the cottages and I just knew I wanted to stay here. Not so large and crowded with guests. I'd have some privacy. And now that—" She paused, not sure if she should continue. But Violet was a good listener, and she could use someone like that right now. "I've recently left my husband. I'm staying here until I can figure out what exactly I want to do."

"I see." Violet reached over and gently touched her arm.

"He… he wasn't exactly faithful to our marriage vows. And it was finally one time too many."

"I'm sorry, that must be painful." A hint of surprise flitted across Violet's face, but none of the pity that Sara Jane feared she might get. She didn't want pity.

"It was. Well, it was the first time I found out. I could barely breathe and it just about did me in. I couldn't believe he'd do that. But he swore he wouldn't do it again. Until he did. Then he promised again. I finally got numb to the whole thing. But we've been married for over forty years."

"It takes a lot of strength to walk away from a life you've shared with someone, even a life with problems like that. But a woman needs to do what's right for herself."

"I'm embarrassed I stayed with him that long. I was so foolish. At first, it was because of Rachel, our daughter. But then she grew up and… I just stayed. I was raised that you live with the consequences of your choices. But I finally just... couldn't. I mean my husband doesn't even like me, much less love me. But his family doesn't believe in divorce. So he just let me take care of his home life and his business parties and..." She dashed away an unexpected tear. "I just never thought this is how my life would turn out. Sometimes I was afraid I'd grow old and just sit out on my front porch, all alone, while Steven was still out running around with one of his women. Was that all I had to look forward to?"

Violet stayed silent, but the support in her silence was deafening.

She looked out into the courtyard with the pretty gardenia bushes and palm trees and one large live oak stretching its limbs out, shading Violet's porch. So peaceful. If only she could hide out here forever.

She turned back to Violet. "Sometimes I dream about what it would be like to meet some man who saw me for who I really was and liked me just like that. Didn't want to change me or correct how I do things. Who thought I was pretty." She shrugged. "Who is going to think that now that I'm in my fifties, with a bit of a menopause paunch, and my hair is graying?

Well, it would be if Steven hadn't insisted I color it."

"It sounds like you had a lot to deal with."

"Sometimes it just exhausts me thinking about my life. I have a lot of if-not-for-Steven type thoughts. That's probably not what most married women think. Or do they? Do you think a lot of women settle for a marriage that doesn't make them happy? Are you really *allowed* to be happy? Is your happiness more important than your family's? I just don't know anymore. But I do know I can't go on like things were."

Violet leaned forward, looking directly into her eyes. "I believe we're all responsible for our own happiness. We have to make the changes we can to better our lives. Some things we can't change. Some we can, though. If you go through life looking at the if-onlys but doing nothing about them, then you miss a lot of chances for happiness." Violet smiled and sat back again. "If I hadn't jumped in and bought this place—against the advice of everyone, mind you, especially my brother—I couldn't be as happy as I am with my life right now. I hope you can find your happiness. Find some peace. And please, stay here as long as you need."

"Thanks for listening to me."

"Sometimes we just need to talk it out, don't we?"

And they sat there in the warm afternoon, sipping their tea, and talk turned to lighter subjects. But she'd never forget Violet's words. "If you go through life looking at the if-onlys but do nothing about them…" Well, she was determined to do something about them. Determined to change the path her life had been on. Find some peace. Find some happiness.

She was divorcing Steven and planned to never step into their house again. She needed nothing from it. She was leaving with a clean slate. She sucked in a deep breath of the fragrant air, feeling alive and energized. Uncertain of what her future looked like, but not at all frightened to find out.

11

Gabe showed up right on time for their antiquing expedition dressed in jeans and a t-shirt. His hair was still a bit damp from his shower, and he smelled slightly of a fresh, evergreen woodsy scent. He stood in the doorway with the light streaming around him, silhouetting his muscular frame. "Morning. I'm all set. My back is ready to haul your furniture finds." He grinned at her. "At your service," he said with an exaggerated bow.

Lizzie laughed. "Come on, then. You and your back. I have a long day planned. There are a couple of towns a few hours away that are known for their antique shops."

They chatted as she drove to the first town. She told him all about her plans for her business. He talked about moving back to town with his mother. "She thinks my move is just a temporary one. But I really don't like to think of her living alone anymore. She's getting forgetful. She had a bad run of pneumonia that put her in the hospital. I just… well, I'd like to help her out and take care of her. Not that she lets me much." He laughed. "And there's always the possibility she'll throw me out when she gets tired of having me underfoot. But if that happens, I'll probably try to find a place of my own nearby."

"I doubt she'd throw you out."

"You never know with Mom. She likes to stay pretty independent. Except for driving. She got lost going to familiar places a few times. I think it really shook her up. She doesn't like to drive at night, either. So I drive her where she wants to go or run and pick things up for her." There wasn't any hint of impatience in his tone, and the way he shrugged gave Lizzie the impression it wasn't a big deal to him to be her chauffeur. "So, how about you? Your family?"

"I have one son, Eric. He's away at college. And my parents moved away to South Carolina to a retirement place. I know, most people move south to Florida to retire. My folks? Moved up north. It's a community of modular homes with a community center and a big pool. They like it." And didn't invite her to come visit. She hadn't seen them in a few years. But Gabe didn't need to know all those details. It's not like they'd ever really been that interested in her life. Her mother had been nothing like Sara Jane was to Rachel. Actually, Sara Jane had been more like a mother to her than her own mom.

He looked at her for a moment, a crease between his eyes. "And… your son's father?"

"That would be David. We're divorced. A year now. He's remarried."

Did she see a spark in his eyes? Nah, she was crazy. Guys didn't get interested in her. Never had. Except for David, and that had been… astonishing. She'd been so amazed when he asked her out. You know, after the whole Saving Rachel Incident. Anyway, what did she really know about men?

"Are you guys friends? Enemies?" Gabe shrugged. "Or if you prefer, we can drop the subject."

"We're… I don't know. I don't know how to describe David. He's one of those really good-looking men. The kind who shows up at Eric's soccer games with his suit jacket casually thrown over his shoulder and his tie loosened. He has that impossibly boyish face in a Rob Lowe-type way. I doubt if he'll look old when he's seventy-five."

Gabe nodded and let her continue. She wasn't quite sure why she was explaining all this to him. "Everyone in high school wanted to be his friend. Or his girlfriend. Or at least sleep with him. He took advantage of all of that, but it seemed like no one ever knew they were being used. I still don't know how he does that. Uses people, throws them aside, and they sit there blinking in the sunlight, not sure what hit them. But rarely do any of them get upset with David. Because somehow, someway, they figure it must be their own fault."

"Ah, I've known people like that." Gabe nodded.

"I've seen him be gentle with a new puppy, and I've seen him be absolutely ruthless about things that don't matter. Like a softball game." She paused and concentrated on the road. "But no one was more surprised than I was when he asked me out. My friend Rachel introduced us. Before I became friends with Rachel, I was kind of a nobody at school. But Rachel? She pulled me into her world. Anyway, my first date with

David was magical. He was such a gentleman. None of that reach and grope stuff. We talked. We laughed. It was out at a cookout by the river. I was so nervous. I felt like everyone was looking at me and thinking what is he doing with *her*?"

He frowned. "I can't picture you as a nobody. I mean, you're opening your own business. You seem to have business smarts and know what you want." He smiled. "Plus, you're pretty."

Was he flirting with her? Nah, men didn't do that with her.

She ignored the pretty remark. "You sure you want to hear all this?"

"I do."

She continued, "Anyway, for some reason that I'll never figure out, David fell for me. Hard. He'd bring me flowers and little gifts. Pick me up from work. Sit with me in the library and do homework, always holding my hand. Always paying attention to me. Listening to me. I'd never, ever had anyone in my life who'd listened to me like that. Certainly not my parents." She hadn't meant for that to slip out.

He raised an eyebrow but let her continue.

"We dated for two years in high school. Then he went off to college while I stayed home and worked and did some classes at the community college. Business classes mostly. I so wanted to go away to the university, but as it was, I had to pay my way through the community college. And pay rent to my parents for living at home. David came home at least once a month and I lived for those weekends. I dreamed about what his life must be like, living in a dorm. The freedom. The parties.

"But when he came home he was always with me. He acted like nothing had changed, even though I could see the changes in him. I was sure he was going to dump me. His visits became further apart. And honestly, I figured the end was near."

"But it didn't end. You two married."

"Yes, that. I got pregnant. There was no way I was going to tell my parents and no way I wanted an abortion." She glanced over at Gabe, then back at the road. "I dreaded telling David. Dreaded his reaction. Dreamed about how he'd react when I'd tell him. But I never dreamed his reaction would be...tears. He said his life was ruined. I felt my heart shred, honestly just shred inside of me. I got up and walked away from him then. I couldn't fix it for him. And somehow, the look in his eyes blamed me. Like it was all my fault. It wasn't. And he knew that."

Why was she telling Gabe this whole long story? She sucked in a deep breath, feeling like she'd been talking for ages.

"You can't leave me hanging like this. What happened next? Unless, of course, you don't want to keep going."

She let out a long sigh. "He came by later that weekend, seemingly a changed man. And we never talked about his first reaction. We ran off and got married before we even told my parents I was pregnant. I moved off to the university, and we moved into married student housing. It was crappy, but it was mine. I painted the walls. Some neighbors gave us a crib and highchair. I thought life was wonderful. I worked, cooked, cleaned, and tried to make everything as smooth as possible for David. I started down a long slope of always being the one who did everything. Made it easy on David. He never had to get up with the baby. He never cooked, cleaned, or anything. I did it all. I was just so grateful that he still wanted me."

She paused for a moment, remembering those days. They'd been hard, but wonderful. She glanced back over at Gabe. She still didn't know why she was telling him her whole life story. Well, most of it anyway. "And we were happy back then. He graduated business school and got a great job. We finally had some decent money."

But she left out the next part. The part where she got pregnant again. David had actually picked her up and swung her around when she told him the news. He was happy. Everything was going his way. He actually said one of the reasons he got his job was his employer thought he was a serious, responsible guy with a family. So adding another kid, well, it just added to his whole persona.

But then… she lost the baby. She was inconsolable, and David just… pretended the whole thing hadn't happened. Told her to snap out of it when she ached so much for the child that would never be held. But she couldn't tell that to Gabe. It was too painful.

She continued on, "Then we started years of the same dance. I thought he was fairly happy. I was. I had more than I'd ever hoped for. A great son, a handsome husband who made good money, a really, *really* nice house after about five more years. I got swept up in PTO and volunteering and driving Eric to sports. Always sports. David climbed the corporate ladder. I learned how to throw a dinner party from Sara Jane—that's my friend Rachel's mother. Rachel took me out shopping for clothes. I have terrible taste in clothes, she told me. I always accepted her help. I wanted David to be proud of me."

She stared at the road in front of her, the white line flying past her. A lone hawk swooped across the road. Gabe sat patiently waiting for her to continue when she was ready.

She glanced over at him. "Then one day, without the slightest bit of warning, he came home and said he didn't love me and he was moving out. I mean, I know they say that most women will sense that something is wrong, something is coming. But I sure didn't. Not. At. All.

"A month later I saw them out at the mall. I couldn't believe it. She looked only a handful of years older than Eric. Young, cute, perky. Hanging on his arm. I saw them from afar before they saw me, and I could tell in the way he looked at her that I had no more chance with David Duncan. He'd moved on and cut me out of his life." She shrugged. "And that was that."

"I'm sorry. That must have been hard."

"It was. And I have no idea why I just told you my whole story about life with David."

"I was glad to listen. Sometimes it helps to talk."

"You're probably never going to ask me another question." She sent him a wry smile. She should feel uneasy about spilling all that out, but for some reason, she didn't. He was a good listener. Comfortable to talk to. She could just be herself, though really, she was finished with trying to be the person someone else wanted her to be.

"Nope. I'm pretty sure I'll still ask questions. It's part of my job. It's what I do as an author. Like asking who could have done this crime? And why?"

"The characters that are going to talk to you again if we find you the perfect desk?"

"Those very same ones." His mouth curved into a friendly grin.

Friendly. Is that what they were going to become? Friends? She could use another friend in her life. Especially someone who wasn't as high maintenance and needy as Rachel.

Then she immediately felt guilty for the thought. Because she loved Rachel, she did. Couldn't imagine her life without her friend in it. But an easygoing friendship with Gabe didn't sound so bad either.

———

Gabe marveled at all Lizzie had shared with him about her life with David. The guy was a fool. Lizzie seemed smart and talented, and she really was beautiful in that way that some women had and they didn't realize it. It hadn't escaped him that she'd ignored his compliment when he said she was pretty.

He was surprised she'd shared so much, but he had asked the questions. Maybe she'd just needed to talk. Everyone was always telling him that he was a good listener. Maybe he actually was. Anyway, he enjoyed getting to know her better. Maybe they could become friends. He wouldn't mind a friend in town.

They arrived at the first stop and, to his surprise, they found the perfect desk right away. A heavy wooden desk with wood worn smooth from use and the word *believe* scratched into the inside of one of the drawers by someone's penknife years ago. It was large and perfect and almost broke his back as he wrestled it into the van with the help of a two-wheeler hand truck.

Lizzie found a coffee table, a few frames, and an old mirror.

They went on to the next town and searched the stores there. She searched with intense concentration, standing back and looking at each item she was considering. She pursed her lips, and creases crept between her eyebrows as she thought. After observing her process with the first few items, he could easily tell if the item was a yes by the pleased smile that spread across her lips or a no by her shrug.

He was having an altogether grand time shopping. And he wasn't really a shopper by any stretch of the imagination. But it was fun to hear Lizzie's take on different items and what sparked an interest for her.

After hours of shopping, they finally had a van full of items and headed back to Wind Chime. They unloaded the items she'd bought, and he hauled them into the different rooms of her shop. "Now, we should head to your place and deliver your desk," Lizzie said as they placed the last table in an upstairs room of her shop.

She followed him back to his house and pulled into the drive. She got out of the van, laughing. "Hey, the road really does have three bends in it. I've lived here my whole life and never really thought about it."

"Hence, the name. Three Bend Road." He grinned, amused by her delighted realization.

They walked up the front steps as she looked all around. "Wow, your house is beautiful. When do you think it was built? Love the architecture."

"I have no clue when it was built, but I agree, it is a rather great house. Too large for just the two of us, really. But it's home to Mom and that's what counts." He opened the door. "Mom, I'm back."

His mother walked into the front room carrying a dishtowel and drying her hands. "Hello." She wiped her hand once more before holding it out to Lizzie. "I'm Martha."

"Hi, Martha. Nice to meet you." Lizzie took his mother's hand. "I love your home. Look at these lovely hardwood floors. I bet they're the originals."

"Thank you." His mother smiled at the compliment. "It's the only place that's ever felt like home to me. I'm glad to be back."

"I found the perfect writing desk. I'm going to go get the two-wheeler and haul it inside to the den."

"Let me help you," Lizzie offered.

"Nah, I've got it." At least he hoped he did.

"I just put on a pot of tea. Would you like some?" his mom asked.

"I would. Sounds nice to get off my feet for a bit. We did a lot of shopping today."

"Then come. Follow me. And Gabe, join us when you're finished."

He hauled the desk inside and leaned against it when he finally had it in place in the den. He faced it looking out the windows toward the orchard. At least he'd have a nice view. Maybe it would help him figure out who was the actual bad guy in his book…

He found his mother and Lizzie seated at the kitchen table.

"Lizzie was just telling me all about her shop. You'll have to take me to see it when she opens. It sounds like it will be a lovely place to find some items for the house. Look, she hung those two pictures. The ones we had leaning against the wall because I couldn't decide where they would look good. I love them there, don't you?"

"They look nice." They did look good on that wall. He had no eye for stuff like that, but he knew when things looked nice when someone else did the figuring out. "And I will take you to her shop when it opens." He grabbed himself some ice water and sat beside his mom.

"So where do you live, Lizzie?" his mom asked.

"That's a hard question to answer. I have a house over on Oak Street, but I just put it on the market. I need to find a new place. Something small. Maybe an apartment. I'm not really ready to buy another house." Lizzie shrugged. "I want to put all my money into the shop to get it up and going."

"Well, you'll have to find somewhere to live." His mother's eyes shone with concern.

"I've been looking, but places are either out of my price range or just… a dump. I'm putting some things in storage for the time being, so I don't need anything very big."

"I'm sure you'll find the perfect place." His mother's brows wrinkled and looked suspiciously like she was up to something.

Lizzie stood. "I should go. I have to return the van and then I'm headed back to the shop. Thanks for your help today, Gabe."

"Thanks for helping me find the desk. It's perfect."

"Hope it helps you discover the bad guy."

She gave him a sassy grin, then turned to his mom. "And it was so nice to meet you."

"You come by any time, dear."

He walked Lizzie to the door. "I guess I'll be seeing you around? Maybe I'll drop by in a few days to see how the shop is coming along." *That sounded lame, didn't it?*

"Sure, that would be great." She gave him a quick smile and headed to the van.

She pulled away down the driveway, and he stood there for a while just staring down the long drive, lost in thought.

"Gabe, you going to shut that door? You're letting out all the air-conditioning," his mother called out.

He grinned. Some things never changed.

He walked back to the kitchen, and his mother still sat at the table. "You okay, Mom?"

"What? Yes, of course." She frowned slightly. "I was thinking… this house is so big for just the two of us."

"I know it is, Mom. That's what I said when you told me you wanted to come back here," he answered patiently.

"I think we should take in some boarders. It would help with the bills, and we sure don't need all this space."

Strangers in the house? No way. That's not what he'd signed up for. He looked closely at his mother. "Mom, you want to let out rooms to strangers?"

"No, just people I feel are... good people. Take Lizzie, for instance. She's good people. I feel it in my bones. And she needs a place to live. We could offer her the bedroom on the third floor. It's nice and large and light. Wouldn't have to charge her much. Maybe it will help while she gets on her feet and opens her store."

So that's the scheme she was hatching. It was so like his mother to want to help someone out. Though he was sure by the time his mother talked to Lizzie that Lizzie would think she was doing his mom a favor. "Are you sure, Mom?"

"Yes, I'm sure." She stood and grabbed the empty teacups. "I think I'll have you drive me to town tomorrow and we'll talk to her."

"If you're sure that's what you want." He wasn't exactly certain about the whole idea himself. Someone else living in the house with them? But if they were going to have someone else living here... Lizzie wasn't such a bad choice.

12

Things were falling into place for Lizzie for once. The shop was coming along nicely. She'd started a simple website, though it needed a lot of work. Now if she could just find a place to live, she'd be set. She'd called Eric and told him she was selling the house. And if she'd thought he'd be upset about her selling his childhood home, she was wrong. Dead wrong. He told her to pack up his things and he'd just stay with David when he came to town. She'd hoped he would come home and pack his own things and decide what to keep and what to pitch, but he said he was too busy with school. How long had it been since she'd seen him? Two months?

Okay, a place to live and to figure out a way

to get back on good footing with Eric, and *then* she'd be all set.

The bell over the door to the shop jangled, and a thrill raced through her. Yes, the bell she'd found on her antiquing trip yesterday was perfect. She hurried to the front room to find Gabe and Martha standing there.

"I know you're not open yet, Lizzie, but I just had to come see your shop. Gabe was headed to town, so I tagged along." Martha swiveled around and looked around the front room. "Look at this. So cleverly decorated."

"I still have a lot more I want to do, but it's a start. I need work on my website, but I do have a presence on Pinterest."

Martha laughed. "That's like some foreign language to me, but I'm sure you'll figure out what needs to be done."

"How'd you move that armoire all the way across the room? I swear we put it on that wall yesterday." Gabe nodded toward the newly placed piece of furniture.

Busted. She had moved it. "Oh, I've long discovered the magic of sliders. I just slip them under the feet of the furniture and shove it where I want. I'm always moving furniture, trying to find the best spot for everything."

Martha walked over and ran her finger over a side table. "This is so pretty. Look at the wood."

"It's cherry. It is pretty, isn't it?"

Martha turned to her. "So… I wanted to ask you something. A favor of sorts. You don't have to say yes, but I hope you do."

"What is it?"

"Gabe and I have been talking about taking on some boarders. Help a bit with covering the bills. Plus that big old house seems so empty with just the two of us."

Lizzie eyed Gabe, then looked back at Martha.

"Gabe thinks we should give this boarder thing a trial run first. And… well, you need a place to stay. Do you think you'd consider staying with us? We have the whole third floor you could have. There are three bedrooms and two bathrooms up there. Gabe told me you have a son. If he comes to visit you, he's welcome to stay there, too. It would make me feel so much better if our first boarder was someone we knew." Martha looked at her expectantly.

Lizzie looked from Gabe to his mother and back to Gabe. Had they just offered up a solution to her living situation nightmare? At least for now? "Are you sure?"

"We're sure," Gabe chimed in. "I'd feel a lot better about Mom's new venture if her first boarder was... well... you." His infectious grin began to melt away any reasons she could possibly have to say no. She did need a place to live and was running out of time to find one.

"You'd be free to use the kitchen, of course. We'll clear you a cabinet and a shelf in the fridge. And you're always welcome to eat with us."

"Mom loves to cook," Gabe added, still with that encouraging smile.

Lizzie could hardly believe her good luck. "Well, if you're sure, I'd love to."

"You don't even want to see it?" Martha asked.

"No, I'm sure it will be wonderful. And the timing is perfect. I already got an offer on the house. Actually, two different families put in offers, so this comes at the best time."

"I can help you move your things in if you want," Gabe offered.

"That would be great. Some things are going to storage until I decide on a new house, but we could move my bedroom suite, and I have a small desk."

"We could move Eric's things into the extra bedroom," Gabe suggested.

"Ah… he's going to just stay with his father when he's in town. I'm going to pack up his things, and David is coming by to pick them up. I do have a sofa bed we could put in the extra room, just in case he does decide to visit."

"He's always welcome." Martha reached over and grabbed her hand. "I'm so pleased. This will be wonderful. Thank you for helping me out."

She walked them to the door. "So, I'll call you and set up a time to move in?"

"Perfect." Martha bobbed her head, a satisfied look on her face. "We'll see you then."

They left, and she softly closed the door behind them and leaned against the doorframe. Was she really helping out Martha, or had the woman just felt sorry for her? She seemed genuinely grateful that she'd accepted the offer to live there. She shook her head. She hadn't even asked about the rent… What kind of businesswoman would she be if she didn't even ask about rent for her room?

Her phone rang and she answered it. "Hey, Rach."

"Lizzie, you need to come over tonight." Rachel's voice was filled with... something. Surprise? Excitement?

"I can't. I really need to go home and work on the website. I have so much to do." And pack, now that she had a place to move to.

"No, really. Can't you come over tonight? I have something to tell you."

"Can't you just tell me now?"

"No, in person."

She didn't know why Rachel was sounding so mysterious, and she didn't want her to feel like she didn't have time for her. She smothered an exasperated sigh. "Sure, I could come over for a bit."

"That's great. Five?"

"Is six okay?" She had so much to do.

"I guess. But come earlier if you can."

"Is Ronnie away?"

"Of course. But he'll be home later tonight."

"Okay, I'll drop by." She hoped Rachel picked up on the *drop by*. She really couldn't stay for hours and hours.

"Perfect. I'll see you at six if not before." Rachel hung up the phone.

Right. If not before. Because it wasn't like she didn't have a million things to do before the store opened, but that didn't occur to Rachel. And her friend always got what she wanted. She let out the long sigh she'd held in. It's a good thing she loved her friend so much.

She wanted to do kind of a soft launch of the shop and open up in about two weeks, then have a grand opening a couple weeks after that. *If* she could get everything ready. Her long must-do list taunted her. Going over to Rachel's instead of home to work on the website was not going to help. She promised herself that she'd just stay for one quick drink, hear what Rachel wanted to tell her, then head home for a couple hours of work before bed.

A grand opening of *her own shop*. It still surprised she was doing this. A shop. A design business.

She slowly, ever so slowly, circled around, looking at the shop. The warm hue of the walls. The sun streaming through the large, sparkling front window. The items she'd found and arranged in the room. It gave off a welcoming vibe, and pleasure and pride ran through her with what she'd accomplished so far.

And it was *all hers.* And hers alone. Now if only she could make a success of it.

13

Sara Jane slowly strolled along the beach near the cottages. She couldn't remember the last time she'd gone to the beach even though they lived so close to it. The gulf stretched out before her in the most beautiful shades of turquoise and emerald green. A soft breeze ruffled her hair around her shoulders. This morning in the bathroom mirror, she'd noticed the beginnings of gray at her roots. Maybe she'd get her hairstylist to do something to blend them in and let her hair go to its natural color—probably mostly gray now under all that dye. She could do that now. It was her choice, and hers alone. She spread out her arms and twirled around at the water's edge, grinning.

It had been over a week now since she'd left Wind Chime Beach. Steven had sent texts and left nasty phone messages the first week. She just deleted them without reading or listening. But the last few days there had been not a word. She wasn't sure if that was a good or bad thing but really didn't care. He knew she was alive and fine. Rachel let him know that much. She owed him nothing more. For all she knew he'd thrown all her things out onto the street. No, he wouldn't do that. People would talk. She didn't put it past him to hire someone to come and discreetly haul her things away. Though, to be honest, she didn't have many things that were *hers.* And the revelation that there really wasn't anything she wanted or needed from the house startled her. How had she gotten to that point? But to her, it was all just *things.* And she didn't need things. She needed freedom. She needed acceptance. She needed room to breathe. All of which she'd found here in the lovely town of Moonbeam.

Violet had let her extend her stay at Blue Heron Cottages. She'd fallen into a nice routine of lazy mornings with coffee and a good book, then exploring the area in the afternoons. She'd tried new restaurants for dinner, enjoying small cafe-type places that Steven would never consider going to. He wanted fancy tablecloths, sparkling silver, and crystal. They usually just went to the club in town or drove into Sarasota or Tampa for one of the nicer restaurants there. This was such an enjoyable change.

She'd eaten delicious hamburgers, fried grouper sandwiches, and hushpuppies dipped in melted butter... all fabulous and nothing that would ever be served at the usual restaurants she'd frequented. She had a beer right out of the bottle. Tried fried green tomatoes. And on Monday she hadn't even *considered* red beans and rice. If she had her way, she'd never eat them again.

She'd found a delightful small bookstore, Beachside Bookshop, and browsed there for a new book each time she finished the book she was reading. The owner, Collette, now recognized her and had suggestions ready each time she went in, which was about every other day since she was a quick reader. She'd forgotten how much she enjoyed reading.

She and Violet often had a cup of tea out on the porch in the evenings before bed. A pleasant, easy friendship had developed between them. They talked about their days, or the book Sara Jane was reading, or Violet regaled her with stories of all the difficulties she'd had opening the cottages on her own. Just companionable conversation and so enjoyable. She hadn't really had friends in her life since marrying Steven. He didn't like any of the friends she had before they met, and she was embarrassed to admit, she'd let them go to the wayside in the whirlwind it had been dating and marrying Steven.

Here she was just Sara Jane. Not Mrs. Benoit. Not plain Sara. Not Steven's wife, not Rachel's mother. Just… Sara Jane. And she liked that.

A lone blue heron stalked along the water's edge, and she stood and watched its majestic yet awkward steps. When had she last paused to do something like watch a bird or stare at the waves or just enjoy the simple moments?

These simple moments were extraordinary, enough to take her breath away as she reveled in them.

She did have to get back to real life soon, though. Whatever real life would look like now.

She had to talk to Rachel and tell her the decision she'd made. The divorce papers would be ready to be served soon. She needed a place far away from Steven when that happened. Rachel would be so upset. It would upend her perfect little world. Rachel didn't deal well with upheaval—not that she'd had much of it in her life to deal with.

Maybe she'd get a place here in Moonbeam. It was far enough from Wind Chime that she wouldn't run into Steven. A bonus was Moonbeam was really not his type of town. Too quaint. No modern, high-rise hotels. It actually was perfect for her. She'd find a job. Though what kind of a job would she find? She hadn't worked. Ever. Unless you called planning dinner parties work.

Rachel would be upset that she wasn't right in Wind Chime, but it was only an hour's drive away. She'd make a point to still visit Rachel regularly or have her come to Moonbeam and stay overnight when Ronnie was out of town.

She'd talk to Violet to see if she knew of a small house to rent. Then she'd pick out just what furniture she wanted for it. Excitement rushed through her at the very idea of having a place of her own, decorated just like she wanted. Being on her own for the very first time.

She'd call Rachel and let her know... just as soon as she found a place. She'd rather everything be a done deal before telling her because she knew Rachel would pressure her to move back to Wind Chime Beach, and everyone gave into Rachel's pleading. But this was one time she wouldn't give in. She loved her daughter dearly, but she knew she'd spoiled her. But Rachel had been such a bright spot in her life, it had made dealing with Steven worth it.

She'd made Rachel's life so easy. Tried to protect her from anything difficult. And by doing that, Rachel had become—and it pained her to say it—but Rachel was *almost* as self-centered as Steven. Just not mean about it. She just wheedled and coaxed and begged until she got her way. It was just easier to give in to her.

She couldn't change how she'd raised Rachel now, but she could stand up for herself. Explain that this is what she needed. Rachel would just have to learn to deal with it. Maybe it would even be good for Rachel not having her there all the time doing things for her, taking care of her, dropping her plans when Rachel wanted her to do something. Maybe it was time for both of them to learn some independence.

With that decided, she continued her beach walk, enjoying the salty air, the call of the gulls, and the fluffy clouds drifting above her. A peace she'd rarely experienced settled over her at the rightness of her decision.

14

Lizzie was annoyed at herself for giving into Rachel's pleas. She would rather be sitting at home, working on the website. She had so many plans and ideas. Just one drink. That was all she was having, no matter how much Rachel begged. Then she'd hurry home.

Rachel answered the door and grabbed her hand, tugging her inside. "I thought you'd never get here."

She glanced at her watch. Six o'clock, just like she'd promised.

"Come on, let's go in the family room. It's too hot to sit outside. The heat is bothering me today. I made us some sweet tea. Does that sound good?"

"Sure." It actually did sound good. She'd

rather have tea than a glass of wine since she planned for a long night of work.

She followed Rachel to the family room, and her friend flounced down dramatically into a chair. "I've had quite the day." Rachel's cheeks were flushed.

Okay, then. She'd get the tea for them since it was obvious that Rachel wasn't going to. Lizzie poured them each a glass of tea from the pitcher on the side table and handed one to Rachel.

She sat down, took a sip of the tea, and eyed Rachel, waiting for her big news.

Rachel leaned forward and set her tea on the coffee table with a dramatic flourish, her eyes shining with excitement. "I have something to tell you. I'm going to burst if I don't tell someone."

"So… tell me."

"I… I can't believe it… I just found out today… I'm pregnant."

Lizzie set down her drink with a clatter and jumped up to hug her friend. "Rachel, that's such great news. I'm so happy for you."

"I can't believe it. After all this time." Rachel's face held a dazed expression. "I know I should have told Ronnie first, but I want to tell him in person and he's not coming home until tonight. I had to tell someone."

"And I'm glad you did. This is fabulous."

"I'm already two months along. I think with Mom being gone and everything, I just wasn't paying attention. But the last few mornings I felt a little sick." Rachel laughed. "You'd think after years of trying I'd be more on top of things. It took me a couple of mornings to figure things out and schedule an appointment with my doctor. Then I just didn't want to believe it was true. Not until I had proof."

"Ronnie is going to be so excited." Happiness swirled through her for Rachel and for Ronnie.

"I know. I can't wait to tell him. I called him this afternoon and told him I was lonely. He said he'd squeeze in a quick visit home tonight but has to leave in the morning for the rest of his business trip."

Lizzie was truly happy for Rachel. She'd wanted this for so long and had almost given up hope. But then, Rachel always got what she wanted in the end. Truly a charmed life. "And Sara Jane will be thrilled, too."

"If she ever comes home. I'm pretty sure she caught Daddy cheating again. But why did she pick this time to leave?" Rachel frowned slightly. "I'll call her tomorrow after I tell Ronnie tonight. I'm sure she'll come home then. She'll want to be here, I know she will."

Rachel was probably right that Sara Jane would want to be here for her daughter's pregnancy.

"I'll have to talk to Daddy and tell him to just let Mom come home. Not to be a jerk about her taking some time to herself. He'll listen to me. Though he is really, *really* mad right now."

"What if she doesn't want to move back in with your dad?"

"Don't be silly. Of course, she'll come back home." Rachel shook her head as if the very idea of Sara Jane not moving back in with her father was ludicrous.

"Maybe she'll want a place of her own. Some time to herself. Your dad… well, he'd be hard to live with. He cheats on Sara Jane. Regularly. You know that."

Rachel sighed. "He does. I know. But Mom seems to just look the other way. They've worked it out in their own way."

Lizzie wasn't so sure about that, but she didn't want to upset Rachel. Especially now.

Rachel patted her belly. "I think it's a girl. That's what I want."

She had to keep from laughing. Rachel probably would get a girl just from pure force of will.

"And I need you to help me make the cutest nursery ever. I can't wait to go shopping for furniture and oh! Clothes. Baby clothes. Lots of them. We're going to have so much fun, aren't we?"

They would have fun, but she couldn't devote all her time to Rachel's project like she used to do. She had a shop to open. She'd have to explain that to Rachel, but not today when she was so thrilled and delighted.

"Ronnie will be excited. Maybe he'll stay home more now that we'll have a baby. He's going to be a great dad."

"I'm sure he will be." She was less sure he'd be staying home more. His job that paid for the big house and all the shopping and trips that Rachel loved kept him away quite a lot of the time. But to be honest, Rachel would probably rather have Ronnie around more than any of those things. "Maybe you should talk to him about cutting back or finding a new job that doesn't require so much travel."

Rachel chewed her bottom lip. "I think I will. Surely he can find something new with less travel."

"I hope so." Rachel was so lucky. She and Ronnie were so in love, so compatible, and now they were going to have the baby they'd wanted for years. How did one person get such a corner on the good luck?

She felt slightly guilty at the thought. She was glad her friend was finally pregnant and going to have a baby. Even with her problems with Eric right now, she couldn't imagine not having him in her life. She loved him fiercely. But spreading some of the luck around might be nice. Like maybe over to her and Eric finding their footing again?

Rachel leaned forward. "I think I heard the doorbell. There. I hear it again." She jumped up. "Come with me. I'll answer the door, and then I want to show you what I bought." She laughed. "I couldn't help stopping at the baby store and buying some clothes on the way home from the doctor."

She trailed behind Rachel and paused in the foyer while Rachel answered the door. Two uniformed officers that she didn't recognize stood in the doorway.

"Mrs. Morrow?"

"Yes? May I help you?" Rachel beamed at the men, her happiness spilling all around her.

The younger man shifted from foot to foot and glanced at the older officer. The older man stared at Rachel for a moment. "Ma'am, your husband has been in an accident."

Rachel leaned against the doorframe and Lizzie hurried up to her side, her heart pounding.

"Where is he?" Rachel's face turned an ugly shade of ash gray, and she grabbed Lizzie's arm.

"I'm sorry. He's... He didn't make it, ma'am. He didn't survive the accident."

Rachel gasped, stepped back, and paled to a ghostly white. Then her eyes started to roll into her head. Lizzie watched in horror as, almost in slow motion, Rachel fell to the ground with the frightening thud of her head hitting the tile.

Lizzie dropped to the floor beside Rachel and patted her cheek. "Rachel?" Nothing. "Rachel. Talk to me." Fear swept through her. The younger officer knelt beside her. She touched Rachel's head and saw blood when she took her hand away. She looked at the officer. "Call 9-1-1. She's bleeding from her head. And tell them she's pregnant."

15

Sara Jane sat on the porch with Violet, sipping on lemonade, enjoying the evening. The sun hadn't quite set, the birds were calling to each other, and the fragrant scent of gardenias lofted on the air.

"Do you know how much longer you're going to be staying here?" Violet asked as she sipped her drink.

"I wanted to talk to you about that. I've been thinking of finding a small house to rent here in Moonbeam. I think I'll stay here a while. I need some distance from..." She shrugged. "From everything."

"We could talk to Donna. She owns the Parker General Store and knows everyone here in town. She might know of a rental for you."

"That would be great."

"It will be nice to still have you around. I'd miss our chats if you headed back home."

"I think distance is for the best right now. Especially while going through the divorce. Steven can be—" She stopped, not wanting to say what she was thinking. That Steven would be furious and looking to exact revenge at the very least. Best to be far away.

"Wind Chime's loss is Moonbeam's gain."

"I do love it here. And it's nice not to just be known as Steven's wife." Really nice. It had been a long time since she'd been her own person. Free to make her own decisions.

"We'll have to find you the perfect place to live. Though, you're welcome to stay here until you find a place."

"Thank you." She took a sip of the lemonade and pressed the glass against her forehead. The heat and humidity clung to her with no breeze stirring a thing tonight. The calendar might say spring, but the weather wasn't paying any attention to it.

Her phone rang and she ignored it. There was no one she really wanted to talk to now.

"You can get that," Violet nodded to her phone sitting on the table between them.

"No, that's okay. I can call back whoever it is."

The phone rang again and she frowned, glancing at it. Lizzie? Maybe Rachel had asked Lizzie to call to coax her back home. She held up a just-a-minute finger to Violet and quickly tapped the phone to answer it. "Lizzie? Hi."

"Sara Jane. You need to come home." Lizzie's words came out in a rush.

She'd been right. Rachel had enlisted Lizzie to talk her into coming home. "Lizzie, I'm not ready to come home. I've actually decided to stay here for a while. Find a place to live." There, she'd let the news out. And the freedom that swept through her was intoxicating.

"No, you don't understand." Lizzie's voice cracked. "You have to come home. Right now. Rachel is in the hospital."

"Why? What's wrong?" Sara Jane clutched her chest. The heady freedom exploded, and all the air whooshed out of her lungs.

"She fainted. She hit her head. Oh, Sara Jane," Lizzie sobbed into the phone.

"Lizzie, tell me what happened." She tried to fight off the growing fear. "She hit her head?"

"Yes. She got bad news. And fainted."

"What news? Tell me."

"It's Ronnie. He's been in an accident." Lizzie sobbed again.

Sara Jane held her breath. "And?"

"And he… he didn't make it."

"Oh, no." Sara Jane leaned back in her chair and closed her eyes. "Oh, no, no, no."

Lizzie cleared her throat. "Rachel fainted when the police came and told her. And like I said, hit her head on the tile. There was so much blood."

"Is she…" She didn't even know what to ask.

"She's okay. They said it's a concussion. But they are keeping her in the hospital overnight for observation."

A tiny bit of relief crept through her. At least it sounded like Rachel would be okay physically. But her poor daughter. Losing Ronnie.

"And there's more, and I hate for you to find out this way…"

What else could there be? Was something wrong with Rachel besides the fainting and the concussion? "Lizzie, tell me."

"Rachel… she's pregnant."

The phone slipped from her hand and landed on the porch. Her daughter was finally pregnant—something Rachel had dreamed of for years—and her husband was dead? Life couldn't be that cruel. It couldn't.

Violet reached over and scooped up the phone, concern in her eyes, and pressed it back into her hand.

"Lizzie, you still there?"

"Yes, I'm here."

"I'll be there as soon as I can. I'm coming right now. Tell Rachel I'll be there."

"I will."

The phone went dead and she turned to Violet. "I have to go."

"I heard. It's your daughter?"

"Yes, she's in the hospital with a concussion… and she's pregnant. She didn't tell me that." Sara Jane closed her eyes. "But the worst thing is her husband… he died."

"Oh, no." Violet grabbed her hands and squeezed them. "I'm so sorry."

Sara Jane nodded then stood. "I've got to go. Right now."

"Of course."

"Violet, thank you for… for being a friend. I don't know what is going to happen now, but I have to go to my daughter."

"Of course you do. Go pack. Just leave the key in the cottage."

She hurried to her cottage, throwing things into her suitcase and finally giving up and just dumping clothes and things willy-nilly into the trunk of her car. Time enough to sort that out later.

She headed back to Wind Chime Beach— the last place in the world she wanted to be, but the exact place she needed to be.

16

Rachel opened her eyes, grimaced at the pain in her head, and promptly closed them again. Where was she? She squinted and peered at the dimly lit room. Her mind spun in circles of confusion.

She glanced to her right—wrong move—a stab of pain shot through her. She thought she saw Lizzie standing by the window.

Then she remembered. That's right. Lizzie had pulled her out of the river. That's why she was here in the hospital. Lizzie had saved her from drowning. She'd have to thank her for that.

Why had she been so foolish to go swimming alone? Her mom was going to kill her. She'd probably be grounded for life. Where *was* her mother?

Her thoughts swirled around and she closed her eyes and surrendered to the darkness.

Later she tried to open her eyes again. The room was quiet. Dark. But there was Lizzie, still here. Sitting in a chair beside the bed now. Wasn't Lizzie's mother worried that she was still here? And where had she gotten a change of clothes? She'd been in her swimsuit at the river.

Thoughts tumbled around her brain, but she couldn't sort them out.

"Lizzie?" She croaked out the name.

Lizzie jumped up and came to stand beside the bed, taking her hand. "I'm here."

"You saved me." Gratitude swept through her.

A deep frown etched her face. "I... I didn't. I couldn't catch you in time. You hit your head."

"My head? No... I was drowning."

Lizzie's eyes widened. "No, Rach, that was... that was a long time ago."

"But I'm in the hospital." She moved her head to the left just the tiniest bit. Definitely in a hospital room.

"You fell. You hit your head on the tile. There was a lot of blood. The doctor thinks you have a concussion. You need to stay here overnight."

"Where was I?"

"You were at your house."

"Is Mom mad about her tile? Is she there getting the blood cleaned up? Is that why she's not here?"

"No, Rachel, not your mother's house. *Your* house."

"I have a house?"

"I'm going to call the doctor to come see you." Lizzie's face clouded with worry, and she pushed the call button.

She closed her eyes, trying to concentrate. She had a house? When did she get that?

Vague memories of a big, white house clouded her memories. A nice patio out back. Pretty furniture inside. And Lizzie had helped her pick out the furniture. She opened her eyes and stared at Lizzie. She was… older.

She reached up to touch her head, and as she pulled her hand away she saw a big sparkly diamond on her left hand. And a… wedding band.

Memories wove back and forth, confusing her. Ronnie. That's right. She'd married Ronnie. They lived in the white house. She licked her lips. "Where's Ronnie?"

"He's, ah…" Lizzie looked around in a panic.

The door to the room opened, and a man in a white coat hurried in. "Ah, she's awake. Good."

"She's… confused." Lizzie glanced worriedly at the man.

"That's not surprising. She took quite a fall."

"Lizzie… where is Mom?"

"She's on her way. She'll be here soon."

Lizzie's hand touched her face—it was so warm. Lizzie pushed back a lock of her hair. She reached up and grabbed her hand.

"And Ronnie? Where's he?" Shouldn't her husband be here?

"Uh… he…" Lizzie looked questioningly at the doctor.

"Do you remember your accident?" the doctor asked.

"No." She thought back. She really couldn't remember anything about today. All her thoughts swirled around in a big quagmire of flashes of memory. Her first date with Ronnie. She'd fallen in love with him on the very first date. Her wedding day. She remembered it. A huge affair with lots of flowers. She'd loved her dress. Lizzie had been her maid of honor. But today? She couldn't remember today.

"I was over visiting you," Lizzie stared at her, eyes hopeful.

She didn't know what Lizzie wanted from her. She was doing her best to remember. That's right. Lizzie often came over when Ronnie was out of town. Ronnie was always out of town. She remembered that. But he was coming home tonight. She was certain of that. Surely he'd be here soon.

Ronnie…

She sat straight up in bed as her memory cleared and every horrible detail of the evening crashed down over her. She looked wildly around the room, refusing to believe the thoughts cramming into her mind, struggling to breathe.

She howled and screamed, clawing the air around her.

But all the memories were back, firmly clinging to her mind.

The doctor was standing over her on one side and the nurse on the other, with Lizzie hovering beside her. She willed herself back into the darkness. Slowly the memories began to fade, though she thought she still heard someone screaming.

Then blessed darkness descended on her again.

17

Sara Jane stood at her daughter's bedside. Rachel was sound asleep, and there was no way she'd wake her to let her know she'd arrived.

Her daughter was going to have a baby.

And Ronnie was gone.

The two thoughts swung back and forth like a pendulum.

Lizzie walked into the room and pressed a cup of coffee into her hand. "Here, you look exhausted."

"Thank you." She took a grateful sip of the scalding liquid.

"She looks pale, doesn't she?" Lizzie stood at the bedside, looking down at Rachel.

"She does." Deathly pale were the words

that came to mind, but she refused to acknowledge them.

"The doctor said that she can probably go home tomorrow. But she was so upset tonight. Screaming. It was… horrible." A shudder wracked Lizzie's frame.

She set down the coffee and carefully took her daughter's lifeless hand. Lifeless. No reaction to her holding it in hers. "I should have been here for her."

"I'm not sure anything would have helped her tonight. But she'll be glad to see you when she wakes up."

"When she wakes up to knowing that Ronnie is gone." Hot tears tracked down her cheeks. Ronnie gone. It was hard to imagine. He was such a vibrant force in their lives. His laugh. His overindulgence of anything Rachel wanted. His fierce love for her. And Rachel loved him back just as fiercely.

"And the baby? Did they check the baby?"

"They did. They said that everything seems okay."

"Did someone call Steven?" She dreaded the answer. Dreaded facing him.

"I did. He's flying in from Los Angeles.

Taking the red-eye. He won't be in until early morning."

She glanced at her watch. At least she had a few hours here with Rachel before he got here. A hint of quiet in the middle of the storm.

"Lizzie, why don't you go home? You look tired."

"I don't want to leave you here alone. And... I don't want to leave her. I want to be here when she wakes up. She's going to need all the support she can get."

Sara Jane nodded. There was no use arguing with Lizzie. And she understood how Lizzie felt because she felt the same way. There was no way she was leaving Rachel's side tonight.

The hours crept by in an endless stream of nurses coming in and Lizzie bringing them more coffee. Lizzie finally drifted off to sleep, curled up in a chair in the corner. But Sara Jane wouldn't let herself go to sleep. What if Rachel opened her eyes? She had to be the first person she saw. Be there for her.

She paced beside the bed, back and forth. How was Rachel going to cope with all of this? The loss of Ronnie? Being pregnant? Her daughter had never had to deal with any kind of problem of this magnitude.

About five in the morning, the door swung open and light flooded into the room from the hallway.

And there he was. Steven.

She sucked in a quick breath of steadying air. Only it didn't help much.

He stalked into the room, glared at her with undisguised fury, and stepped beside the bed, willing her to step aside with his angry look. But she stood there unmoving, unwilling to leave Rachel's side.

He looked down at their daughter with such a look of tenderness that she almost gasped. Somehow she'd forgotten, in the hardening of her heart against the pain he brought to her, that he did love his daughter without reservation, in his own Benoit way.

"What did the doctor say?" His voice was steely cold, barely controlled.

"He said she'll be okay. She's... traumatized. But physically she'll be fine. She has a concussion."

"How long does she have to stay here?"

"She might be able to come home today.

They'll check her when she wakes up. She was… hysterical… last night." She paused, then continued. "They think the baby is fine, though."

His eyes widened in surprise. "The baby?"

She closed her eyes for a moment. She thought he'd been told. Obviously not. Lizzie stepped up to her side and gave her an apologetic look. "I… didn't tell him when I called."

She glanced at Steven, knowing they'd now share a grandchild. Just something else to connect them when what she wanted was to be far away from him. But this was her new reality. "She just found out."

"Today," Lizzie added. "Well, yesterday."

"She must be so…" Steven shook his head. "Poor Rachel."

Rachel stirred in the bed.

Sara Jane leaned over and touched her face, not wanting Rachel to wake up just yet. The longer she slept, the longer she had until she'd have to face the truth of what her life was now.

Steven left after an hour or so of furious glares at her. He said he'd go grab a shower and clean clothes and be back. Lizzie still refused to leave. The two of them sat silently beside Rachel's bed until she finally began to stir. A tiny moan. More rustling. She glanced over at Lizzie, whose face reflected the fear she herself felt.

She stood and moved beside the bed. Rachel's eyes fluttered open, then closed again. She took her hand. A small smile crossed Rachel's face, and she drifted back to sleep.

She stood there, holding Rachel's hand, wondering what the morning would hold when her daughter finally woke up. Finally remembered.

A while later, Rachel stirred again and tears began rolling down her cheeks. She opened her eyes, bursting with pain to their very depths. "Oh, Mom." Her voice was barely a whisper.

She leaned over and gathered Rachel in her arms, wishing there was anything she could do to take away her daughter's pain. Long, wracking sobs came from deep inside Rachel, and she clung to her.

"Sh, it's going to be okay." She patted Rachel's back. "It's okay."

"It's not okay." Rachel finally gulped out the words. "It will never be okay again. Ever."

"We'll figure it out." Find some way to move forward. Find a way for Rachel to accept that Ronnie was gone.

Rachel finally pulled back, pain and horror etched on her features, and whispered, "It's all my fault."

"No, it's not. It was an accident"

"But I told him I was lonely. Lizzie's been working so much and you were gone." Rachel let out a sob. "He changed his schedule to squeeze in a night at home before he had to leave again. Changed his plans. Don't you see? It's my fault. He was on the road because of me."

Guilt hammered through Sara Jane. No, it was her fault. If she'd been here in Wind Chime, Rachel wouldn't have been so lonely. Then she wouldn't have asked Ronnie to come home. She'd only been thinking of herself. She knew Rachel got lonely when Ronnie was away, so she always planned to do things together with her daughter. Go out to lunch or have her over for dinner. But no. She'd run away to Moonbeam. All she'd thought of was getting away from Steven. Not the effect it would have on Rachel. If she'd been here, maybe none of this would have happened. The what-ifs hammered down on her.

Steven's voice interrupted her thoughts. "It's not your fault."

"Daddy." Rachel pulled away from her and held out her arms to her father.

Steven nodded for her to move away, and she reluctantly did as Rachel held out her arms to Steven. He wrapped her in a long embrace. "No more nonsense about it being your fault. Do you hear?"

Maybe Rachel would listen to him.

"Now, we need to get a doctor and get you out of here. Use the call button," Steven commanded Lizzie.

"But… I can't go to my house. I can't face it alone."

"Of course not. You'll come home. To your old room."

Rachel lifted a tear-streaked face to her. "Mom, come home, too. Please. I can't bear to live at my house now. Not without Ronnie. Can't you and Daddy make up? Please? I want to move back home with you. I can't… I can't be alone. Please," Rachel pleaded with her.

Lizzie shot her a sympathetic glance.

"Daddy, Mom should come home, right? It's okay. Everything can just go back to normal at home, right?"

Steven had no more resistance to Rachel's pleas than she did. "I suppose she could. We can just forget about this whole mess of her silly little trip."

She gritted her teeth. And can we forget about the silly little thing of his affairs?

"See, Mom. You'll come home, right?"

She gave Rachel a tiny smile, with her own heart plummeting. "I could come back for a while. Just until you're better."

"You're not coming and going. You won't embarrass me again. If you're coming home, you're home to stay. This will never happen again." Steven shot the words at her.

Lizzie stood frozen in place, watching her.

She could not move back in with Steven and pretend nothing had happened. Move back and start their ridiculous dance again. But she couldn't say no to her daughter. She just couldn't. Now was not the time. But he could not command she stay.

"Mom?"

"I'll come home," she said quietly as

resentment crashed over her. She'd been so close to her freedom. Her chance to have the life she wanted. But that choice was selfish now. She needed to help Rachel deal with her grief. Help her through her pregnancy. Help her with the baby. And as much joy as she felt about having a grandchild, the idea of being trapped back in that house with Steven threatened to bury her under a mountain of hopelessness.

But it all came down to the fact that Rachel needed her.

Tears rolled down Rachel's face. "Good, we'll all go home. But... nothing will ever be right again. I just can't go on without Ronnie."

"Of course you can. You'll find a way."

Steven stood. "I'm going to find a doctor. Have him check her out, and if she's okay, we'll head home." He turned to Lizzie. "You can go." He dismissed her as he stalked out of the room.

Sara Jane balled her fists and mouthed an I'm sorry to Lizzie.

Lizzie leaned over and kissed Rachel's forehead. "I'll be by soon to check on you."

Rachel just nodded.

"Thank you." She walked Lizzie to the door. "I'm so grateful you could be here with her."

"Are you going to be okay?" Lizzie said quietly as they stood just outside the door.

"I'll have to be. Rachel needs me."

"But... I kind of thought that this time was the last straw with Mr. Benoit."

"It was. I'd made plans. I... I started divorce proceedings. I made plans to move to Moonbeam. Close enough to see Rachel often, but far enough from Steven."

"I'm not surprised."

"But I'll put all that on hold. Rachel needs me. It will be good for her to be back in her childhood home. She's right that the memories in her house right now would just be so hard."

"I could run over to her house and get some of her things."

"That would be helpful. She has a few things at the house for when she decides to stay over sometimes when Ronnie was out of town." Even saying Ronnie's name stabbed her heart.

"I'll go do that and drop them off later this afternoon."

"Thank you. Why don't you try to get some sleep in first?"

"Probably a good idea. It was a long night. You should try and get some sleep, too." Lizzie squeezed her hand, pulled away, and headed down the hallway, her steps echoing on the tile.

Somehow she didn't think sleep was in the plans for her anytime soon. She needed to get Rachel home and settled in. She'd just gut her way through her exhaustion. And figure out a way to make all of this work.

18

Lizzie headed over to Rachel and Ronnie's house. No, just Rachel's house now. Grief gripped her in a vice hold as she slowly pulled into the drive. The large white house stood there as if nothing had happened. As if Rachel and Ronnie would just walk back inside, holding hands and laughing. But they wouldn't. Rachel might walk back in, but she'd never have Ronnie by her side.

The air whooshed out of her lungs as she walked up the porch steps and unlocked the door with the key Rachel had given her when they first moved in, insisting she needed it. And she had needed it quite a few times to let Rachel in because Rachel was always forgetting her own key.

She stepped inside and quickly stepped back out, standing in the doorway. The pool of blood on the floor brought last night's memory hammering back.

So much blood. She closed her eyes for a moment, willing the memory away, but it clung firmly to her mind. But the blood was still there when she opened her eyes.

Determined, she hurried to the kitchen to get supplies to clean up the mess. When she'd finally made it look like nothing had happened last night—though she was acutely aware it had —she went back to the kitchen and rinsed the rag she used and the gloves she'd worn until there was not a sign of blood. Then she carefully put away the cleaning supplies.

She walked through the house straightening and picking up things. Rachel's shoes kicked off by the sofa. A stack of magazines on the table. A dead bloom from a floral arrangement in the hallway. Trying to put order to the house, but nothing helped because it was deathly quiet and empty. Ronnie wouldn't be bursting through the door to kiss his wife and tell her how much he missed her. His laugh would not ring out with one of his endless corny jokes.

Trudging upstairs, she went to Rachel and

Ronnie's bedroom. She pulled out a suitcase from the back of the closet and started to pack things Rachel might want. Her favorite sweater. A couple of nightgowns and the robe with tiny pink roses she loved to wear. She gathered toiletries from the bathroom, refusing to look at Ronnie's razor and aftershave sitting beside Rachel's favorite makeup in the cabinet.

She walked into the guest bedroom by the master. Baby clothes lay on the bed, and she left them there, unable to touch them. The guest room Rachel planned on making into the nursery. Surely when Rachel adjusted to the shock and had some time to grieve, she'd want to come back here. She loved this house. Though Ronnie was everywhere, she'd give Rachel that.

Leaving the nursery-to-be, she grabbed the suitcase and dragged it down the stairs. With one last look at the house, she pulled the door closed, locked it, and left. Maybe Rachel was right. The house was smothered in memories of Ronnie. But time would help, wouldn't it? She had no idea because she'd never lost someone she'd loved as much as Rachel loved Ronnie.

She went back to her own house. The stacks of boxes in the hallway taunted her. Somehow, in the midst of all this—of helping Rachel, of opening her store—she had to move out of her home. And she needed to spend more time with Rachel now. Make it a priority. How was she going to deal with all of this?

But she couldn't face any of that right now. She'd just take a quick nap. Set an alarm. Then get up and take Rachel her things. Ignoring the boxes, she went to her bedroom and collapsed on the bed, too tired to even strip off her clothes. Within minutes, sleep took her in its welcoming arms and away from reality.

Lizzie felt much better after a long nap and a quick shower. She headed over to Rachel's. Mr. Benoit answered the door and said Rachel was sleeping. It was obvious he wasn't going to ask her in, so she left the suitcase with him. Glancing at her watch, she contemplated either going back home and packing more things or heading to the store to get a bit of work done.

The store won because she dreaded the packing. In spite of her dour mood and the overwhelming sadness clinging to her, the jangle of the bell over the door when she entered the store brought a tiny smile to her lips. Sunlight streamed in and she swept her glance around the room. A few boxes sat in the corner, ready to be unpacked. She'd start there. Set up that corner. After she did that, maybe she'd feel like she'd accomplished *something*. She carefully unwrapped a teal vase and set it on the table beside a comfortable, overstuffed chair that just screamed "come sit here." She placed a decorating magazine beside it that had the same shades of teal on the cover.

The bell jangled and she spun around. Gabe stood in the doorway, framed in light. "Mind if I come in?"

"No, sure. Come in."

He stepped inside. "Mom wanted me to check with you. Set up a time when I could help you move."

She closed her eyes for a moment, then opened them. "I... I have to give it some thought. Things are a bit..." What? Horrible? Terrible? Devastating? She cleared her throat. "My friend, Rachel... I told you about her. Well, her husband was just killed in an accident."

Gabe stepped forward, his eyes filled with genuine sympathy. "I'm so sorry."

"And… she just found out she's pregnant."

"Oh, wow. That's rough."

"And she fell and hit her head, and she was in the hospital, and I was there with her all night, and just everything is…" The words tumbled out, and then she couldn't help herself. The tears she'd been holding in cascaded out, scorching her cheeks.

With one quick step, Gabe was at her side and pulled her into his arms, simply holding her as she sobbed. She took comfort from his strong arms, holding her tight. When she finally settled down, he released her and stepped back. She walked over to the desk she planned to use as a consultation station and pulled some tissues out of the drawer. She wiped her eyes, her face, and looked at Gabe, feeling like she should be embarrassed for falling apart. But somehow, she wasn't. Not with him.

"So, what can I do to help? Anything at all."

"I don't think there is anything you can do."

"How about I unpack those boxes over there?" He pointed to the half-opened boxes in the corner. "Then you can put the things out where you want them."

Okay, maybe he could help. Just a little. And

honestly, she didn't feel like going home alone to her house. "Okay, yes. Thank you."

They worked side by side in friendly silence, only speaking a few times.

"Here's another vase."

"Thanks."

"Where do you want this?"

"Over there."

They finished with the boxes and Gabe stood. "Now how about you let me come help you pack up your house?"

"I couldn't ask you to do that."

"You didn't ask. I offered. Please, let me help. You have so much on your plate right now."

As much as she was firmly entrenched in an independent I-can-do-anything streak right now, she was tired. And overwhelmed with everything. She nodded and gave him a small smile. "I'll gratefully accept your help. Thank you."

"Fine. How about I come over in the morning? You look tired. You should go home."

She was exhausted. A good night's sleep would help. Maybe. If she could turn off all the thoughts racing through her mind.

They walked out of the shop and she locked the door behind her.

"You're okay driving home?"

"I'm fine." She gave him a weak smile hoping to convince him, convince herself.

"I'll see you tomorrow morning then. Oh, wait. I need your address." He handed her his phone.

She typed in her address and handed it back. "Thanks for helping me. Here and tomorrow."

"I wish I could do more." He nodded at her, slipped into his car, and drove away.

She stood there on the front steps of the shop. Her shop. She should be so excited and happy... but grief pounded down on her. Ronnie was gone. And Rachel... poor Rachel.

Gabe returned home and went in search of his mother. He found her standing in the middle of her kitchen. "What are you doing?" He frowned.

She turned around and gave him a little laugh. "I... I don't know. I came in here for some reason, but I can't for the life of me remember why." She shrugged and walked over to the stove. "I'll put a kettle on. Why don't you sit and we'll have a cup of tea."

He settled into a chair at the kitchen table and watched as she efficiently bustled around the kitchen. She brought over a mug of tea for him, and hers in one of her beloved china teacups, and settled in the chair across from him.

"So you were gone longer than I thought with your errands." She blew on her tea.

"I stopped by Lizzie's shop and helped her for a while. She's going through a rough time right now. Her best friend's husband was killed. I guess Lizzie was up most of the night in the hospital with her friend. Rachel, that's her name. Rachel took a bad fall when she heard the news."

"Oh, that's terrible."

He nodded as he dunked his tea bag up and down in his mug. "It is. And I guess Rachel just found out she's pregnant, too. Just a really bad situation. So I offered to help Lizzie pack up her house tomorrow. She looks exhausted."

"That's a good idea. I'll come and help, too."

"You sure?"

"Of course, I am. Don't start treating me like an old lady just because I had a momentary lapse of memory."

"Yes, ma'am." He knew better than to argue with his mother.

19

Lizzie woke up the next morning and smiled at the sunshine tumbling across her bedroom, feeling refreshed and ready to get to work at her shop.

Until... she remembered.

Remembered everything. The weight of the knowledge suffocated her. She dragged herself up to lean against the pillows she kept piled against her headboard—bought after David moved out because he hated throw pillows on a bed—and scrubbed her hands over her face.

She should get ready, but she sat and stared at the beams of dancing sunlight. Gabe would be here soon to help pack.

Get moving.

She slid her legs over the side of the bed, and her bare feet hit the wooden floor. One step at a time, that's how we do the hard stuff. Sara Jane often quoted that. Said it was something her grandma had always said. She hoped Sara Jane's grandma was right.

Lizzie answered the door a half-hour later to find both Gabe and Martha standing there.

"I hope you don't mind, dear. Gabe told me about your friend. I'm so sorry. That is so tough. Anyway, I made us breakfast. Cinnamon rolls. And a thermos of coffee." Martha and Gabe stepped inside. "So how about we have something to eat, then get started packing? I'm an expert packer. We'll get things all sorted and packed in no time."

Gratitude swept through her. She didn't really like accepting help, but this was one time she was going to put that aside. The sooner she was packed up and moved, the sooner she'd have more time to spend with Rachel.

"I've packed the dishes… but I kept out paper plates. I have some mugs. Somewhere…" She pushed boxes around and spied the mugs. "Here they are." She held them up triumphantly.

The cinnamon rolls were sinfully delicious,

and she realized she never ate dinner last night, just dropped into bed exhausted. They talked about the weather and Martha's new recipe she found for peach cobbler. Just normal, everyday conversation. Avoiding talk about Rachel, though she was right there in the front of her mind. She'd go over and see her later today.

"How about I pack up the rest of the kitchen?" Martha offered when they'd finished. "Since you won't need your kitchen things at our house, I'll box it all up. Label each box so you'll know what's inside."

"Thank you, that would be great."

"What can I help with?" Gabe asked.

"The garage? I have some tools out there, and things like rakes, hoses, a weed eater." Not much, really. David had taken most of it. "The movers are coming in three days to move things to storage. The timing is horrible, but I need to think about getting out of here before closing. The buyers wanted a quick close— they're paying cash—and I didn't see any reason to delay. But if I'd known about Rachel—"

"Don't worry. We'll get you all packed up. We'll move what you want to our house and have the rest ready to be put in storage," Gabe assured her as he walked out to tackle the garage.

She went upstairs to Eric's room. She'd already packed up most of her own things but hadn't been able to face her son's room yet. She stood in the middle of his room, slowly turning around. There was his favorite bat in the corner. He was quite the baseball player but had decided not to play at college. A poster of a hockey player holding the Stanley Cup was held up by only three tacks now, with one corner curling down. She briefly wondered who the player was. She knew nothing about hockey.

Eric had taken his favorite clothes to school, so all that was left were clothes he rarely wore. She methodically took each item out of the closet, carefully folded it, and placed it in a box. The t-shirt he'd gotten when his team won the state championship in junior high. Too small for him now, but she couldn't bear to toss it. Scores of soccer shoes and baseball shoes, too small for him. In the back of his closet she found half a dozen shirts she'd bought him for college, the tags still on them, balled up in a box. Obviously he hadn't been thrilled with her choices.

Time to get ruthless. She packed up two large boxes to take to the thrift store where the proceeds actually went to the charities they claimed they supported. That made her feel a bit better. She'd done her research on that after finding out many thrift stores were actually for-profit and deceived people dropping off donations. At least these items would go to a good cause. She put the new-with-tags shirts in the donation box, too. It was too bad it was too late to return them. She could have used the cash…

She stripped the bed that she always kept made just in case Eric would come stay. Which he hadn't in months. She piled the bedding to wash and pack away.

She finally took down the poster, unsure if Eric would still want it.

Martha entered the room. "I've finished the kitchen. You doing okay in here?"

"I think so. Just about have it all done." She stood there, holding the poster, still undecided.

Martha nodded to a large box beside the bed. "I bet the poster would fit in there."

She nodded, grateful to no longer waver on the decision. She packed it up, and if Eric ever decided to go through his things, he could make the decision himself. Martha helped her tape the box shut, and she wrote on it in big block letters. Eric's things.

"It's hard to pack up a house you've lived in a long time, isn't it? It's sad. So many memories." Martha's eyes shone with empathy.

"It is." She hadn't realized just how hard it would be. She'd been busy with the shop and ready to start her new life… but so much of her life had been here in this house. Raising Eric. And she'd thought she had a good life with David until he wanted out. So why was it so hard to leave? She was ready. She was. But it was still painful. Change often was.

"Why don't you come downstairs and take a break? I left out the teakettle, and it's on the stove, heating up. Let's sit and have some tea. Take a break."

"That sounds great." She scooped up the bedding and followed Martha out of the room, taking one last look at Eric's now bare room.

Gabe was in the kitchen when they got downstairs. "Garage is finished."

"You two have been so helpful. I never would have gotten all this done without you." She went to the laundry room, threw in the bedding, and returned to the kitchen where Martha had three cups of tea waiting.

She sipped hers, grateful to sit for a bit. "I just have the coat closet by the front door and a few things in the dining room to pack up."

"How about I rent a van and we move your things tomorrow? Then all that will be left is the things for the movers to put into storage."

"You don't have to do that. I'll rent one."

"Yes, he does. Friends help friends when they need it." Martha leaned over and took her hand. "And we're friends now. Just let us help you."

She nodded, swallowing back tears, grateful for the help and support. "You know what? Running into Gabe at the hardware store was a lucky day for me. And getting to know both of you."

"Sometimes things work out like that. The universe knows what we need when we need it." Martha's eyes shone with warmth as she nodded.

She glanced at the clock on the wall. *That needed to be packed up, too*. "I should probably go and check on Rachel. See if she needs anything. I texted Sara Jane earlier — that's her mother — and she said Rachel was sleeping. She's probably up by now."

"We'll be heading out, then." Martha stood.

"Gabe will be over in the morning with the van. And I'll be glad to have you in our home. I'll cook something special for tomorrow night to celebrate the move."

"You don't have to do that."

Gabe laughed. "You'll soon learn that Mom finds every excuse to cook a big meal. It's her thing."

"I do enjoy cooking for people. Too many years of just cooking for myself, so indulge me in cooking tomorrow's dinner."

She nodded. "Okay, I accept."

Gabe winked at her. "Better learn quickly that you'll never win an argument with Mom."

"Stop it," Martha protested with a grin as she took Gabe's arm. "Come on. Let's get out of here and let Lizzie visit her friend."

***

Lizzie drove to the Benoits' and pulled up the long drive. The Benoits had one of the largest houses in Wind Chime Beach. Something like eight bedrooms, seven baths, along with a living room, family room with a den off of it, and a huge formal dining room. Then there was Mr. Benoit's office. And the sunroom that Sara Jane liked so much. Not to mention the pool and the huge backyard. All that, and not a single person living in the house was happy…

She'd been shocked the first time she went inside the house. At sixteen, it had seemed like a palace to her. A place a person might get lost in. But Sara Jane had welcomed her warmly. Hugged her and thanked her repeatedly for saving Rachel. And somehow, over time, Sara Jane had become more of a mother to her than her own mom.

She walked to the ornate front door with huge cut-glass windows and knocked. Unfortunately, Mr. Benoit answered the door. She'd hoped Sara Jane would. Or at least their housekeeper. She forced a smile. "Hi."

"Elizabeth, what are you doing here?" He glared at her with the most unwelcoming stare.

Lizzie, she silently corrected him. "I just came to see Rachel. Check on her." What did he think she was doing here? She was Rachel's best friend. Rachel needed her.

"You shouldn't have wasted the trip. Rachel is sleeping. We don't want to wake her, do we?"

"Ah, no." She stepped back. "But you'll tell her I stopped by? Tell her to call me."

He nodded dismissively and abruptly closed

the door in her face. Okay then. She'd try calling Rachel in a little bit. She headed back to her car to drive home and finish up the last of the packing so she'd be ready when Gabe came tomorrow.

20

The next morning Sara Jane awoke to light streaming in the windows. She tilted her head from side to side, stiff from sleeping in a chair all night. She'd spent the last two nights sleeping in a recliner in Rachel's room. Well, not sleeping, really. Rachel woke up screaming time and again and she'd rush to her side to calm her down.

The only time she'd left the house was to go to the funeral home and talk to them about Ronnie's funeral. Rachel had turned her head away when she'd asked her what she wanted to do about his funeral, so she'd taken on the task herself, hoping Rachel would be okay with her decisions. Who knew there were so many decisions to make? Type of casket. How long for visitation. Arrange with the pastor to speak at the service. Did she want music? What songs? It had exhausted her, but she'd plodded her way through it. One step at a time, just like her grandma had said.

She pushed out of the chair to check on Rachel. Sound asleep. That was good. Maybe she'd have time to grab the shower she so desperately needed. Then she'd come back and sit with Rachel. She was a bit surprised that Lizzie hadn't stopped by to see Rachel. Not like her, but maybe she was busy with her shop. She'd text her later to see if she could stop by. Maybe that would perk Rachel up. Maybe she could convince Rachel to get up and shower and get dressed. All her daughter wanted to do was sleep.

Speaking of sleep, she promised herself that tonight she'd sleep in a bed. She craved one. Just one night's sleep. Was that too much to ask? Of course, Steven hadn't offered to help. Hadn't offered to take a night sitting by Rachel's side. But tonight she was determined to go to sleep in the guest room next to Rachel's room. At least she'd be in a bed. And she'd be able to hear Rachel. She just wanted... a bed. A pillow. A few uninterrupted hours of sleep on a flat surface.

And today she was going to tackle moving her things into the guest room that was going to be *her* room now. Most of her things were still tossed in the trunk of her car. There was no way she'd go back and share a bedroom with Steven. No way.

The thought of how close she'd been to her freedom taunted her. Her plans to move to Moonbeam, get her own place. She pushed the thought from her mind. Rachel needed her. She was a mother, and when your child needed you, no matter what their age, you were there for them.

The last two days she and Steven had passed each other in the hall or the kitchen, or when he came to check on Rachel, but never said a word. He would walk into Rachel's room and speak to his daughter if she was awake... which wasn't often. But he never said a word to her. Which actually was pretty okay with her.

After one last look at Rachel, she left the room. First coffee, then a shower, then she'd face the day.

She wandered down to the kitchen, surprised

to see Steven sitting at the table. He usually left for work before now or at least was busy working in the den. He stared at her as she poured a cup of coffee. She could feel his gaze boring into her back. She ignored his stare, took the cup, and turned to leave.

He caught her arm as she walked past and she struggled to keep the coffee from spilling. "Are you making red beans and rice for dinner?"

Her mouth dropped open. What was he asking? And was it Monday? The days all blurred together right now. She shook her head. "We're not having red beans and rice. I'm never making it again. And I'm not going to cook for you either. I'll make something for Rachel, but you're on your own."

"Don't be ridiculous." He stared at her for a moment. "Of course you'll be making meals and taking care of the house. And you need to quit sleeping in Rachel's room. Come back to our room like it was before. And we'll just forget that nonsense of you disappearing. It never happened. We'll go back to how we were. And you won't ever do that again. I won't have it. I told people you were off visiting an aunt. Stick to that story. Do you understand?"

She pressed her lips together, exhausted and annoyed. Maybe he'd always gotten his way, but no longer. She wasn't going to put up with his demands, his commands. "No, that's *not* how it's going to be. I'm not cooking for you. And I'm moving my things to the guest suite next to Rachel's room."

"You can't do that. You'll upset Rachel. That's nonsense."

"What is *nonsense* is you thinking that I'm coming back and sleeping in a room with you. That's not going to happen." She wrenched her arm from his grasp

"You're being ridiculous," he said dismissively and flicked his hand at her as if swatting away an annoying fly.

She tried counting to three... or three hundred. It would never be enough to calm her anger. "You are a cheater and I'm finished with it. Do you understand *that?* Finished."

"Don't be so dramatic. That woman didn't mean anything to me."

"How nice for her," she said dryly. "Does she know that?"

He glared at her for her impertinence.

"I'll be here for Rachel. Do anything to help her. But this is not permanent, this move back to this house. This is just for as long as Rachel needs me."

"That's not how it's going to be. I told you if you moved back in—"

She held up her hand, certain she'd never interrupted Steven in her entire life. "It is how it's going to be. I'll be here for Rachel. That is all. You've always gotten your way. You're spoiled and self-centered and think you can just keep doing whatever you want. But I'm over it. I will not stay married to a cheater."

"I'll throw you out of the house." His words thundered through the room.

"If you want to do that to Rachel, upset her, that's your choice. I could always find a place to stay and have Rachel move in with me."

Steven jumped up, his chair clattering to the floor behind him, his eyes flashing in anger.

Without waiting for his answer, she whirled around and hurried out of the kitchen. She doubted Steven would throw her out. He would be worried about what would people think. He was *always* worried about what people thought. So she'd stay as long as Rachel needed her. Though the anguishing thought of just how long that might be crushed her very soul. Through the pregnancy? While the babe was an infant? Could this drag on for years? Just how long could she do this?

She trudged up the stairs, hoping the caffeine would revive her. Steven slammed the door behind him as he left, and relief swept through her just knowing he was out of the house, if only for a while. She paused and sank onto the top stair, unable to keep moving.

Anger toward Steven overwhelmed her. Steven, a man who she'd once thought she loved. She didn't hate him now. Not exactly. *Hating people was wrong.* But she despised him. Loathed him. Couldn't stand the sight of him.

And yet, she was stuck here in this house with him for the foreseeable future.

21

True to his word, Gabe showed up early the next morning, and he and Lizzie moved her bedroom set, desk, and boxes of clothes, along with a sofa bed to put in a room for Eric. If he ever came to stay…

It didn't take her long to unpack her things and get settled in. She hung her favorite picture on the wall. One of her and Eric at the beach when he was a young boy, clinging to her hand, watching the waves tumble to shore. Life had been so much simpler then.

She hung up her clothes in the large walk-in closet. They'd moved the dresser with her clothes still in the drawers, so there was nothing to do with that. It didn't take long for her to transform from a woman living in a large house to someone living in a single bedroom.

But she loved the room they'd given her. Finished with her unpacking, she stood in the middle of the room and took in the space. It was flooded with light and had the original hardwood floors. The bathroom had a big old tub, but a gleaming, white-tiled shower had been added sometime along the way. White curtains with a tiny bit of lace hung in the windows, though Martha told her she was free to change them if she liked. Or paint the walls. But she loved their soft, pale green color. Gabe had hauled up a wooden rocking chair for her that Martha insisted she needed for her room.

She walked over and sank into it. Martha was right. It was comfortable and just what she needed to sit in by the large window that looked out on the garden below. She rocked back and forth for a few moments, savoring the quiet and a few moments of doing absolutely nothing.

She reached for her phone. Time to let Eric know where she was living now. The phone rang and she was certain she'd have to leave a message. He rarely picked up.

But this time he did. "Mom?"

"Eric, hi." It was so good to just hear his voice.

"What's up?"

"I just wanted to let you know that I found a place to live. I've moved in."

"Really? Where?"

"It's a room in a lovely large house off Three Bend Road."

"A room?"

"Yes, they were looking for a boarder. It's really lovely."

"Does Dad know?"

"Where I live doesn't really concern him." She defended herself. It wasn't any of David's business.

"You're just living in one room? At a boarding house? You don't have a place of your own?"

She ignored his criticism. "There's a room here for you, anytime you want to visit. We have the whole top floor. Two bathrooms, too."

"I'm not staying in some stranger's house."

"They're not strangers… they are my friends." And they had become her friends. They were helping her through a terrible time right now.

"I won't be staying there. I'll just stay with Dad when I come to town."

Her heart sank, but she wasn't surprised. "Well, the room is always here for you. I... I miss you."

An awkward silence clung to the air.

"Uh, I've got to go to class."

"Wait. I need to tell you something."

"What?" There was no avoiding the impatience in his voice.

"I have sad news. Ronnie died in an accident. His funeral will be this weekend. I thought you'd want to come and pay your respects." After all, he'd spent hours with Rachel and Ronnie when he was younger. Ronnie even went to a lot of his sports games to cheer him on. Eric spent hours hanging out with them at Sara Jane's pool.

"I'm... sorry." He did sound sincere.

"It's been quite a shock."

"Tell Rachel I'm sorry."

"I will." If Mr. Benoit ever let her in the house to see her.

"So you'll come home?"

"I can't, Mom. I have exams next week. I need to stay here and study."

"But Eric, they're like family."

"Mom, I can't. Hey, I have to go. Gonna be late." He hung up the phone.

She sat there staring at her phone. What had she done with raising this child? Funerals were not fun, but they were a part of life. You went to them to support the people who lost someone.

She considered sending him a strongly worded text. But really, did she want him to come to the funeral with an attitude? She needed to concentrate on Rachel. Be there for her. She'd just have to sort her relationship with Eric out after she got through the next few weeks. Helping Rachel. The funeral. Opening the shop.

Her phone rang. Ah, Sara Jane. Hopefully reporting in on Rachel. "Hello?"

"Oh, good. Lizzie, I caught you."

"You did. I just got moved into a new place out on Three Bend Road."

"Oh, I didn't know you've found a place. Well, good. I guess you've been busy, so that's why you haven't been by, but I was wondering if you'd have time to stop by and see Rachel today."

"I have been by. I've tried to visit Rachel each day. But Mr. Benoit hasn't let me in. Didn't he tell her that I'd stopped by?"

"No… he didn't." The anger in her tone crackled across the airwaves.

"I can come over now. Is she awake?"

"She is. Kind of. I'm worried about her. All she does is sleep. She wouldn't do anything to plan the funeral. I hope I made the right choices about everything."

"Oh, I'm sorry. I should have come and helped you with that."

"No, that's okay. It's all decided now."

"I saw it posted on the church website that it's this weekend."

"It is."

"Just let me get cleaned up, and I'll come over and visit with her for a bit. See if that helps."

"Thank you, Lizzie. I do hope it will cheer her up. Maybe you can even convince her to get up and shower? Get dressed?"

"I'll do my best." She hung up the phone and headed off to shower off the grime of the move. Then she'd head directly to Rachel's and see what she could do to help. The stack of the shop's bookwork sitting on the desk mocked her. Yes, that, too. She needed to pay for some orders and still had a few official forms for the town to fill out. But she ignored all that because Rachel needed her.

Within thirty minutes she was headed downstairs, her damp hair hanging about her shoulders, feeling slightly revived. She found Martha in the kitchen. "I'm going to head over to Rachel's for a bit."

"Good idea. I'm sure she'll love seeing you. She'll need all the support she can get now."

"Sara Jane said Rachel hasn't even gotten out of bed. Not that I blame her. Sometimes hiding in bed seems like a good solution."

"But we can't really hide from our problems, can we?"

"No, we can't." And she couldn't hide from her own problems and responsibilities either. Opening the shop. Helping Rachel. And eventually figuring out how to reach out to Eric and fix that, too.

"I'll see you back here for supper? We eat about six."

"Yes, I'll be back. Thank you."

"Hope you like fried chicken."

"I love it."

"Perfect. I'll see you this evening. Go spend time with your friend."

Thankfully, Sara Jane answered the door when she got there. Sara Jane grabbed her hand and pulled her inside. "It's good to see you. I'm sorry about Steven. I should have known that you'd be by to see Rachel."

"I texted her, too."

"I don't think she's even charged her phone." Sara Jane shook her head.

She followed Sara Jane up the familiar stairs to Rachel's room. Memories of high school floated around her. Laughing and racing up the stairs to listen to their favorite music and gossip about classmates. Getting ready for dates. Rachel always had her over to get ready for the many double dates they went on. Lizzie with David, and Rachel with whoever she was dating at the time. That is until she met Ronnie. Then it was always Ronnie.

They walked down the hallway, and as they passed the guest room next to Rachel's, she saw items on the dresser and a purse on the floor by a chair. She glanced at Sara Jane, who nodded. "Yes, I moved into that room."

She wasn't certain if Sara Jane had moved into the room to be closer to Rachel or to avoid

Mr. Benoit, but she didn't quite have the nerve to ask.

They walked into Rachel's room, and Sara Jane went over to the window to open the blinds. "Rachel, honey, look who's here."

"Close the blinds." Rachel pulled a pillow over her head.

Sara Jane ignored her daughter's words. "Lizzie is here."

Lizzie sat down on the edge of Rachel's bed and gently pulled the pillow away. "Hey, Rach."

Rachel rolled over. "I'm tired. Can you come back later?"

Sara Jane looked over at her hopefully so she continued. "How about you get up for a little bit? You could sit in the chair by the window. Or how about a shower?"

"Too tired."

"Rachel, I know that you're devastated. But you need to get up and eat something. If not for you, then for the baby."

Rachel propped herself up on her elbows. "For the baby? The *baby*? If not for the baby, Ronnie would still be alive. I wouldn't have asked him to come home. This baby has ruined everything. Now, go. I'm tired." She slumped back down in bed and pulled up the covers.

Lizzie sat there with her mouth ajar. Was Rachel actually blaming the *baby* for Ronnie's death?

She glanced over at Sara Jane and saw the tears threatening to spill from her eyes. She tried one more time. "Rach, you don't mean that. You've wanted this baby for… well, forever. The baby is a blessing."

Rachel ignored her.

Sara Jane nodded toward the door. "Come on. We'll leave her to rest."

They headed out of the room, Sara Jane pulled the door closed behind them, and turned to her. "Oh, Lizzie. What are we going to do?"

They went downstairs and sat outside by the pool in the cool shade of a group of trees. "I don't know what to do. I keep trying to get her to eat. She's only had a few bites since she's gotten home." Sara Jane leaned back in her chair and took a sip of the sweet tea she'd poured for both of them.

"She has to eat."

"I've tried bribing her with all her favorite foods. Nothing works."

"I'd say to give it time, but it can't be good for the baby with her not eating." A flash of pain and disbelief swept through her. "And she blames the baby…"

"I can't believe she said that. I'm sure she didn't mean that." Sara Jane's eyes clouded with concern.

Rachel sure sounded like she meant it, but there was no need to worry Sara Jane more than she already was. "I'm sure it's just the shock talking," she said to ease Sara Jane's mind.

"Maybe." But she didn't sound convinced and let out a long sigh. "She refuses to talk about the funeral. I'm not even sure I can get her up and dressed to go to it."

"She wouldn't miss Ronnie's funeral." Would she? At this point, she wasn't certain about anything regarding Rachel.

Sara Jane leaned forward, looking tired and older than her years. There were wrinkles beside her eyes and her shoulders sagged with the weight of everything going on now. "I need to go over to Rachel's house and get her something to wear to the funeral."

"Oh, let me do that for you. I'll grab a couple of her dresses to choose from."

Sara Jane's eyes filled with gratitude. "Thank you. I don't really want to leave the house with Rachel so…" Her voice trailed off and she stared at her glass of tea, swirling the ice around in a slow, rhythmic pattern. "My heart just hurts for her. She's in so much pain and I don't seem to be able to do anything to help."

Not being able to help your child—no matter their age—was a hard cross to bear. She reached over and took Sara Jane's hand. "You're doing a lot. You moved back here to take care of her. That had to be hard."

"It was. It is. Steven's being... difficult. We had quite a row this morning. He seems to think everything can just go back to how it was." She shrugged. "But it can't. Not for Steven and me. Not as a family. I can barely stand the sight of the man."

"I'm so sorry." Sympathy crept through Lizzie. Sara Jane had gone through so much with Mr. Benoit. His caustic words, his cheating, the way he was so dismissive toward her. And now she had to move back in so she could take care of Rachel. Life had a way of throwing cruel twists at you when you weren't expecting them.

"It just is what it is." Sara Jane let out a long, drawn-out sigh.

"I don't really have advice to give you about

you and Mr. Benoit." She shook her head. "But give Rachel some time. I'm sure she'll pull out of this. I mean, it will be hard, but Rachel is tough. She can handle this."

"Is Rachel tough?" Sara Jane cocked her head to one side, her eyebrows drawing together, lips pursed. "We've always done everything for her. She's had an easy life. A charmed one. How does a person who's never encountered trouble in her life deal with a blow like this?"

How *would* Rachel handle all this? Sara Jane was right. Rachel didn't deal well if life threw *small* problems at her. Now she had all of this to figure out. "It's only been a handful of days, though, since she found out about Ronnie. She needs time to deal with it."

"She does. But there's the baby to think about now, too. She can't just refuse to eat. Refuse to get out of bed. She needs to get up, eat, walk around, get some exercise and fresh air."

"I'll come back every day. I promise. We'll work on her."

"But you're so busy opening your shop."

"I'll move back the opening. Rachel is a priority now." And just like that, the decision was made. She would move back the opening. Somehow she'd figure out the financing to wait a bit to open. She needed to be here for Rachel and for Sara Jane.

"You don't have to do that."

"Of course, I do. Rachel is my best friend," she assured Sara Jane. "It will be okay. Let's just get Rachel through this rough time."

"You're a good friend to her, Lizzie. A very good friend."

22

The next day Sara Jane waited until mid-morning to carry a bowl of soup into Rachel's room. Her daughter was sleeping—or pretending to. She looked down at her stringy hair and pale face, and her heart ached. But something had to change. For the baby's sake at the very least.

She walked over to the windows and opened the blinds. Sunlight streamed into the room. Rachel rolled over, turning her back to the light.

"Rachel, it's time to wake up. I brought you some soup."

"Not hungry." The pillow muffled her words.

She walked over and took the pillow away. "Rachel, you're going to eat. You're responsible for another human being now. It breaks my heart what you're going through, but you have to take responsibility for this child. Eat right. Get out among the living. It's not just all about you now." Her words were forceful but needed. She'd always let Rachel get her way. Protected her. Made things easy for her. But now was not the time to give in to her. She needed to eat. Provide nourishment to the baby growing inside of her. She'd made a lot of mistakes with Rachel, but she was determined that now wasn't going to be one of them.

Rachel sat up partway in the bed and glared at her. "Leave me alone. You don't understand. Ronnie is dead. He'll never hold his child. I wanted to raise a child with Ronnie, not alone."

It was impossible to miss the pain in Rachel's eyes, and her voice. But she had to stay strong for her daughter. Make her see that she needed to eat. She hardened her heart against Rachel's pleading eyes. "Well, alone is the hand you've been dealt. It's not easy, but you'll have help. I'll help you. Lizzie will help you. But you have to help yourself, too."

"I… I just can't do it. I don't want to do it." She said the words more like a petulant child than a grown woman.

"It doesn't matter what you want, Rachel. You have to find it inside yourself to keep going. When that baby is born and you hold her... or him... in your arms, then you'll know it's all worth it. You will."

"I can't."

"You have to. You're a mother now."

"Leave her alone." Steven's cold words sliced through the air. "She needs time to grieve."

She whirled around to see Steven standing in the doorway. "She needs to eat. For her. For the baby. She needs to get out. At least go sit outside. Rejoin the world. Because she has a life to take care of now. A baby." She dared defy Steven.

"We'll hire someone to help her with the child."

Of course, that would be Steven's solution. "The baby needs her to eat. To get out of bed." She stood firm.

"Quit nagging her. She's doing the best she can." He threw the words dismissively at her as he strode into the room and sat down on the bed beside Rachel. "Don't worry, sweetheart, it's going to be okay."

"Oh, Daddy, it's never going to be okay." Rachel collapsed into his arms.

"You know…" Steven pulled back slightly. "You're not very far along with this pregnancy… we could find a doctor to… ah… terminate it."

Sara Jane let out a shocked gasped, her mouth wide open. What had he just suggested? "Steven!"

"Well, it's an option." He shot the words back at her.

She stared at Rachel. Surely she wouldn't want to get rid of this baby that she'd wanted for so long?

Rachel looked at her, then Steven. "I… I don't know."

"You don't have to decide right now, honey." Steven pulled her into his arms again, looking over her shoulder with a smug look as if this was some kind of competition.

"Rachel you've wanted a child for years. It's been your dream." She watched Rachel's face closely, looking for any sign that she thought Steven's suggestion was outrageous, too.

"Leave her be," Steven commanded.

Surely Rachel wouldn't decide to end the pregnancy. She was just tired and confused.

Stuck in a spiral of grief. She'd dreamed of this baby for years, of being a mom.

Rachel pulled back from Steven's embrace. "Daddy... I don't know..."

Sara Jane held her breath.

"I don't think I can do that. Get rid of it like that."

Sara Jane sighed with relief at her daughter's words.

"You still have time if you change your mind," Steven assured Rachel.

"Steven, just shut up."

His eyes widened, then hardened into a glare. "You can't talk to me like that." He spat the words at her.

"Mom, please don't fight with Daddy."

As if this was all her fault somehow. She just nodded at Rachel. "You should eat something." She turned around and left the room. It wasn't going to help to get into an argument with Steven in front of Rachel. But her daughter had to eat. And it just might be time to show her a bit of tough love. Because it wasn't just about her now. There was a baby involved.

Unless she listened to her father's suggestion...

Lizzie drove over to Rachel's house and used her key to let herself in. At least there was no pool of blood facing her this time. She stepped gingerly around the spot where the blood had been and headed upstairs.

She paused in the doorway of Rachel and Ronnie's bedroom, feeling like she was breaking into some kind of inner sanctum now. The bed was made, which was unusual for Rachel. She always said that making a bed was a waste of time since she was just going to get back into it. Ronnie had laughed at that and indulged her, though he usually made the bed if he was home. Not that he'd ever be home again…

Everything had been a blur the last time she came here to get things for Rachel. Now every little detail smacked her in the face. Walking into the room, she tried to ignore the clutter on top of the dresser and three pairs of Rachel's shoes scattered in the room. The book beside Rachel's side of the bed where she'd inevitably turned down the corner of the page to mark her place no matter how many bookmarks Lizzie tried to give her. Rachel cracked the spine on books too, something she'd never understand.

She resisted the urge to straighten the room and pick up Rachel's shoes. Just get the clothes and run. That was a better plan. Leave this house haunted by Ronnie's presence. Shaking her head at her bouncing thoughts, she walked into the large closet and flipped on the light.

A smile crept over her face as she realized Rachel's side of the closet spilled over into Ronnie's. His portion was neatly organized with suits together, pants together, and a section of shirts. Dress shirts first, then more casual ones, then ending with the Hawaiian print ones he loved to wear to casual parties. Rachel's side-plus-more was a jumbled mess. Dresses mixed in with blouses, mixed in with slacks.

She shuffled through the clothes and grabbed two black dresses and a beige one, uncertain what Rachel would want to wear to the funeral. Rachel could rock a simple black dress like no one else. But did a person want to rock a dress at a funeral?

She collected a pair of shoes and went back out into the room to find the black flats she'd seen kicked off near the bed. She spied a string of pearls on the dresser and grabbed those, too, uncertain on just what Rachel might want.

Suddenly she couldn't bear to be in the

house any longer. Too many glimpses of Ronnie, too many echoes of his laughter, too many memories of Rachel and Ronnie, holding hands and glancing at each other with that special look they had for each other.

Hurrying down the stairs with the outfits, she walked out the door, locking it behind her. Locking out the memories as she headed to the Benoits'.

Thankfully, Sara Jane answered the door again this time. The red, swollen eyes betrayed the fact she had been crying. "Are you okay?"

Sara Jane pulled her inside. "I... I don't know." A lone tear trailed down her cheek. "Come into the kitchen. Steven is upstairs with Rachel right now."

Sara Jane reached for the clothes and put them in the hall closet. Lizzie had no desire to run into Mr. Benoit, so she followed Sara Jane through the house.

"Coffee?"

"Yes, please." She sat at the table and Sara Jane brought over two steaming cups.

"So... Steven..."Sara Jane settled in a chair across from her. "He offered to help Rachel get... to get an abortion."

Lizzie gasped. "He didn't."

"He did."

She frowned. "What did Rachel say?"

"She said she didn't think she could go through with it. But Steven insisted she still think about it."

"But Rachel has wanted this baby for years."

"She's afraid of raising the child alone."

"It will be hard, but you'll help her. I'll help her."

"I told her that but—" Sara Jane stopped abruptly at the sound of Mr. Benoit coming down the stairs.

"Oh, Elizabeth. I didn't know you were here," he said as he walked into the kitchen. "Rachel is resting now. Don't go up and bother her." His tone sounded like he was talking to a tiresome toddler.

She nodded but had no intention whatsoever of leaving without seeing Rachel.

"I have to go to work for a bit. I'll be home for dinner." He turned and walked out the door.

"And I won't be making that dinner," Sara Jane whispered softly to herself.

Lizzie grinned in spite of herself.

"And we'll go up and see Rachel when we

finish our coffee," Sara Jane said. "He can't tell me when I can see my own daughter."

She kind of liked this new version of Sara Jane. Ignoring her husband's commands. A spunkier version. A stronger version.

They finished their coffee and went upstairs. Rachel was sleeping, yet again.

"She didn't touch her soup." Sara Jane frowned.

"Why don't you take it downstairs and heat it up again? I'll sit here with Rachel."

Sara Jane left and Lizzie pulled a chair up beside Rachel's bed. "I know you're awake."

Rachel didn't move.

"You're a lousy faker. Sit up and talk to me."

Rachel opened her eyes and glared at her. "Leave me alone."

"I won't leave you alone. I miss you. I'm worried about you."

Rachel let out a long sigh. "I'm tired. Too tired to chat about inconsequential things."

Inconsequential like anything going on with her own life as compared to Rachel's? She ignored the request. "So, how about we talk about things that matter. I brought over clothes for you to wear to Ronnie's funeral."

Rachel turned her head and stared out the window, not answering.

"And when your mother comes back with the soup, you're going to eat the whole bowlful. Do you understand?"

"I'm not hungry."

"It's not always about you, Rachel." She tried to rein in her frustration. "It's about the baby." Her friend could be so self-centered sometimes. Yes, she was in pain, she was grieving, but it wasn't just about her.

"Daddy said…" Rachel turned and looked at her. "He said… he could arrange… to… end things."

"You mean have an abortion. Say the word, Rachel, if you're considering it."

Rachel just stared at her for a long moment. "Don't you see? I'm always going to resent this baby. If I hadn't gotten pregnant… Ronnie would still be alive. I could get rid of it and move away. Start a whole new life somewhere else. Somewhere away from all the memories."

"I'm not even going to get into a discussion of pro or anti-abortion. It's not about that. I'm just going to say that you've wanted this child for years. Wished for her. Longed for her. Or him. The baby is a part of Ronnie. You don't want to lose that connection, do you? This last part of Ronnie?"

"But if I hadn't gotten pregnant, hadn't begged Ronnie to come home so I could tell him the news…"

"It isn't your fault or the baby's fault. It's just one of those cruel things that life sometimes throws at us." Or life sometimes threw at other people. Never Rachel until now.

"I… don't think I can do this." Rachel looked down at her hands.

Lizzie looked at Rachel's hands resting in her lap. The polish was chipped. She wasn't sure she'd ever seen Rachel with chipped nail polish. Or the straggly hair that rested on her shoulders. "You can do this. You can."

"But… I don't want to."

Rachel's soft words were like a hard slap of reality. Rachel just couldn't imagine doing the hard stuff in life. Lizzie sucked back a sigh of annoyance. Yes, it was terrible about Ronnie. Devastating. But… Rachel needed to think of the baby. She took Rachel's hand in hers, hoping to give her strength. "You're going to have to find a way to do it. Sara Jane and I will help. It's going to be okay," she assured her friend.

But would it? Would Rachel find the strength to handle everything that had been thrown at her?

Sara Jane walked in with a bowl of soup and some crackers.

"Here, give me that. I'm going to help Rachel eat it." She reached for the tray and settled it in front of Rachel, nodding at the bowl "Go ahead. Eat some soup."

Rachel sighed and picked up the spoon. "I'm just doing it so you'll quit nagging me."

"Whatever it takes." Lizzie nodded as she watched Rachel take her first sip of the soup. Sara Jane looked over, her eyes filled with gratitude.

Lizzie sat there until Rachel finished the bowl of soup and looked up with a petulant glance. "Now will you leave me alone?"

"Don't you want to get up and take a shower now?"

"No, I don't." Rachel slid down in the bed and pulled up the covers. "I just want to sleep."

Well, at least she'd eaten something. That was a start. She and Sara Jane slipped out of the room.

23

Sara Jane called Lizzie early Saturday morning. "Rachel says she's not going to the funeral." Exhaustion and defeat were clear in her voice.

Lizzie closed her eyes. She had to admit she, too, was exhausted from all the work of coaxing Rachel to do what was best... for her and the baby. She was tempted to just tell Sara Jane to leave Rachel at home. But she knew that eventually, Rachel would be sorry if she missed Ronnie's funeral. She sighed. "I'll be over as soon as I finish getting ready."

Within twenty minutes she was standing at the Benoits' front door. Unfortunately, Mr. Benoit answered. But this time she didn't let him make the decision. She stepped inside, uninvited. "I'm here to help Rachel get ready."

"She doesn't want to go. She doesn't have to go." He glared at her.

Sara Jane appeared on the stairway behind him. "Lizzie, come on upstairs."

She sidestepped Mr. Benoit—still glaring at her—and hurried up the stairs to Rachel's bedroom. Rachel was sitting in a chair by the window, staring outside. Her hair was wet, so Sara Jane must have at least convinced her to shower. That was a step in the right direction.

She walked over and knelt beside her. "Rachel, hon, it's time to get ready for Ronnie's funeral."

Rachel shook her head.

Lizzie reached out and took Rachel's chin, turning her head to face her. "Rachel, I know you. Listen to me. Someday you'll regret it if you don't go to the funeral. Let's get you dressed. Trust me. Please. I swear if you get there and want to come back home, I'll bring you back here."

Rachel bobbed her head slightly. Lizzie took her hands and pulled her to her feet. "Let's pick out a dress."

She and Sara Jane helped Rachel get dressed in a simple black dress. No jewelry.

Black flats. Rachel sat in a chair while Lizzie blew dry her hair, and pulled it back in a simple silver clip. Rachel shook her head when Lizzie said she'd help with makeup. Okay, then, no makeup to cover her pallor.

Mr. Benoit came to the doorway. "So, you're going?"

Rachel nodded.

Lizzie quickly jumped in. "I'll drive her and Sara Jane."

Mr. Benoit's forehead creased with a frown, but he nodded. "I'll meet you there." He turned and disappeared.

Sara Jane mouthed the words "thank you."

They each took Rachel's arms and slowly walked down the stairs. A duo of strength for Rachel.

Thank goodness Lizzie had offered to drive. Sara Jane didn't know if she could have tolerated going to the funeral with Steven. Who knows, he might have even tried to talk Rachel out of going. But Sara Jane truly felt that if Rachel didn't go, she'd regret it someday. She just hoped she'd made the right decision on persuading her to go.

She and Lizzie walked Rachel up the steps to the church. Twelve steps. She counted each one. Rachel's face paled—if it were even possible to pale more—as they stepped into the dimness of the church.

Rachel clutched her arm and looked at her, her eyes wide.

"It's okay. We'll be right here with you."

They walked right up to the front pew of the church and sat down, with Rachel sitting on the end looking like she might make an escape at any moment. Music played, but it wouldn't register in her mind what the tune was. Something she'd picked out. Steven came to the end of the pew and motioned for them to scoot down so he could sit by Rachel.

So there she sat with Rachel sandwiched in between her and Steven. The model of a supportive family. Like two normal parents helping their daughter through a terrible situation.

Only…

Nothing was normal anymore.

The service passed in a blur. Friends of

Ronnie's got up and paid tribute to him. Finally, Lizzie rose and went up front.

"Ronnie was…" She paused and closed her eyes, then opened them and cleared her throat. "He was a very special person. His laughter was infectious. His smile brought light to everyone. And… he loved Rachel so very, very much."

Rachel stiffened beside her and looked away from Lizzie. Sara Jane took her hand and squeezed it, but Rachel didn't react.

"Ronnie will be missed. But he would want all of us… Rachel… all of us… to go on living. To take each day as the blessing that it is and live life to the fullest. That isn't to say he won't be missed. He will. Greatly. But by living life fully, we honor his memory."

Lizzie came back to the pew and they moved their legs to let her scoot past them to her seat. Sara Jane wiped away her tears and gave Lizzie a small smile. She'd paid a wonderful tribute to Ronnie and his life.

She glanced at Rachel who had not shed one tear today. She'd actually not cried for the last few days. Always just the stony, silent, blank look on her features.

The pastor said a few words, more music

played, then thankfully the service was over. They rose and walked back down the aisle. The very aisle that Rachel had walked down with Ronnie at her wedding. The irony didn't escape her.

24

Lizzie stood in the large fellowship room of the church. Nodding at people. Accepting their condolences since everyone in town knew Rachel was her best friend. Her mind flashed back to that day she'd saved Rachel's life. Saved her from drowning. Now her friend was drowning again, and she wasn't sure how to save her this time. Or if she even could.

She looked around the room, searching for Rachel, wanting to make sure she was doing okay. Or at least surviving the day. Her eyes flew open wide as her gaze reached the entrance. Eric stood in the doorway dressed in slacks and a nice dress shirt, peering into the room. He looked ever so handsome. And older in some way. His hair was a bit longer than usual. His shirt was a light blue, the color that brought out the blue flecks in his eyes. She waved to him as he looked her direction, and he nodded, then threaded his way through the crowd.

She reached out her arms and pulled him into a hug, letting the assurance that her son was safe and right here wash over her. He felt so good in her arms. It had been so long since she'd seen him, hugged him. "Oh, Eric. I'm so glad you came."

"Yeah, well, I was talking to Dad and then Kiera got on the phone. She said she thought I should come. You know, since… Rachel and Ronnie are… were… well, you know…"

So he was listening to his stepmother more than his own mother these days? She shoved the jealousy away. At least he'd come. That's what was important.

"I saw Rachel out in the foyer. She looks horrible. Shaky. Pale." Eric's brow furrowed.

"It's been a big shock to her."

"Yeah, I bet. Ronnie was pretty cool."

"He was," she agreed.

"I've never been to a funeral. It was… strange."

"You should have come sit by me."

"Nah, you were up front with Rachel. I just ducked into a seat in the back."

"I'm glad you came. I'm sure it means a lot to Rachel and Sara Jane." It meant a lot to *her*.

Eric loosened the tie at his neck and shifted from foot to foot, looking every bit like he was going to launch his escape. She wasn't ready for him to leave. Who knew when she'd see him again?

"Would you like to go out to dinner with me tonight?" She ached to see him for more time. This whole thing with Ronnie made it crystal clear how fragile life was. Maybe if she and Eric went to dinner they'd have a chance to talk. She stared at his face, memorizing every detail, every change. A hint of a beard like he hadn't shaved this morning. The curl of his hair near his temple.

Eric shook his head. "Nah, I have to get back to school. Going to head out now, actually. Change clothes and go back. Gotta study."

"Okay." Disappointment surged through her.

Suddenly there was a glimpse of the old Eric. A look in his eyes. A look of compassion. A glimpse of the old Eric who cared about her feelings. "But maybe I could stay. Just for tonight. I could head back early morning."

"That would be wonderful." Gratitude swept away the disappointment. More time with her son. A chance to work things out.

"So, I'll meet you at Seaside Cafe at six? I'm going to go home and change," he said while glancing at the door, ready to make his escape.

She ignored the fact that David's house was now *home* to Eric. "Yes, I'll see you there."

She watched him disappear into the crowd. At least she'd have dinner with him tonight. She clung to that thought like a lifeboat as she looked around the room filled with people and their condolences and their looks of pity tinged with relief that it wasn't one of them holding the funeral for one of their loved ones.

Funerals were such strange, awkward events. She was ready for this one to be over. She swept her gaze around the room and saw Sara Jane talking to some ladies from the church, but no sign of Rachel. She'd better go find her.

Rachel had to get away from the crowd. If one more person told her how sorry they were. One more person hugged her. One more person told her how fabulous her husband had been… well, she was going to scream. Her jaw ached from clenching it and her fingernails had made red indentations on her palm from her tightly balled fist.

She knew how fabulous Ronnie was. Was, not *is*. She did. And every single fiber of her being was aching to have him back. To be in his arms. To see his smile. Just one more time.

No, that was a lie. One more time would never be enough.

She walked past a table of photos of Ronnie. One of him as a young boy with an impish grin. One standing beside his first car. A wedding picture where they'd been cutting the cake. And her favorite photo of them taken on the beach on their honeymoon. Her mother or Lizzie must have put this together because she, herself, had had no part in planning the funeral. She wanted no part in planning this final goodbye to her husband. As if it were even possible to say goodbye.

She stared at the photos as if they were someone else's life. They *were* someone else's life… because they'd never be her life anymore. Not without Ronnie.

She fought back the tears because she knew if the first tear fell, she'd never be able to stop crying again. Ever. The sobs would wrack through her, tearing her apart. And there was so little of her left now as it was. She felt like a ghost walking through a room, not really existing.

Would she ever truly exist again?

A faint nausea crept through her but she ignored it, just like she kept ignoring the fact she was pregnant, although her mother and Lizzie weren't making that easy. Anyway, she thought women were supposed to get morning sickness in the *mornings*, not late afternoon.

She looked wildly around the room fighting for breath, whirled around, and ran blindly out the nearest door, bending over as she reached the sunshine, struggling to catch a breath in the never-ending hot, humid air.

Lizzie appeared at her side, touching her back, patting her. When she could finally breathe—at least a little bit—she stood back up and looked at Lizzie.

Lizzie's eyes were full of sympathy, brimming just on the edge of tears. She closed her eyes. She couldn't see Lizzie cry. She'd lose her tenuous grasp on any semblance of control.

Lizzie's hand was at her elbow, warm, comforting. "Come on, I'll take you home."

She nodded gratefully, unable to talk. It was just like Lizzie to know when she needed her. Know that she needed to escape. She grasped Lizzie's arm and let her lead her away from the nightmare that was her husband's funeral.

"I'll text Sara Jane and let her know we're leaving. I'm sure she can catch a ride with someone."

"Will you stay with me?" Rachel whispered the words, afraid to be alone, a change from her leave-me-alone stance of the last week.

"Of course I will."

"You can stay and have some supper with me. I promise I'll eat if you stay." Suddenly she was desperate to have Lizzie with her. Maybe they could talk and pretend all this didn't happen. Pretend there was really life left to live.

Lizzie's eyes held a strange reluctance, but she nodded in agreement. "Of course. Whatever you need."

25

Gabe walked down the sidewalk in The Village area, hoping that maybe, just maybe, Lizzie might be at her shop. She hadn't come home after the funeral should have been long over. He was worried about her. Funerals were hard. But then, maybe she'd stayed at Rachel's house for a while. But there was always the chance she'd come to her shop to unwind.

At this point, he considered her a friend. He wasn't sure when that had happened. It just did. He didn't have many friends in his life since he'd moved around a lot. Hadn't really made any friends except Lizzie back here in Wind Chime. He'd been too busy getting the house ready and taking care of his mom. Though his mother did seem to be doing better now that she was back in her old house.

He continued down the sidewalk, peeking in the windows. Many of the shopkeepers looked like they were getting ready to close up soon. Shops sure didn't stay open late here in town.

He smiled when he saw faint light spilling out from Lizzie's shop. Just like he'd thought. She'd escaped to the shop. He knocked once and opened the door and stopped in surprise when he saw a young man standing there. "Oh, I was looking for Lizzie."

"She's not here." The young man looked at him closely.

"Oh," he said, wondering why the young man was here if Lizzie wasn't.

"Lizzie is my mom."

"Oh, you must be Eric."

Eric frowned. "I am. And you are…"

"Gabe. Gabe Smith. Lizzie moved in with my mother and me. A boarder at our home."

"Ah."

"Are you meeting Lizzie here?"

Eric looked around guiltily. "No… I just… I wanted to see the shop. She keeps going on and on about it when she calls. It looks pretty nice." His voice held grudging admiration.

"I think she's done a great job. I bet she'll be very successful." He didn't know why he was defending Lizzie so strongly to her son. He'd become protective of her since he'd gotten to know her. Her son should be very proud of all she'd done to get the shop ready.

"Anyway, I was pretty sure this key would work. Mom always likes to key things to what she calls the pink key." Eric held up a key. "Well, my copy isn't pink, but hers is."

He remembered seeing the pink key when she'd locked up. "Do you know where she is now?"

"She's with Rachel. She was supposed to meet me for dinner at Seaside Cafe, but she texted and said that Rachel had asked her to stay with her for a while."

"That's too bad. I'm sure she would have loved having dinner with you."

Eric shrugged.

"You know, your mother has had a long day. And I bet she'd love to see you again when she comes home. Do you want to follow me back to our place? You could wait for her at the house?" He knew that Lizzie had been missing Eric.

"I don't know." Eric frowned.

"I'm sure it would mean a lot to her. She's

probably had an emotionally draining, long day." Maybe he could do this small thing to improve Lizzie's day. Let her see her son this evening.

Eric shrugged again, wavering. "I guess I could. I can't imagine she'll be at Rachel's much longer. She's not much of a late-night person."

"Great. Let's lock up and you follow me. We're out on Three Bend Road."

Eric turned out the lights and carefully locked the door, then followed him back to the house.

He led him inside and called out as he entered. "Mom, I've got company. Eric, Lizzie's son."

His mom walked out of the kitchen with a towel in her hands, drying them as she walked. "Eric, so nice to meet you. Lizzie talks about you often."

"Ma'am." Eric nodded.

"Oh, you should call me Martha. But I can see your momma has raised you right. You hungry? I've got a stew on the stove. I was just waiting to eat until Gabe got home."

"I'm kind of hungry."

"Then come on. Let's get you fed. I've got

cornbread muffins to go with it and I made a chocolate cake for dessert."

Eric's eyes lit up. "That sounds great."

"Follow me." His mother led the way to the kitchen.

Gabe's stomach rumbled at the mention of the dinner. And now they'd get a chance to get to know Eric a little bit. Lucky chance, stopping by Lizzie's store and finding Eric. Hopefully, Lizzie would be home soon. And hopefully, she'd be pleased with the surprise he'd brought home for her.

Lizzie slowly walked out to her car. Sara Jane had found a ride home with the pastor's wife and shown up not long after she got Rachel settled back at home. And as promised, Rachel had eaten a few bites of supper, not much, and had finally drifted off to sleep. She looked at her watch, annoyed that she'd had to text Eric and cancel dinner. Aggravated and sad she'd missed her chance to have dinner with him since she saw him so rarely.

So much of her life was being put on hold

for Rachel. Opening the store. Spending the time with Eric that she desperately wanted. But Rachel needed her. She knew that. The thing was… Rachel always needed her, and to be honest, when she needed Rachel… well, the favor wasn't always returned. But even thinking that thought, the night of Ronnie's funeral, made her feel like a traitor. A lousy friend. A crummy human being.

She started the car and glanced up to see Sara Jane looking out, illuminated in the window. Poor Sara Jane stuck there in the house with Mr. Benoit. He'd come home from the funeral and made a remark about dinner, but Sara Jane had ignored him while the tension crackled between them. Sara Jane must be miserable living there. But she too, put her life on hold for Rachel.

She waved at Sara Jane but doubted she could see her. Exhaustion crept over her with each mile, concentrating on the white line on the center of the road. Making the turns automatically without really thinking about them. The headlights cut a wide swath illuminating the gravel drive and she was surprised to see she'd reached home without consciously knowing she'd gotten there. She was just as surprised that she thought of Gabe and Martha's house as *home*. She parked the car and slowly climbed the porch stairs. Each step taking an enormous amount of effort. This day would never end.

She scrubbed her hand over her face, trying to brush away the exhaustion. She was too tired to think straight tonight. As she entered the house, voices drifted in from the kitchen. She'd just duck in and say goodnight to Gabe and Martha and head upstairs and collapse into bed, ready to say the day was done. Finished. Over.

She entered the brightly lit kitchen and stopped short. She was so tired she was seeing things. She imagined that Eric was sitting at the table eating with Gabe and Martha. That made no sense.

Gabe jumped up. "Lizzie, you're home. Come, sit down. I ran into Eric and invited him to wait here for you."

"But how..." She looked at the three of them as confusion took hold. Eric was really here?

"Let me get you a plate." Martha rose and went over to the cupboard.

Lizzie just stood there trying to understand. "Eric?"

"Mom, sit. You look tired."

She did as he asked and sank onto the chair beside him.

"I was looking at your shop and Gabe came by at the same time to see if you were there. Anyway, I told him about you having to cancel our dinner so he asked me if I wanted to come wait for you to get home. Then Martha had this dinner all made." He grinned. "I can't pass up a free meal."

"I see." Though she hardly did. She glanced over at Gabe who smiled at her. She couldn't even put into words how much this meant to her. Seeing Eric after the horrible day she'd had. She'd been so sure that she'd missed her chance when Rachel had insisted she stay with her.

Suddenly her appetite roared in with a vengeance and she reached for a helping of stew and a muffin. Conversation swirled around her. Eric talked about his classes, answering Gabe's many questions. Martha urged Eric to eat more and he took another helping. Eric actually smiling and laughing. When was the last time she'd seen that?

Martha served them all big slices of chocolate cake, and it was probably the best cake she'd ever eaten. Or maybe it was just because she was enjoying herself so much. A simple dinner with friends and her son. Her son *smiling and laughing*.

Gabe pushed back from the table. "Mom, you've outdone yourself."

"It was really great," Eric added as he, too, pushed back.

Martha stood. "How about Gabe and I do the dishes and you two go talk for a bit. I'm sure you have some catching up to do."

She held her breath, sure that Eric would say that he needed to rush off.

"You sure you don't need help with the dishes?" Eric offered.

She smiled in spite of herself. At least he'd learned his manners well.

"No, you two go on. Gabe will help."

"I'd kind of like to see your room, see your setup here, Mom."

Delight swept through her as she stood. "Follow me."

She led him up to the top floor and down the hallway to her room. "That's a room for you, whenever you want it." She nodded toward the room they'd set up for him.

Eric peeked in, then continued to follow her down the hall and into her room. He slowly looked around, taking it all in. "It's nicer than I thought. I mean the room is huge and you have lots of your own stuff in here."

"It is nice."

"You got the whole top floor?"

"Basically."

"And does Martha cook like that all the time?"

She laughed. "She does. I keep telling her she doesn't have to cook for me, but she doesn't listen. I'm going to go to the store and buy up a bunch of her favorite foods and staple items. That's the least I can do. She says she loves having people to cook for."

Eric sank onto the edge of the bed. "You happy here?"

She almost broke into tears. The old Eric, sitting here. Asking how she felt. Caring about her. She swallowed back the tears. "I am. It works for now. I'll worry about finding a house after I get the shop up and running."

"I used the pink key and went in and looked at the shop. It's really nice."

"You did? You went inside?" That surprised her that he'd even be interested in the shop. He never asked questions and always seemed to want to end any conversation when she tried to talk about it.

"I knew the pink key would open it." Eric grinned.

"Ah, you know me so well." She sat down on the bed beside him and crossed her legs. "So, school is going well?"

"Better. I…" Eric looked down at his hands. "I moved out of the dorm this semester. Got an apartment with this other kid I know."

So she hadn't even known where her son lived? What kind of mother was she?

"The dorm had too many distractions. I know my grades have fallen."

That was an understatement, but she didn't say a word. She waited for him to continue.

"And… I met this girl. She's smart. And studies a lot. We study together all the time. I think it's helping my grades."

"That's good." He had a girlfriend? For how long? Another fact she didn't know about her son.

"Her name is Michelle, but everyone calls her Chelle. She… She told me I was being rude for not coming back to the funeral. That it was important to pay your last respects. That I was acting like a spoiled kid."

So it hadn't just been because Kiera suggested it. It made her feel strangely better that Chelle had been an influence, too.

"I'd love to meet her."

"Uh, sure. We could do that."

At least it hadn't been a no way.

"And Chelle said that I'm being a jerk to you, too. That family is important. She comes from a big family. Her parents, and two brothers, and two sisters. Her grandmother lives with her parents, too."

She was liking this Chelle more each minute.

"I know I've been… busy. Haven't seen you much. I brought Chelle home with me last time I came to town. She thought you were out of town or something since I didn't come see you. Then she was really mad at me after we got back to school, when I admitted to her you actually were in town." Eric shrugged. "I've been lame. It was so confusing when you and Dad divorced. I felt torn. I knew he was the one who wanted the divorce. I know he hurt you."

She adjusted her seat on the bed, utterly surprised at the words coming out of Eric's mouth.

"But still, it was easier to be at Dad's

because… well, he doesn't really ask questions. Doesn't have rules. And you just seemed so angry all the time. And sad."

"Oh, Eric. I'm sorry. I was angry. I felt lost and didn't know what I was going to do with my life. I'm sure it was hard for you." She took his hand. "But I've worked through it. And now I have my shop and have figured out what I want to be when I grow up." She gave him a small smile.

"I'm sorry if I hurt you."

"No, I understand. Everything you knew got blown apart, too. I should have handled it better." She should have been concentrating more on Eric and done less wallowing in her own pain. "I'm just glad you talked to me now and we sorted things out."

"Yeah, I hate being on the outs with you."

He smiled at her and her entire being filled with contentment. As if rightness filled her soul. The rightness of having her son with her. The sadness and incredible stress of the day began to ebb away. She pushed back a lock of hair at his temple.

He laughed. "Yeah, Chelle said I needed a haircut, too."

"No, I—" She laughed. "Okay, I was thinking that."

"So, how about you? When are you going to open the shop? Soon?"

"I was. But then Ronnie died and Rachel needs me. So I've put off the opening for a while."

Eric rolled his eyes. "Mom, you know I love Rachel, but she *always* needs you. She's just one of those kinds of people, always puts herself first. What kind of best friend is that, really?"

"But—"

"No, really. You're always dropping everything to do what Rachel wants. Now it's your time to open the shop. Do what you want. What makes you happy."

"But Ronnie just died. She's lost right now."

"I know it's not the same thing, but when Dad divorced you, did she drop everything to be there for you?"

No, she hadn't, but this was different. Right? "But I have to help her through this."

"You do. She's your best friend. But it doesn't mean you have to push back opening the shop or stop everything you need to do. Just make some time for her, but don't let it take over your life."

"How did you get so wise?" She squeezed his hand.

"I had a very smart mom. Well, except when it comes to Rachel." The familiar impish grin she loved so much spread across his face.

"And I have the best son ever."

26

Lizzie woke up to sun streaming in the window. How long had she slept? She rolled over and glanced at the clock. Way too long. Must have needed the sleep after yesterday.

She'd talked with Eric for over an hour last night, then he'd left, but not before promising to bring Chelle for a visit soon. It had been a heck of a day. Emotional in so many ways.

But today felt like a fresh start. She jumped out of bed and hurried to get dressed. She'd go check on Rachel, then go to the shop and get busy. Eric was right. She could be there for Rachel but not put everything on hold. She'd sit down at the computer, look at what still needed to be done, then set a grand opening date. Excitement skittered through her at the very idea of actually opening the shop. Something of her own. Something she'd worked hard to create.

She went downstairs and found Gabe and Martha at the kitchen table.

"Blueberry muffins on the counter. Just out of the oven. Coffee's made." Martha nodded toward the counter.

"You know, you don't have to keep feeding me." Although, she snagged a muffin and mug of coffee and sat down. "But I sure do enjoy your cooking."

"You look rested this morning. I was worried about you last night. You looked exhausted." Martha's forehead wrinkled with concern.

"I was until I got my surprise visit from Eric." She turned to Gabe. "I can't thank you enough for making that happen."

"Glad I ran into him." Gabe's smile was as warm as his hazel eyes.

"Did you get a chance to talk to him?" Martha asked.

"I did. And I think we sorted everything out." She took a sip of the welcomed coffee and set the mug back down. "And he told me he has a girlfriend."

"Well, that's nice."

"He's going to bring her to meet me soon. I already like her." She grinned. "Chelle—that's her name—seems to have a positive impact on his studying, and she encouraged him to come back for the funeral. She's from a big family and told him family is important."

"I agree with the girl. Gabe and I aren't a big family, but family is important."

"That's what my mom always tells me." Gabe winked at Martha.

"So what are your plans for today?" Martha asked as she went over to grab the coffee pot to refill everyone's mugs.

"I'm going to drop by and see Rachel. I know yesterday was horrible for her. But at least the funeral is behind her. There is some relief in that. Then, I'm heading to the shop. I want to pick a date for the opening."

"Oh, that's good news. And Gabe and I will be there for the opening, won't we, son?"

"Wouldn't miss it." Gabe nodded. "Is there anything else I can do to help you get ready?"

"You've already helped enough." She looked over at him. "And shouldn't you be back at your writing? Now that you have that perfect desk and everything."

A guilty look spread across his face. "I

should. I'm just having a bit of writer's block so I've been avoiding it."

"I'll go into work at the shop, and you go try to get some words on the page. Or the computer screen. Figure out whodunit."

"Lizzie is right. You've been so busy helping me. It's time you got back into a routine. Get back to your writing."

Gabe let out a long, exaggerated sigh, but his eyes twinkled. "I can't argue with both of you." He rose. "I'm going to grab another cup of coffee and head to my office." He grinned at Lizzie. "As ordered."

"You run along, too, Lizzie. I'll rinse up the breakfast dishes. I hope you get a lot done at the shop. And I'll see you for dinner tonight. I'm making meatloaf, mashed potatoes, and some fresh green beans."

"You don't have to feed me every meal."

"Don't try to argue with Mom. You won't win." Gabe laughed as he left the kitchen.

"But I enjoy it. Six o'clock work for you?"

"I'll be here."

"And take some muffins with you. Maybe Rachel will be tempted by them."

She hugged Martha. "Thank you." She hurried out to the car.

As a precaution, she texted Sara Jane that she was on her way over, and luckily Sara Jane opened the door. "Rachel's still in bed. Hasn't budged. I'd hoped that maybe with the funeral behind her, maybe she'd…" She shrugged. "I don't know. I just want to take away all her pain, but I can't."

"Did she eat breakfast?"

"Not a bite."

"Let me try. I brought some blueberry muffins Martha made." She held up the muffins carefully wrapped up on a plate.

"Martha, she's the one you moved in with, right? How's that working out for you, boarding with them?"

"It's wonderful. You'll have to meet her. I adore her. And her son, Gabe. You should meet him, too." And she realized that Rachel had never met Gabe or Martha either. They were so important to her life now and her best friend hadn't even met them.

They went upstairs, past the room Sara Jane had taken over, and into Rachel's room.

"Hey, Rach, I brought you the best blueberry muffins."

"Not hungry."

"Eat one anyway." She set it on the dresser and went over and threw open the blinds.

"That's too bright," Rachel grumbled.

"It's a beautiful day today," she said agreeably, ignoring Rachel's complaints.

"And I have some tea for you. It's in that thermal pot. I'm sure it's still hot." Sara Jane poured a cup of tea for Rachel.

"You know, we could go sit outside," Lizzie suggested. "It's not hot yet. A nice breeze this morning."

"No." Rachel shook her head.

"Okay, we'll put your tea and muffin over here by the chair by the window. Come eat."

Rachel muttered something under her breath but slung her legs off the side of the bed. Sara Jane snagged a robe and handed it to her. Rachel slipped on the robe and shuffled over to the chair, plopping down with a scowl on her face. She took one sip of the tea and a tiny bite of the muffin.

Lizzie perched on the bed beside Sara Jane. "So, after breakfast, how about you get dressed? You could go out and sit by the pool. Or even take a swim."

"I don't think so."

"Rachel, honey, you can't stay in your room

forever." Sara Jane frowned, her eyes filled with worry.

"I just lost my husband. I can do whatever I want," Rachel said peevishly.

"You did lose Ronnie and it's a terrible, terrible blow. But you need to think of the baby." She frowned at Rachel and her attitude of ignoring the baby's needs.

"Would you two just leave me alone?" Rachel screamed out the words, throwing the teacup across the room where it shattered into tiny pieces.

"Rachel." Sara Jane jumped up.

"Really, just leave me alone." Rachel leaped up, raced past the broken pieces of china, and headed into her bathroom, slamming the door behind her.

Lizzie got up and gathered the pieces of china. "I didn't mean to upset her."

"I know. She's grieving. It's just going to take time."

"But staying in bed all day, day after day, isn't going to fix her pain. Nor is it good for the baby."

Sara Jane wiped a lone tear that trailed down her face. "No, it isn't. But I'm at a loss with Rachel right now. Let's just give her space."

She put the broken pieces in the wastebasket and walked over to the bathroom door and knocked. "Rach, I'm leaving. I'll be back tomorrow."

No answer. She turned to Sara Jane and shrugged. Sara Jane closed her eyes for a moment, then opened them. "Come on. I'll see you out."

She trailed behind Sara Jane to the front door, wishing she could do more. That she could help. But at some point, Rachel was going to have to decide she wanted to help herself. And nothing she or Sara Jane said to Rachel would change that.

"Thanks for coming, Lizzie. I really do appreciate it." The lost look on Sara Jane's face tore at her heart.

"Can I do anything for you? Anything to help *you*?"

"No, I'm not sure what will help at this point. Maybe just time."

Lizzie slipped out the door into the lovely weather she'd tried to get Rachel to enjoy with no success. Sara Jane stood in the open doorway, watching her drive away. Probably avoiding going back inside to what her life had become now.

Sara Jane watched Lizzie's car disappear down the road. With a sigh, she turned and went back inside, looking around the formal foyer. She didn't like one thing about it. From the ugly vase of flowers to the dark paintings on the wall. And Steven had insisted on pulling up some beautiful old hardwood floors that had originally been in the house and putting down cold, impersonal marble. Her footsteps echoed as she crossed the floor and headed to the kitchen. It was almost lunchtime and she wanted to make a sandwich. Maybe she'd even make one for Rachel, even though she doubted her daughter would touch it.

She walked into the kitchen and stopped short. Steven sat at the kitchen table with a file open before him. Why wasn't he working in his office? Suddenly she wasn't as hungry as she thought she was. She started to turn around and leave.

"I'm having a dinner party for some clients." His voice interrupted her departure.

She didn't answer him. It was none of her concern.

"Friday."

"It's inappropriate to have a party now." She didn't even bother to turn around.

"They are coming in from London. I have no choice. I'll need you to plan a small dinner. About twelve people, maybe a few more."

"I'll give you the name of a caterer. That's all I'll do for you." She turned back around to face him.

"No, you'll plan the party. Cook one of your meals. My new assistant has already called and invited everyone." His cheeks turned fiery red and his eyes flashed.

Assistant. Is that what he was calling his new conquests now? She shook her head. "No, I won't."

"Yes, you will." He jumped up and stalked over to her, grabbing her wrist and twisting her arm behind her, pulling her close to him. "You're my wife. It's what you do. This nonsense will end. Now. I'm tired of it."

She forced herself not to close her eyes. To just stare into his fiery glare. "I'm not doing it, Steven. I refuse." And the wild thought that she'd like to stick out her tongue and tell him he couldn't make her flittered through her mind.

He took a step forward, pinning her between him and the counter, staring into her face with such fury that she held her breath. "Move out. Move out of my house."

"But Rachel…"

"She'll be fine. I'll hire a nurse until she snaps out of this. I'm tired of her sulking, too. And you'll not be allowed to enter the house. Do you understand? This is the choice you're making."

"You're saying if I don't throw your silly dinner party, that you'll keep me from seeing our daughter?" She couldn't believe that even Steven would stoop this low to get his way.

"Your choice." His eyes flashed in triumph, sure he'd get his way.

"No, this is your choice, Steven," she said softly. "Yours, and yours alone." She wrenched her arm free of his grasp, ignoring the pain in her shoulder when she did it. "I'll pack my things."

"You're leaving Rachel?"

"No, actually, I'm packing Rachel's things, too. Especially since you're tired of her *sulking*. We'll both be moving out."

"You can't take her."

"Watch me, Steven. Just watch me."

He reached out to grab her arm again and she sidestepped him. "I've had enough of your bullying. Enough of your commands. Enough of your cheating and lying."

He moved closer and grabbed her chin, forcing her to look right into his face, just inches from him. "This isn't over. You haven't won."

She grabbed his arm and tugged his hand from her face, her heart pounding in a riotous rhythm. "This isn't a contest where someone wins or loses. It's just the way it is. Your choice. Do you want Rachel and me to leave?"

"You can stay," he growled. "But only because of Rachel. I don't want to upset her. But this isn't over. You'll see."

She turned and walked out of the kitchen in slow, measured steps to make sure it didn't look like she was running away. But she wanted to run away. Far away. As far away from Steven as she could get. She needed to figure out a plan because it was clear things weren't working now. She no longer felt safe staying here in Steven's home.

She went to her room, rubbing the arm Steven had twisted. She stood in the middle of the room. Already this guest room seemed more like her than any other room in the house. After tossing the dark, striped bedspread, she'd ordered a bright floral one. She'd placed a rocking chair near the window. She'd taken down the dark curtains and just left the wooden blinds up, thinking she'd order some pretty curtains when she had time. She'd waited until Steven was gone to work one day and found a box of her things in the attic. A favorite vase from her grandmother. A small wooden box she'd found years ago and had on the dresser in her and Steven's room until he'd announced it was tacky and to get rid of it. She put both the vase and wooden box on the dresser in this new room of hers. Then she'd found an old afghan her grandmother had knitted, carefully packed away in a trunk, and placed it on the back of the rocking chair.

But really, none of this mattered now. Her small stake in making something, anything, in this house her own. Because now... she just didn't feel comfortable here.

Maybe she should pack a small to-go bag, just in case she had to leave in a hurry. Things she might need, but not think of if she was rushed. She carefully packed the bag and set it in the very back of the closet.

She headed to Rachel's room to check on her but stopped short when she saw Steven in the room.

"Mom, I was just talking to Daddy. He says he needs to have a business dinner for some important people coming in from London, but you said it was inappropriate. It's okay. He should have the dinner. I don't want Daddy's business to suffer because of… of me."

She eyed Steven warily.

"Great, then it's decided. I'm sure your mother can plan something in time. She always has."

"Steven, I told you I'm not throwing a dinner party for you."

"Of course you will. Rachel said it would be fine." Steven smiled at her triumphantly.

Rachel looked up at her, then over at Steven. "No, Mom, really it's okay."

"It's not okay, Rachel. I'm not going to plan a dinner, and cook for it and… I'm not." She shrugged.

Steven's jaw clenched and the triumphant smirk was replaced by a steely glare.

"I told your father that if he wants the dinner, I'd give him the name of a caterer and he can handle it himself." Or he could have his *assistant* arrange it all…

"But, Mom. You always do the dinners. Not

some caterer who doesn't know what Daddy likes."

"Not this time." She stood firm.

"Mom, don't be like that. Dinners like this, it's what you do best."

Ouch. That hurt. She stared at Rachel for a moment. "No, I'm not doing this one," she said softly, but assuredly.

"Then you can move out." Steven jumped up and roared at her.

Rachel burst into tears. "Mom, please. Don't do this. I don't want you to leave again." Rachel begged her, tears streaming down her face. "Don't fight with Daddy."

So *she* was fighting because she said no to throwing his silly dinner party? Somehow this had all become her problem? She stood looking at Rachel, then over at Steven who was grinning in victory again. She always gave into Rachel. Always. Steven knew it. And Rachel needed her now. She'd just lost Ronnie. And there was the baby to consider. If she didn't coax Rachel to eat, who would?

She alternated her gaze between Steven and Rachel. Wavering in her decision. Torn. Hating being put in this position.

27

Lizzie escaped to the shop, guilty that she was so glad to be away from the Benoits'. Away from Rachel and her insistence that she couldn't do anything. That life was over, even though she had a baby to consider now and the wonderment of motherhood ahead of her, albeit without Ronnie.

Guilty relief and pleasure swept over her as she opened the door to the shop. It was starting to feel familiar. Like it was hers and she belonged here. It had been a long time since she felt she truly belonged anywhere.

She went over to the big desk that held her computer—one that would do double duty as the checkout register—and sat down. The computer hummed to life as she switched it on, illuminating the worn desktop. She trailed her finger along the wood that gleamed with the polish she'd applied to it when she'd coaxed it back from tired and banged up to lustrous and vibrant. Once the computer started up, she instantly got lost in numbers. She finally clicked on the calendar and stared at it. When would be a good day for her opening?

Maybe the Thursday before the annual Beach Days Festival? That gave her three weeks. Then it would be open that weekend for the crowds the festival usually drew to town. With the decision made, she added the date to the calendar. Then she printed out a sign for the window. Grand Opening with the date. A fancier sign would be better, but this would have to do on her limited budget.

She added the opening date to the front page of her website, then remembered a chalkboard sign she'd picked up. She rummaged around until she found it and used fancy lettering to announce the opening. That class she'd taken on calligraphy came in handy these days. She set the sign out in front of the store and walked back inside.

Turning her efforts to a display in the corner next, she kept moving things, trying to get every detail exactly right. She must have put a dozen items on the side table, but nothing seemed exactly right. Maybe the lamp on the table was wrong? She stood back, tilted her head, and tried to see it from a new perspective.

The bell over the door jangled and she turned around. Great, just great. Just what she needed. "David, uh, hi."

"Eric said he came by to see the shop. I thought I'd come by and see it, too."

Why? Now that would be the bigger question. "Oh?" Like he was interested in anything having to do with her life now?

He eyed the room. "Looks a little crowded, doesn't it?"

She stared at him in disbelief. The man knew nothing about decorating. Nothing about color. She swept her gaze around the room, mad that David made her doubt herself. "No, I think it's perfect."

David shrugged. "Whatever. How'd you get the money for all of this?"

"That's really not any of your business, is it?"

"Eric said that you're living in a boarding house. Really, Lizzie?"

"David, do you need something, or did you just come to criticize me?"

"I just don't want to see you screwing up your life like this."

"My life is fine. Great, even."

"Whatever you say." David held up his hands. "Don't say I didn't warn you. I think you've taken on more than you can handle."

The bell over the door jangled again and Gabe walked in.

"She's not open yet. Can't you read the signs?" David frowned.

Like David had any right to kick someone out of *her* shop. Ignoring David's rude words, she walked over and tugged on Gabe's hand, pulling him into the shop. "Gabe, this is David. My ex. David, this is Gabe. I live at Gabe and his mother's home now."

Gabe stuck out his hand. "Nice to meet you."

David eyed Gabe carefully, obviously sizing him up, then slowly shook his hand. "Likewise."

"David was just leaving, weren't you? I'm pretty sure we were finished."

David looked at Gabe again. "I guess we were." He turned around and strode out the door, closing it firmly behind him.

Gabe looked at her closely. "You okay?"

Leave it to Gabe to know her well enough to see she was upset. "Yes. No. Argh, he makes me so mad sometimes." She threw up her hands. "I can't believe I let him get to me. That's on me. Ridiculous." Why did she let him bother her? Make her second guess her decisions?

"I'm sorry he got you upset."

"No, really. My fault. I let him get me upset. A habit that I need to break, because, really, I don't care what he thinks anymore." She let out a long breath and shook her hands, jiggling away the tension, and put on a deliberate smile. "See, all better."

"If you say so. You looked pretty mad."

"I'm over it." Or she would be over it. Soon. Like when she never had to see David again. But of course, that would never happen. They had a son together and they lived in the same small town. But a woman could dream, couldn't she?

"I was at the hardware store and thought I would drop in and see if you needed any help. Like my brawn to move some furniture or something." He held up an arm and squeezed his muscle, grinning.

"Or, maybe you're still avoiding your writing." She laughed at his antics.

"Maybe." The corner of his mouth quirked up in a grin.

The bell jangled again. Who knew she could have so many visitors before it even opened. She turned to see Sara Jane standing in the doorway. "Oh, Sara Jane. Perfect. You can meet Gabe." She paused and took note of Sara Jane's frazzled expression. "You okay?"

"What? I'm fine." But her words didn't convince Lizzie. Sara Jane walked over and took Gabe's hand. "So, you must be Gabe. I've heard so much about you and your mother."

"Nice to meet you." Gabe bobbed his head.

"I read one of your books. You had me fooled to the very end. I never guessed who the killer was." Sara Jane smiled at Gabe.

He laughed. "I'm not really guessing who the killer is in this book I'm writing either."

"Sara Jane is Rachel's mom." Lizzie rushed to explain but was sure Gabe remembered that fact. He remembered lots of little details about lots of things. He always listened so carefully to her.

"I'm sorry about your loss, ma'am."

"Thank you, but please, call me Sara Jane."

She looked around the shop. "I just needed to get out of the house for a bit, and thought I'd come by and see your shop. It looks lovely, Lizzie. So inviting. You have such a great eye for this."

A bit different than the way David had appraised the shop. "Thank you. That means a lot to me."

"If Lizzie doesn't need my muscle, I think I'll duck out now and leave you two ladies to chat."

"Thanks for stopping by. I'll see you at dinner."

Gabe disappeared out the door and Sara Jane turned to her. "I thought I saw David leaving the shop as I was coming down the sidewalk."

She let out a long sigh. "You did. He came by to—as near as I can figure out—tell me what a mistake I'm making and how I'm not arranging things here in the shop correctly."

Sara Jane shook her head. "He always let you decorate the house. I didn't even think he cared or had an opinion on anything like that."

"It appears he does now. Along with my business decisions. He basically told me I was going to fail."

Sara Jane walked over and took her hands. "He's wrong. I think you're going to make a big success of this. You're very talented."

"Thank you."

"So put what he said out of your mind."

"Okay, I will. But now you talk. Something's wrong. I can see it in your eyes. What is it?"

"Everything," Sara Jane said, then laughed quietly. "Now, I sound just like Rachel, don't I?"

"A bit." Lizzie smiled but knew that something had really upset her.

"I'm so annoyed with myself." Sara Jane collapsed into a chair. "Oh, this is comfortable." She ran her hand along the arm of the chair. "And nice, soft fabric."

"Thank you. It is. But that's not what we're going to talk about. Why are you annoyed?"

"It appears I'm throwing a dinner party for Steven Friday night."

"You're what? How did that happen?"

"I told Steven I wouldn't, but then he did an end-run around me and talked to Rachel. She said I should do it. Plan the party. Cook." Exhaustion emanated from Sara Jane.

"But you shouldn't do it if you don't want to." She sank onto a matching chair beside Sara Jane. "These *are* comfortable."

"So… Steven said if I didn't do the dinner party, he'd throw me out of the house."

"He wouldn't really. Would he?" She raised an eyebrow. "But would that be so bad? To be away from Mr. Benoit? Though, there is Rachel. Mr. Benoit would never make her eat or make her do anything. She might just stay in bed the rest of her life." Maybe that was a total exaggeration, but then, maybe not.

"I told him that I'd pack up Rachel and take her with me, but…" Sara Jane looked down at her fingernails as if just noticing they were in need of a manicure, which they were, then looked up at Lizzie. "But I'm not sure she'd move with me if I move out."

"Oh, I bet she would." She wanted to sound supportive, but she wasn't sure Rachel *would* move with Sara Jane.

"Anyway, I decided it was easier to throw the silly dinner party than upset Rachel. She has it so hard now. I don't want to unsettle her even more. And really, Ronnie's funeral was just yesterday."

"But a dinner party? Now?"

"I know. I told him it was inappropriate, but he won't listen. Got Rachel to side with him on how *important* it was to have the dinner."

What Mr. Benoit wanted was always important. What other people wanted or needed? Not so much. "I'm sorry."

"Sometimes it's easier to give in to Steven than to fight him. And I really don't have the energy to argue with him right now. Especially once he got Rachel on his side. I already sat down and planned the meal. Ordered in the groceries to be delivered tomorrow."

"I could come help you get things ready on Friday."

"No, you have enough with the shop."

"You have Rachel and the baby to worry about and now this stupid dinner."

Sara Jane's mouth slipped up in the tiniest of smiles. "I'm not making any of Steven's favorites. And I'm not making anything that takes much time to prepare. I couldn't care less what these people from London think of me, the dinner, or Steven's business affairs. I even ordered a bakery pie and store-bought rolls. I'm not making those."

Well, that was a change. Sara Jane was known for her excellent baking skills. "Good for you." She eyed Sara Jane wondering if she should say what was on her mind or keep quiet.

Sara Jane laughed. "Go ahead and say it. I can see you want to say or ask something."

She gave in. "You know. When Rachel gets a bit stronger and gets her footing, you really need to have a heart-to-heart talk with her. Explain you were getting ready to leave Steven. Do you still plan to leave him?"

"I do. When I can." Exhaustion swept across Sara Jane's face and seeped into the corners of her eyes. "But I just can't see that it's going to be very soon."

"Rachel will get stronger. She'll get her feet under her. I expect her to start getting excited about the baby again any day now." Or at least she hoped Rachel would. And it sounded so positive to state it with certainty. As if just saying it would somehow give Rachel strength.

"I hope so." Sara Jane rose, sliding her hand along the fabric of the arm of the chair one last time as if bidding it goodbye, unwilling to leave it. "I should head back now. Check on Rachel."

She jumped up. "How about we go for ice cream first? Doesn't that sound decadent? That new ice cream shop just opened down the street. Let's do our best to support a new business."

A bit of the exhaustion slipped from Sara

Jane's features. "Oh, let's do that. You know, if only to support a new business."

They walked out of the shop, arm in arm. She could use a bit of escapism and downtime herself. Plus, rumor had it that the shop had the best butter pecan ice cream ever. She'd love to see if the rumor was true.

28

The week passed in a blur for Lizzie as she settled into a routine. Go see Rachel on her way to the shop and try to coax her to eat. Head to the shop to work long hours, often until late evening, before heading home. Martha left her dinner in the oven on warm each night even though Lizzie kept insisting that she didn't have to do that. But Martha insisted just as strongly that she did.

She bought an old van to use for deliveries. Gabe had checked it out for her and said it was in good mechanical condition and she'd gotten quite a deal on it. That was one more thing checked off her miles-long to-do list.

She glanced at her watch on Friday night, surprised to see it was after nine. She wondered how the dinner had gone for Sara Jane. Maybe she could drop by and check on her. She could park down the street, go around back, and peek in the back door from the pool. If the dinner was over and Sara Jane was in there cleaning up, she'd knock and see if she could help. No way she was going to the front door.

She passed by the Benoits' and there were no cars in the driveway. Great, the dinner must be over. She parked down the street and took the familiar back pathway to the pool area. The one she and Rachel used to take when they were young.

She was glad to see light spilling out of the kitchen window as she approached. As she got closer to the door, loud voices spilled outside. Mr. Benoit's. She peeked in the window and gasped. He had ahold of Sara Jane's arms, clenching them tightly, then smashed her backward against the wall.

She rushed to the door and threw it open. "What's going on?"

"Elizabeth. Get out. You can't just burst in here." Mr. Benoit turned, and his angry eyes bore into her.

She ignored him. "Sara Jane, you okay?" An

angry red blotch covered Sara Jane's cheek. "Let her go."

Mr. Benoit slowly released his clamped hands from Sara Jane's arms. "This has nothing to do with you. Leave my house or I'm calling the police."

She ignored him once again. "Sara Jane, you're coming with me. You're leaving. Enough is enough."

Sara Jane stood, rubbing her arms, saying nothing, a look of shock in her eyes.

She turned at the sound of a noise in the doorway to the kitchen. Rachel stood there in her robe, frowning. "What's going on? I heard all the noise. Mom, are you fighting with Daddy again? And why are you here, Lizzie?"

"I came to check on your mother. See if she needed help cleaning up after the party."

Rachel just stood there staring at her.

"When I came in he was hurting your mom. Look at her arms. And he smashed her against the wall." Angry red patches were clearly evident on Sara Jane's bare arms where Mr. Benoit had grabbed her. "And look at her face. See that?" Lizzie pointed at the obvious slap mark on Sara Jane's face. "He hit your mother."

"No, he didn't. Daddy wouldn't do that."

Sara Jane slowly reached her hand up to her head, and when she brought it back, there was blood on it.

"You're hurt." Lizzie stepped forward.

"She's clumsy. Always falling. That's what happened. She was falling and I was trying to catch her."

"That's not what happened. I saw you slam her against the wall." She spit the words out at Mr. Benoit, furious at his lies.

"Lizzie, you're making things worse. You heard him. Mom was falling."

"I wasn't falling," Sara Jane said softly as she reached for a towel on the counter and held it to her head.

"Let me see your head." Lizzie walked over and looked at it carefully. "I don't think it needs stitches but you're going to have quite the bump."

"She tripped," Mr. Benoit insisted again.

Lizzie whirled around to face him. "No, she did not. You shoved her. And what about that slap mark on her face. Did she slap herself, too?" She turned to Sara Jane. "Come on. Let's pack your things and you're coming with me. Rachel, let's get you packed up, too."

"Lizzie, this isn't helping. And I don't want Mom to leave."

"Rachel, you're not serious. Look at her. She can't stay." Even Rachel could see that her mother couldn't stay. Right?

"I'm tired of this nonsense. Leave. I sure don't care. I think it's a great idea. Move out, Sara." Mr. Benoit spun around and stormed out of the kitchen, his steps echoing as he crossed the house and slammed out the front door.

"He's probably going off to visit his newest fling. I heard one of his business associates at dinner saying he was seeing the new assistant he hired." Sara Jane slumped against the counter.

"Mom, don't say that. He told me that he wasn't seeing anyone anymore."

Lizzie turned to Rachel. "And you believed him? Really, Rach? And *anymore?* Like it was okay that he cheated before? Come on. Let's get you two packed up."

"No... I'm staying. I want to stay in my room. It's familiar. It's... I don't know. Mom, please don't leave. Stay here with me."

"Rachel, your mom has to leave. Look at this. What he did."

"But... I can't leave. Can't go somewhere new."

"You can always go to your own home."

"No, I can't do that. I just can't." Rachel shook her head vigorously, her hair bobbing around her shoulders.

She gave up on convincing Rachel, but she had to persuade Sara Jane. She could not be here when Mr. Benoit came back. "Sara Jane, come home with me tonight. You can stay in Eric's room. We'll figure this all out in the morning."

"I'll just get a room somewhere. But you're right. I do need to leave."

"No, you're coming with me." She sent off a quick text to Gabe before Sara Jane could argue any further. "There, it's decided. I'm coming upstairs with you to get your things."

"You can't leave me here all alone," Rachel wailed.

"Rachel, it's your choice. You can come with us or stay. But it's your choice to make."

"I don't want to leave."

"Well, your mother is." She gently took Sara Jane's arm and led her up the stairs.

Rachel trailed behind them, tears starting to fall. "You can't leave me."

Sara Jane paused on the landing and turned. "Rachel… I have to. Please come with me."

"I… I want Ronnie." The tears flowed down her cheeks.

"I know, honey, but he's gone. Things have changed. It's your choice. Pack and come with us, or stay."

Lizzie looked at Sara Jane in admiration. She never really stood up to Rachel. But look at her now. Good for her.

"I can't leave…" Rachel slid past them and up the stairs.

They followed her upstairs and went into Sara Jane's room. She cleaned up Sara Jane's scalp. The abrasion wasn't bad, but a healthy-sized bump was already forming.

When she was finished, Sara Jane pulled out her already packed suitcase, then they filled up another bag with some more toiletries and clothes. At the last minute, Sara Jane grabbed a vase, a wooden box, and an afghan off the back of the rocker.

"Let me try one more time with Rachel," Sara Jane said.

They stood in the doorway to Rachel's room. She was sitting in the chair by the window staring outside into the darkness. "Please come with us," Sara Jane implored her daughter.

"I can't. I'm staying. I can't believe you're leaving me here all alone. You're leaving me. Ronnie left me. Everyone leaves me."

Lizzie pushed past Sara Jane and walked over to Rachel, staring at her for a long minute before speaking. "Rachel, at some point in your life, you're going to have to grow up. Take responsibility for your choices. Think about others... stop being so..." She paused as Rachel's cheeks dotted with red spots and her eyes widened, but she plunged on. "Stop thinking only about what's best for you."

"I'm not—"

Lizzie held up her hand, cutting her off. "Really, Rachel. You need to do some soul searching and figure out how you want the rest of your life to go. You have choices to make. Your future and how you want to live it is up to you." She turned around and walked out of the room.

"Fine, you can leave me too, Lizzie," Rachel called after her. "Just fine,"

Rachel's words followed them down the hall. She glanced at Sara Jane expecting to see tears, but instead, a look of determination settled on her features.

She drove Sara Jane to Gabe and Martha's

in silence. As she pulled into the drive, Sara Jane reached over and touched her arm. "Thank you for tonight. For everything you did. For bringing me here."

"I'm glad I was there to help."

"And, Lizzie? What you said to Rachel? It was something I couldn't bring myself to say to her, but she needed to hear it. I just hope she listened to you and thinks about what you said."

Lizzie wasn't so sure about that. Rachel had been furious when they left. And she didn't know what it would take to ever get Rachel to change.

Rachel sat in the chair by the window, staring out into the darkness. Numb. And angry. So very angry. Her hands trembled as she clenched the armrests. How could her mother just up and desert her now? Right when she needed her most. Ronnie had died. Did no one understand that? He was gone. Gone forever.

She didn't really believe her father could have shoved her mother like Lizzie said. Or slapped her. And Daddy had said that Mom had tripped. That seemed the most logical explanation.

Okay, he did cheat on her mother. She knew that and didn't approve. She wouldn't be surprised if he still was. But hadn't her mother accepted how Daddy was for so many years? Why was it all of a sudden such a big deal? Some men cheat. Everyone knows that. But look at all Daddy had provided. This nice big house. Nice things in it. Fancy vacations. It wasn't like Daddy's cheating really affected how their lives were.

Anyway, it all went back to the fact that her mother had deserted her. Left her here all alone. And her mom knew she hated being alone in this house. Her father had been so mad when he left, she doubted if he would show up again tonight.

And Lizzie. Some friend she turned out to be. How could Lizzie talk to her like that? Say those things. She wasn't selfish. She wasn't. Hadn't she brought Lizzie into her crowd of popular friends back in high school? That had changed Lizzie's whole life. But was Lizzie grateful? No.

And what was Lizzie rambling about anyway? She couldn't just choose her future.

She wanted her future to be with Ronnie. And that couldn't happen.

Her hand slipped down to rest on her belly. And this baby. Why couldn't it have happened sooner? Or later? Or any time that would have changed the sequence of events. Ronnie wouldn't have been on that exact roadway, at that exact time. He'd be here with her.

She'd always thought mothers felt connected to their babies as soon as they got pregnant. But she felt nothing for this baby. It didn't feel real. It was an it. A non-thing. Sometimes she almost forgot it existed.

How had her perfect life turned into such a nightmare? She stared up at the starlit sky, but it refused to give her any answers.

29

Sara Jane woke up with a start, unsure of where she was. Then it all came rushing back to her. The dinner party. Steven. Rachel.

Rachel who had pleaded with her to stay. Only, of course she couldn't. An impossible decision. She'd have to call Rachel in a while. She was not an early riser, so there was no use trying now.

She climbed out of bed and gingerly touched her head. Quite a bump up there.

Tripped. Anger surged through her as she remembered Steven's words.

Thank goodness Lizzie had been there to step in. What would he have done next?

No, she wasn't going to let thoughts of Steven ruin her day. She pushed him from her mind and hurried to get dressed, deciding on a lightweight, long-sleeved shirt to cover the bruises on her arms where Steven had grabbed her.

Steven again. Always there at the back of her mind. Or the front of her mind. She scrubbed a hand over her face as if she could just wash any thought of him away.

She walked over and looked out the window, holding the lacy curtain aside to see the view. Sunshine streamed through the fluffy white clouds dotting the brilliant blue sky. A pretty garden below her soaked up the rays. It looked like someone had been recently working on tidying it up. The job wasn't finished, but parts of it had obviously had some recent love and attention. The whole scene could be painted and plopped into the dictionary beside the definition of peaceful. She stood there soaking it all in, enjoying the serenity.

A knock sounded at the door. "Come in. Oh, morning, Lizzie. I was just looking down at Martha's garden. It's lovely."

"She said she still has a lot of work to do on it. I gather it was quite neglected over the years while she rented out the house. But it is pretty, isn't it?"

"I could help her. I used to love to garden. But Steven insisted we get gardeners and said I would mess things up if I puttered in the garden." *Steven again. Go away.*

"Steven's a jerk."

"He is that." She nodded agreeably. And that was one of the kindest terms she could think of to describe him.

"How are you feeling today?"

"I do have quite the lump on my head. But I'm okay." She deftly moved their focus of conversation off of her. "I wonder how Rachel did last night."

"I don't know. But you could try calling her in a bit. She's probably still sleeping. I doubt she'd pick up a phone call from me right now. Not after how I talked to her last night."

"But you were right to say what you did. She does have to make some decisions." She shrugged. "She needs to grow up. But I blame myself for how she is. We always spoiled her. Always made things easy for her. But the timing of all of this is unfortunate."

"I sure don't mean to be heartless, but she'll have to deal with what life has thrown at her now. I am heartbroken for her that Ronnie is gone, I am. But life is hard sometimes. We don't always get what we want. And she's been given the gift of life, a baby."

"I think the problem is that Rachel *has* always gotten everything she wanted. Always."

"That's true." Lizzie's face clouded. "Anyway, how about we go downstairs and get some coffee? We'll talk after breakfast. Try to figure things out."

More than willing to put her problems behind her, she followed Lizzie down the stairs, drawn to the kitchen by the delicious aroma of cinnamon and freshly brewed coffee. Martha was just taking a coffee cake out of the oven when they entered the room. She turned around, a welcoming smile on her face. "Good morning. Hope you're hungry. I tried a new recipe for coffee cake."

"It smells wonderful," Sara Jane said. "Can I help you with anything?" It was the least she could do for everything Martha had done by putting her up here in her home at the last minute.

"Sure. The mugs are over the coffee pot. Can you pour us all some?"

Gabe joined them in the kitchen. "I couldn't stand it any longer. Mom, that smells delicious."

"You all sit. I'll bring over the coffee cake.

Oh, and Gabe, there's a bowl of fresh fruit in the fridge. Will you grab that?"

They all settled around the kitchen table and dug into the tasty breakfast. She couldn't believe what an appetite she had this morning. Everything was delicious. She turned to Martha. "I sure appreciate you putting me up here last night. I hope I wasn't too much of a bother. And now you're feeding me this lovely breakfast."

"Not at all. Glad to have you."

She hoped Martha was as sincere as her words sounded. "I'll go look for a place to live this morning. I'm sure I can find something." She could even just get a hotel room until she found a new place to live.

Martha set down her coffee mug and touched a finger lightly to her lips. "You know, you could board here like Lizzie does. We have that empty third room upstairs.

"Great idea," Gabe chimed in, nodding vigorously.

"I don't know. I don't want to be a bother."

"You're not. We could use another boarder," Martha assured her.

"That's a great idea. I have another bedroom set just sitting in storage. You could use that." Lizzie grinned, looking pleased. "This will be great."

"Are you all sure?"

All three of them replied with a chorus of yes.

"Okay, it looks like you have a new boarder."

"Perfect." Martha beamed.

"Oh, and my van I bought for the shop. We could go get the bedroom set from storage." Lizzie waved her fork, a triumphant grin on her face.

"I'll help with that," Gabe offered.

"Avoiding writing again?" Lizzie teased.

"I resemble that remark." Gabe tossed his head back, laughing.

Sara Jane relaxed at the easy banter around the table. It would be nice to live in a house where tension didn't crackle in every room. Where she didn't have to tiptoe around so as to not upset Steven.

But she did need to call Rachel and check on her, see if she was eating. Though, she wondered if Rachel would take her call, either.

Rachel did not disappoint. She neither answered any phone calls or texts. Sara Jane gave up for a bit and went with Gabe and Lizzie to retrieve the furniture. After they hauled it all up to the third floor—not something any of them would want to do again any time soon— she collapsed on the bed beside Lizzie.

"I've got some sheets for the bed in that box." Lizzie pointed to a box in the corner. "But I'm not sure I have the energy to get up and open it."

"You don't need to do anything else. You've done more than enough. Both you and Gabe."

"I still say he was just looking for a good excuse to avoid his words for the day." Lizzie shoved herself upright. "Speaking of that. I need to head to the shop. You going to be okay?"

"I'm fine. I'll just unpack my things and settle in."

"Rachel still not answering you?"

"No, not yet."

"She will. She just needs some time."

Maybe, but Sara Jane wasn't so sure.

Lizzie left and Sara Jane made the bed. Then she unpacked her bags, hanging up clothes and putting things in the hall bathroom. She carefully placed the vase and the wooden box on the dresser. She folded the afghan at the end of the bed and ran her fingers along the familiar pattern. There, it felt a little bit like home.

Maybe she'd drive over and see if she could get Rachel to answer the door. But what if Steven was there? Then she realized she didn't have her car anyway. She sank on the edge of the bed and rested her head in her hands. How had things gotten so messed up?

She wallowed in her pity party for a few minutes, then sat up straight. Enough of that. She'd made the decision to move out. She was going to call her lawyer and continue with the divorce. Her life was changing, but she vowed to make it into something…

Into what?

She had no idea. But she was going to make it into one she was proud of. Find a job. A permanent place to live, although Martha's house was lovely for now.

She sent one more text off to Rachel.

I'm worried about you. Please answer me. I want to see you. And even if you're mad at me, please try to eat something.

She stared at the phone screen, hoping for a reply. After a few minutes she gave up.

She jumped off the bed. She'd go find Martha and see if she wanted some help in her garden. That would keep her busy and productive. And maybe keep her mind off of Rachel, though she doubted it.

Three days later Sara Jane was crazy with worry about Rachel. Was she eating? Was she doing okay? She helped Martha cook and worked side by side in the garden with her, trying to keep busy.

Late that morning, while she was kneeling beside a gardenia bush, weeding below it, she heard the ping of a text. She stripped off her gloves and grabbed her phone.

Daddy's gone out of town on a business trip. Your car is here. Do you want to come get it?

"Is it Rachel?" Martha paused her hands full of mulch.

"It is. She says Steven is gone and I can go get my car."

Martha stood and pulled off her gardening gloves. "Let's go talk to Gabe and get him to take you over."

"I don't want to take him from his work."

Martha laughed. "Haven't you figured it out yet? He's having a bit of writer's block. He'll take any excuse to take a break. Text her back that you'll be over in just a bit."

She hurried upstairs, got cleaned up, and met Gabe downstairs. "I really appreciate you taking me."

"No problem. Besides, Mom has a list of things for me to pick up from the grocery store. I gather we're having a peach pie for dessert tonight."

Gabe was such a wonderful son. Helping Martha. She'd gathered that Martha didn't drive anymore and was dependent on him for errands and carting her around. But he didn't seem to mind.

"I appreciate you helping Mom out in the garden. She really wants to get it all looking better. Like it was before when we lived here."

"I'm glad to help her. It keeps me busy. And we've been comparing baking secrets, too. I really enjoy her company."

Gabe dropped her off at her home. No, Steven's home. Not hers anymore. He waited in the car while she knocked at the door. Then knocked again, glancing back at Gabe, hoping she hadn't dragged him out here for nothing. Though, she could probably get into the garage and get the car, even if Rachel wouldn't answer.

Finally, Rachel opened the door. Gabe stuck his hand out the car window, waved, and pulled away.

"Oh, Rachel, it's so good to see you. Are you doing okay?"

"Just great." Rachel scowled.

"Are you eating?"

"Did you just come to nag me?"

"Rachel, I'm only concerned about you and—"

Rachel held up a hand. "I know, I know. About the baby."

She stood there, not knowing what else to say. How to mend things between them. She thrust a basket toward Rachel. "Here, Martha packed you a basket of things you might like to eat. There's some soup, her homemade bread, and some brownies."

Rachel's face wrinkled up. "Why would she do that? She doesn't even know me."

"Because she's a very kind and caring person."

"I hate being here alone," Rachel said with a hint of accusation in her voice.

"I know."

"If you apologize to Daddy, I bet he'd take you back."

She stared at her daughter in astonishment. Who was this person standing in front of her? "I don't have anything to apologize for. He struck me, Rachel. He threw me against the wall."

"I'm sure he didn't mean to."

Anger mixed with disbelief surged through her. "Rachel, do you hear yourself? You want me to move back in with a man who abuses me? You can't possibly think that's going to happen."

Her daughter stood there silently, looking forlorn. And looking for all intents and purposes like, yes, she did expect her mother to move back in.

She stared at Rachel again, taking in all the details. Still in her nightgown. Hair not brushed. Not smartly dressed, including jewelry and full makeup, like she was used to seeing. Just standing there waiting for someone else to fix her life for her. To rescue her. But this time, she was the only one who could rescue herself. "I'm going to get my car now. You should eat something. And if you'd like to meet me tomorrow at the gazebo at Sunset Beach, I'll bring lunch. I'll be waiting for you. I hope you come."

She turned around and headed around the house to the garage, hoping that Steven hadn't disabled the car or sold it or something. She went in the side door to the garage, slid into her car, hit the remote opener, and waited for the garage door to lumber open. She held her breath and pushed the ignition. The car purred to life. With a sigh, she pulled out of the garage. As she drove past the front door, Rachel was still standing there in the open doorway.

Clenching the steering wheel, she willed herself to kept driving right past her, out the driveway and onto the street. One of the hardest things she'd ever had to do.

30

That evening after dinner Gabe and Lizzie sat out on the porch, sipping glasses of icc-cold tea. The lazy spin of the ceiling fan above them moved the humid air. Lizzie fanned herself with her hand, then swept her hair off of her neck, trying to cool off.

"Feels like a storm coming in." Gabe rocked back and forth in the freshly painted rocker on the porch. Freshly painted, thanks to Sara Jane, who was doing everything she could think of to keep busy.

"It does."

As if to confirm their guess, lightning crackled in the distance, lighting the sky and illuminating a live oak tree in the front yard.

"With all the planting Mom and Sara Jane have done in the garden, they'll appreciate a good rainfall."

"They have done a lot on the garden. It looks so nice."

"I know Mom loves having the company out there while she works on it."

"Sara Jane is trying so hard to keep busy. At least she got to see Rachel today. Though I take it, it didn't go very well."

"I'm sorry about that."

"Rachel won't answer my calls or texts. I feel terrible. I know I was hard on her that night Sara Jane left. And at a time Rachel was having a rough go of it. But Sara Jane was having a hard time, too."

"I know you didn't say anything, but I saw the bruises on Sara Jane's arm the other day. And what I think was a bruise on her face that she's trying to cover up with makeup. It's not hard to connect the dots," Gabe said quietly.

Lizzie looked over at Gabe's kind face. He probably couldn't imagine a man striking a woman. Heck, *she* couldn't understand it. "Sara Jane is a strong woman. She's going to get through all this."

"I'm sorry she has to deal with it. On top of dealing with Rachel. And losing her son-in-law."

"Life is really crummy sometimes, isn't it?"

"At times." Gabe took a sip of his drink. "But we all have to deal with what life throws us."

There was a faraway look in his eyes, and she wondered what he was thinking. Before she could ask, a crack of thunder boomed, shaking the house.

"You want to go in?" he asked.

"I'd kind of like to stay out here and watch the storm come in."

He stood. "Then let's move over to the glider. It's more protected."

She followed him over to the glider and settled beside him. The rain splattered down on the roof of the porch. Lightning cracked again and again. Thunder raged.

But here on the porch, sitting next to Gabe, slowly gliding back and forth, the fury of the storm was somehow soothing instead of frightening. The storm had also pushed in a welcomed cool breeze as it swooped in around them.

The ice in Gabe's glass rattled as he took a sip. "So how's the shop coming along? Getting things all ready for the opening?" He slowly pushed the glider into motion.

"I am. So close. I'm sure I'll keep thinking of more things that need to be done up until the moment I put the open sign in the window, but really, things are taking shape. It looks better than I had ever imagined." Did that sound like she was bragging?

"I'm happy for you. How's the website coming?"

"I'm getting that finished up, too. I was stuck, but Eric happened to call, and he walked me through how to fix it."

"Pays to have a techie son, I guess." A flash of lightning illuminated his smile. "Glad you two are getting along now."

"So am I. I sometimes—" She stopped. It just sounded too terrible if she put it into words.

"Go on, tell me." His look of encouragement gave her courage. And he was just so easy to talk to. Maybe even easy to bare her soul to?

"I feel like suddenly my life is starting to fall in place. That I've *made* it fall into place. I've worked so hard. And I'm just so content with my life now. It's… it's a strange and unusual feeling for me. This contentment. And I feel guilty that I feel this way when Rachel is so miserable. She's my best friend. And I don't seem to be able to help her."

"I think Rachel is going to have to figure out how to help herself. Maybe she's just so angry right now at what's happened that she can't sort it out yet. You and Sara Jane are safe people to take her anger out on. Like a kid does with his mom sometimes, knowing he won't lose her love when he does."

She stared into his eyes. "Maybe you're right. We do love her. I want to help, but she's pushing me away."

"She's going to have to figure it all out. What her new life is going to be like. I know from experience, we sometimes have to just deal with situations we never dreamed we'd have to deal with."

She looked at him expectantly, but he didn't offer any other explanation. She leaned back in the glider, the gentle back and forth soothing her like a beloved quilt on a cool winter's night. Familiar, comforting. The simple moment was just so perfect.

They sat like that, watching the storm ebb

and flow around them until it finally started to ease.

She looked over at him and caught him staring at her with a peculiar look on his face. She smiled at him and he leaned closer. Her breath caught in her throat and her pulse started to race. Before she could think, do the sensible thing to pull away, his lips settled on hers. Warm. Gentle.

Confusion swirled through her. Pull away? Deepen the kiss? Why was this so difficult?

She jerked back and put her hand up to her mouth. He stared at her a long moment. "I... you okay? I thought..."

"No. I mean..." She jumped up. "I wasn't expecting it."

"I wasn't either. It just felt... right." His gaze bore into her.

She looked away. "I'm not ready for anything like that. I just wanted us to be friends."

The glider squeaked as he moved. "Then that's what we'll be. Friends. Didn't mean to upset you. Won't happen again."

Did his words have a hint of hurt laced in them? "Gabe, I—"

"No, it's fine. Don't worry about it. We'll be friends. I *like* being friends with you."

She turned to look back at him again.

He gave her a warm, reassuring smile. "It's fine."

She nodded—not fully convinced by his words. She walked to the door and slipped inside, hoping it didn't look like she was running away. Though she kinda was. She wasn't ready for anything else in her life now. There was the shop. Rachel. Sara Jane.

Then he had to go and kiss her and ruin everything. Ruined a perfectly good friendship.

Now he'd gone and ruined everything. What had he been thinking? Why in the world had he kissed Lizzie?

Gabe's heart thundered in his chest, mocking him.

He'd just felt so at peace, sitting out there with her watching the storm come in and then slowly slip away. The sound of the raindrops on the porch roof. The cool breeze that drifted in with the storm. The rumbles of thunder and flashes of lightning.

Yet, there they sat together on the glider, safe and sound. *Connected*. Almost like they were the only two people in the world.

And she'd kissed him back. She had. Like she'd enjoyed the kiss.

But then got scared or uncertain or maybe just overwhelmed.

He set the glider in motion again, hoping it would soothe his nerves. The thing was, he cared about her. He did. And he really enjoyed being friends with her. Talking with her. Laughing with her.

And teasing her. He enjoyed that. The way her eyes lit up and a grin would spread across her face. Then… zing… she'd throw a snappy remark right back at him.

He could talk to her about anything. Well, almost everything. There were still some things that were best kept hidden in the past. And honestly? He didn't feel like it was his story to tell.

He stared up at the sky where the clouds were starting to clear and one lone star flickered above.

His timing was terrible. Really, what had he been thinking? She was opening the shop. Problems with her very best friend. She had so much to deal with. Starting up a relationship now would be overwhelming.

He'd just back off and give her space. He could do that. He *would* do that. He'd be cordial and civil and… he'd just try his best to avoid her so she wouldn't feel as awkward as he did.

31

Sara Jane went to the grocery store early the next day and bought all of Rachel's favorite foods. Not that she even knew if Rachel would meet her, but she pushed that thought from her mind. Martha let her use the kitchen and she prepared a feast. Fresh strawberries with a sprinkle of sugar, just like Rachel liked them. Chicken salad made with green olives, celery, and cashews scattered on top. Also a favorite of hers. Sugar cookies boxed up to send home with her. A couple of oranges and apples to make the meal a bit healthier. Lemonade to drink... not too sweet, not too tart. Martha had added in some slices of freshly baked bread.

Sara Jane stared at the huge, neatly packed up basket and rolled her eyes. That should be enough food for the two of them. And about ten more people.

She headed for the gazebo and got there a bit early, wanting it all to look nice for Rachel. She spread out a tablecloth on one of the tables but didn't really know if she should unpack the basket or not...

When Rachel didn't show by noon, she poured herself a glass of the cool lemonade and sat watching a mother play with her young daughter out on the beach. The little girl laughed and raced to get a bucket of water to pour on her sand creation, her pigtails flying behind her as she ran back and forth. She closed her eyes for a moment and a video of similar memories when Rachel had been a young girl played through her mind. How she'd loved to go to the beach, make sandcastles, and collect shells.

At twelve-thirty she set down her glass and kicked off her shoes. She slowly trudged across the warm sand to the water's edge. Rachel was not a prompt person by any means, but being this late probably meant she wasn't coming. Disappointment swept through her as she waded in the foamy froth of the waves. She bent down and picked up a shell. A calico shell. She rinsed it in the water and stared at it in her hand. Delicate dots of purple edged the top of the shell. She slipped it in her pocket and watched as a blue heron walked along the beach in awkward strides. The little girl with the pigtails laughed and raced to the water's edge, startling the bird, and it rose with majestic sweeps of its wide wings and swooped down the beach, indignant at the interruption of its stroll on the beach.

"Mom?"

She twirled around and stared at Rachel in surprise. Dressed in simple shorts and a blue t-shirt. Her hair was freshly washed and bounced around her shoulders. And did she have a hint of makeup on? "Oh, good. You're here." She kept herself from glancing at her watch, sure it was close to one o'clock now, as pleasure crept through her. She'd come.

"I didn't know if I was going to come or not."

"Glad you did," was all she said as they headed back to the gazebo and she started to unpack the basket, not knowing if Rachel would eat, but surely something would tempt her.

Rachel settled on the bench across from her, eyeing the food.

"Lemonade?" She held up a glass.

Rachel nodded. She took a sip of the drink, then reached for a strawberry. "Haven't had these in a while."

She spread out the rest of the food, feeling a bit foolish about the quantity of food she'd brought. But maybe something else would catch Rachel's eye.

She took some chicken salad, placed it on a plate, and set it in front of her daughter, not saying anything. Not *nagging* her to eat.

Rachel took a few bites and reached for a slice of the homemade bread. "This Martha's again?"

"It is. Sourdough this time. She loves to bake."

"She's a good cook. Tell her thank you for me. For this, and the basket yesterday."

"I'll tell her."

They ate mostly in silence then. Watching the birds swoop by on the shore. A lone jogger running past at the surf's edge. The little girl with the pigtails had tired of racing back and forth and sat beside her mother on a bright pink beach towel. The world drifted around them.

But Rachel was eating. That was all that mattered.

Rachel reached for a sugar cookie after she finished her lunch. "Is this the kind with the almond?"

"Sure is. Your favorite."

"Thanks, Mom."

"I made some extras for you to take home. I mean, you should take all this home with you. I brought way too much."

"You did bring quite a lot." Rachel gave her the tiniest smile. Really, only a hint of one. But it made her heart soar.

She looked across the table and saw Rachel had her hand resting on her belly, but she didn't think Rachel really knew she was doing it.

"Ah, more lemonade?" she offered.

"No, I'm good. I think I'll head back home. I'm tired."

"Sure." Disappointed their time was over, she stood and started to pack up the leftover food. The huge amount of leftover food.

"I could probably meet you here again," Rachel suggested softly.

"Tomorrow?" She didn't even try to hide her hopefulness.

Rachel nodded and turned and walked away to her car, carrying the basket with her.

She sat down on the bench as Rachel drove

away. Tears ran down her cheeks. For the first time since they'd found out about Ronnie, she had a glimmer of hope that her daughter was going to be okay. A faint glimmer, but a glimmer nonetheless.

32

Gabe never said a word about their kiss over the next couple of weeks. Not a single word. Though there was an awkward distance between them now that she regretted. She missed their easygoing talks. The quiet evenings they'd spent together or the times he'd drop by the shop. Those times had just vanished with the kiss.

But at least she was too busy to think about it. Well, almost too busy. They settled into a routine. They all had breakfast in the kitchen, then Lizzie headed out to the shop. Gabe went to his office to write. He said the words were finally coming to him, but she wasn't sure they were, or he just used his office as a place to escape from her.

Sara Jane helped Martha clean up the breakfast dishes, do some gardening or cooking, then she'd head out to meet Rachel at the gazebo for lunch. She'd bring Rachel food and just check on her. At least it got Rachel out of her room and up and dressed each day.

The day before the grand opening of the shop, Sara Jane announced that Rachel was coming to dinner that evening. Martha had encouraged her to invite her, and Rachel said yes, much to everyone's surprise.

Lizzie made sure to wrap up her work early that day even though she could have worked long into the evening making sure everything was ready for tomorrow. Adjust yet one more item on a table. Refold the knitted afghan on the back of a chair. Straighten a picture on the wall that probably didn't need straightening. She sighed. She probably should leave before she drove herself crazy.

Anyway, she wanted to be certain she'd be home when Rachel got there. Not that she knew if Rachel was even speaking with her. She hadn't answered her phone calls or texts. But Rachel couldn't just ignore her in person, could she?

She went into the kitchen and found Sara

Jane and Martha busy making dinner. "Can I help with anything?"

"You could set the table. And let's use a tablecloth tonight." Martha motioned to a cabinet. "Lower shelf."

The doorbell rang and Lizzie paused. "You two have your hands full. I'll get it." She headed to the door, ridiculously nervous. She was just opening the door to her best friend.

She tugged open the door, and there was Rachel. She wanted to hug her, something she'd normally do. But nothing was normal right now. So she settled with, "Hi, come on in."

Rachel just nodded as she stepped inside. Ah, still not speaking to her. Okay, then. One thing she'd say about Rachel was the woman knew how to hold a grudge.

But she was relieved to see Rachel was dressed as she used to be when she went anywhere. Smartly dressed in white slacks and a pretty pink blouse. She'd completed her outfit with simple sandals that had probably cost a fortune and a favorite necklace that she *knew* had cost a fortune. Rachel had told her how much when she bought it.

Gabe stepped into the room and broke the awkward silence. "You must be Rachel. I've heard so much about you. Glad you decided to join us for dinner."

Rachel slipped on a smile that only Lizzie would know was hiding some nervousness and reached out a hand to Gabe. "Glad to meet you, too. Both Lizzie and Mom have spoken of you often."

"Come on in. Sara Jane and Martha are in the kitchen." Gabe motioned for Rachel to follow him.

She trailed after Gabe and Rachel, not sure which of them she felt more awkward around. Wasn't this special?

Martha set down the spoon she was using to stir a pot on the stove as they entered the kitchen. She hurried over to Rachel to give her a hug. "I'm so glad to finally meet you."

Rachel actually hugged her back. Lucky Martha.

Sara Jane grinned from across the kitchen. "I made a pecan pie for dessert. Your favorite."

"It smells delicious in here," Rachel said.

"I was just going to set the table." She slipped past Rachel and grabbed the tablecloth, spreading it carefully on the table.

Rachel chatted with Sara Jane, Martha, and Gabe. Still not saying a word to her. Fine. If that's how it was, so be it. She walked over, pulled out the plates and silverware, and proceeded to set the table.

"Thanks, dear," Martha said as she finished the chore. "Dinner is ready. Why don't you all sit?"

Sara Jane and Martha filled the table with platters and bowls of food. Enough to feed an army, but they both looked so pleased. The conversation went on around her as they all dished out generous helpings on their plates.

"So, Rachel. How are you feeling these days?" Martha asked.

Lizzie glanced at Rachel, hoping she wouldn't snap back with an 'I'm so tired of people asking me that' and hurt Martha's feelings.

"I'm feeling pretty good, I guess. Putting on some weight." She patted her stomach, and Lizzie had to keep her mouth from dropping open in surprise

"That's good," Martha smiled at Rachel.

"I went to the doctor today. He said the baby is doing fine. He did an ultrasound, but I asked them not to tell me if it's a boy or a girl. I just… don't want to know. Not yet."

"Back in my day, we never knew until the

baby was born. I see nothing wrong with that." Martha laughed. "We didn't have all these new-fangled techie things back then."

"Hey, but I turned out okay. Perfect, even." Gabe grinned.

"And modest." The words slipped out before Lizzie could catch herself.

"Totally modest." Gabe grinned at her, the first time since… well… the kiss.

"When is your due date?" Now that her awkwardness with Gabe was breaking, she got brazen with Rachel, directly asking a question to see if she'd actually answer.

"I'm further along than I thought. I'm due in October." She didn't look at Lizzie when she said it, but at least she'd answered.

"Oh, an October baby, that's wonderful, honey." Sara Jane's face shone with happiness and expectation.

"That's great you're feeling good. So I assume you're coming to Lizzie's grand opening tomorrow?" Gabe asked.

Rachel glanced over at her and shook her head. "No, I don't think so."

"Oh, but, honey. Surely you can at least drop in for a few moments," Sara Jane added.

"Lizzie's worked really hard on this. We're

all proud of her," Gabe said. "We're all going. We could pick you up on the way there." He glanced over at her and smiled with one of his familiar friendly smiles. She'd missed those during their awkward post-kiss stage.

"No, I can't." Rachel shoved back her chair and slammed her fist on the table. "You don't understand. You've never had your whole life upended like I did."

"Rachel!" Sara Jane frowned and silence fell around the table.

Then Martha leaned forward. "Actually, he has, dear. His senior year of high school."

They all turned to look at Martha.

"After growing up here his whole life, he had to move the beginning of his senior year. To a school where he knew no one. I had to take a full-time job and we lived in the most gosh-awful one-bedroom apartment. Gabe slept on the couch. He worked long hours after school and on the weekends. Had to give up sports, and he was headed for a baseball scholarship before all this happened."

Lizzie glanced over at Gabe. He'd never said a word about this to her. She'd thought she knew all about him.

Martha continued. "He basically lost his

father, too. You see, every so often my husband, Victor, would ask me to make a random delivery for his business when he said his delivery service was unavailable. The last one I did, I tripped and fell and smashed the box open. I knew Victor would be angry so I got another box to put it in and I found…" Martha paused and took a deep breath. "I found drugs in the box. I was so angry. He'd been using me to run drugs. *Drugs!*" Her eyes flashed. "I turned Victor in to the authorities and he ended up going to prison."

Lizzie stared at Martha in surprise.

Gabe reached over and took his mother's hand. "So we had to get out of town after Mom talked to the authorities. We weren't safe here when the people Dad dealt drugs for found out that they lost their shipment and weren't getting any money for it. And the whole arrests of those involved and trial took years before it concluded. But I've never been prouder of Mom for what she did, and what she gave up. Her testimony put Dad in prison and broke up the drug ring."

Rachel frowned. "That's where I knew your name when Lizzie first said it. I knew it sounded familiar. Your father was Victor Smith, head of Wind Chime Bank."

"He was. I mean, he's still my father. I just haven't seen him in years. He won't take my visit. And honestly, I'm still so angry about what he did to Mom that I don't really care. And him helping put all those drugs on the street? It's not something I can forgive him for."

Lizzie sat back in her chair, swiveling her gaze between Gabe and Martha. She was more impressed with Martha now than ever, and that was saying something because she already thought Martha was a remarkable woman.

"When all this happened, all the bank accounts were frozen, so we had no money. It was really tight there for a while. Luckily this house was in my father's name at the time, not mine and Victor's. We'd lived it in for years after my father moved away from town. But we couldn't go live with my father after this happened because I didn't want to bring any danger to him. I inherited the house a few years later when my father passed away and rented it out for extra income."

"Oh, Martha, I didn't know you'd gone through all of that." Sara Jane's eyes were filled with sympathy.

"Well, it is what it is." Martha turned to Rachel. "So you see, life does have a way of throwing things at you when you least expect it. Things you never dreamed you'd have to survive. But you do. You go on. You get stronger. Or you become one of those people who never move on and drown in a miserable life, always blaming that one horrible thing that happened. But we all have the choice."

Silence fell around the table again. Lizzie turned to Rachel, wondering if she'd take Martha's words to heart. "So will you come? Please? I want you there. You're my best friend. And this is important to me." She wasn't sure why she was trying so hard. Was she trying to test Rachel? See if Rachel was as good a friend to her as she hoped she was to Rachel? Or maybe to prove Eric wrong. That Rachel didn't always just think of herself. She held her breath, waiting for an answer.

"No, I can't. Coming here. This… this was the best I could do. Good luck tomorrow. But I just can't come." Rachel jumped up. "Thank you for having me, Martha." She gave Lizzie a look that maybe said she was sorry.

Maybe it said that, or maybe Lizzie was just

hopeful that was what the look meant. Then Rachel disappeared out the door.

"You want to go sit out on the porch for a bit? Have a glass of wine?" Gabe asked after the dinner dishes had been all cleaned up.

She almost turned him down, thinking she'd better just head upstairs since she had such a busy day tomorrow. And she was afraid to mess with the fragile repair to their friendship. But she'd missed their quiet times together. "Sure. For a bit."

They headed out to the porch, and she went over to a rocking chair, avoiding the glider that would have put them both sitting close together, side by side.

Gabe leaned against the porch railing across from her. That clunky friction settled between them yet again. Before she could catch herself, she let out a small sigh.

Gabe looked at her closely, searching her face. "So... I'm sorry about how I messed things up with us. I shouldn't have kissed you. My timing was terrible." He shrugged. "But I miss spending time with you. Talking to you."

"I miss it, too."

"I've tried to avoid you so things wouldn't be awkward between us, but it seems like it just made it more uncomfortable."

"It has been a bit strained." She was glad to get all this out in the open.

"You know, it's okay to ask for what you want. To speak up. To say you just want to be friends. I'm glad you told me."

"It is what I need right now."

"Then that's what you'll get. So, you think we could just start over?" He tossed her an impish grin and stretched out his hand. "Hi, I'm Gabe Smith."

"Nice to meet you. I'm Lizzie. Mind if I live with you and your mom?"

They both laughed, and the tension between them slipped away into the warm night air. Finally.

She'd missed her friend. Maybe someday, when things settled down, it might become more. But for now, she was content to have her friend back. And for that, she was very grateful.

33

Lizzie stood inside her shop. Well, she wasn't exactly standing. She paced back and forth. Adjusting things. Glancing at the teal wall clock and wondering if it was broken because time couldn't really be going this slowly. Ten more minutes until she'd hang the open sign in the window. And in a fit of cooperation, the weather was lovely today. Nice breeze, and low humidity. She planned to prop open the door to encourage more people to come in and browse.

Please come in and browse. Buy something. Or book her for an interior design consult. Just something to make all this seem worthwhile and make her feel like she'd made the right decision to open the shop.

Where had all this insecurity come from?

Though, she'd never done something like this all on her own. Depending only on herself. She'd never been a risk-taker, and this was one big risk.

She hurried up the stairs to check those rooms one more time—adjusting an old book on a side table by maybe a fourth of an inch—then clambered back downstairs, glad she'd worn her most comfortable flats. She might be on her feet all day.

Unless… no one came…

At exactly ten o'clock she hung the open sign and propped the door open. Then waited. And waited some more. A few people walked past the shop and slowed a bit, but no one entered. She took deep breaths to chase away the panic.

She looked up when someone finally entered and smiled when she saw Martha, Gabe, and Sara Jane. Martha walked up to her with a large tray. "I brought cookies."

"And I brought this jug of lemonade." Sara Jane looked around the shop.

Gabe held up a bag. "I have the cups and napkins."

"Oh, that is so nice of all of you." She set up the refreshments on a table by the window.

Maybe the food would attract people to come in...

Sara Jane walked up to her. "Oh, Lizzie, it all looks so nice."

"Thank you. So... Rachel didn't come with you, huh?" Lizzie asked, disappointed.

Sara Jane gave her a quick hug. "I called this morning and tried to convince her. But, no, she's not coming. I'm sorry."

"That's okay." But it stung that her best friend wouldn't come to such a momentous day in her life.

She shoved the thought away when a couple she recognized but whose names she couldn't remember stepped inside. The woman glanced around and exclaimed, "Harry, just look at this shop. See that corner over there? That's exactly what I want to do to my reading nook in the sunroom."

She went over to talk to the couple. Mary and Harry Greenfield. More people came into the shop, browsing around. Martha or Sara Jane greeted them as they came in if she was busy with another customer.

Then it finally happened. Martha walked a woman up to her. "Lizzie this is Mrs. Wall. She wants to talk to you about booking a design consult. She's redoing her front room."

"Mrs. Wall, how nice to meet you." She shook the woman's hand. "Let's go over to my calendar and see if we can schedule a time."

The morning passed by quickly. Martha and Gabe left, but Sara Jane decided to stay. "Let me help you if I can."

She wasn't about to turn down any help at this stage. She had no idea so many people would come into the shop for the grand opening.

Sara Jane brought another woman over to meet her. "Lizzie, this is Violet. I stayed at her resort, Blue Heron Cottages, when I was in Moonbeam."

"Hi, Lizzie. Nice to meet you. Sara Jane told me about your shop and that you did design consults. I have a few of my cottages left that I need new furniture for. I've gotten by for a while with some old furniture, but I'd like to spruce them up a bit. Thought maybe you could help me out."

"I'd love to." Lizzie looked at Sara Jane with gratitude for bringing yet another client to her.

"I've painted some of the old furniture, and a few pieces do look nice. But others just need to be replaced. I'd love to find some older antiques that we could paint in cheerful colors."

"Her cottages are very beachy, and each one is a different color. Very nice. I loved staying there," Sara Jane added.

"Let's book an appointment." She led Violet over to the calendar and found a time to go over to Moonbeam.

People continued to stream in and out. She looked up from wrapping a watercolor painting of a seascape for a couple when she saw more people coming into the shop. She gasped in surprise and handed the painting to the couple before hurrying to the door.

"Eric." She gave her son a big hug. "I'm so glad to see you."

"Mom, this is Chelle."

She smiled at the pretty girl standing beside him. "Chelle, I'm so glad to meet you. Thank you for coming to the opening."

"We wouldn't miss it. Mrs Duncan, it's so nice to meet you."

"Lizzie, please, call me Lizzie." As far as she was concerned, Kicra was Mrs. Duncan now. And in that moment she suddenly decided to file paperwork to take back her maiden name. No more Duncan. Lizzie Timmons. That felt like the right thing to do for this new life she'd created for herself. A foolish grin spread across her lips and she didn't care. "Feel free to browse around and make sure to grab a cookie and lemonade. Martha brought them."

"If Martha made them, I'm sure they're delicious." Eric grinned and took Chelle's hand.

She waited on more customers while Chelle and Eric walked around the shop. They stopped and Eric introduced Chelle to Sara Jane, then they disappeared upstairs. So far this day was turning out perfectly.

After a bit, Eric and Chelle came back downstairs. "Mrs. Duncan—I mean Lizzie—your shop is wonderful."

"Thank you." She beamed at the compliment.

Eric looked around the shop. "So, did Rachel come?"

She shook her head. "No, she said she… couldn't."

Eric scowled. "Hm."

"But that's okay." She put on a wide smile to cover her hurt, but she was sure Eric saw through it.

"We should probably get going and let you get back to your work. But Mom, I'm so proud of you." Eric gave her a quick kiss on the cheek. "Congrats on the opening."

Chelle reached out and took her hand. "I'm so happy it's going so well for you. Look at all the people coming and going."

"And I've booked some consults already. I am pleased."

"We'll come back to town soon, when you're not so busy."

"That would be nice. I'd love some time to sit and chat."

They walked out the door, hand in hand, and Eric leaned closed to Chelle, saying something, and she nodded. Then Chelle reached up and kissed him. Lizzie smiled, thrilled that Eric had met such a nice young woman. And it warmed her heart that both of them had come to her opening.

Yes, so far the day was just perfect.

Rachel wandered around the empty house. Her father was out of town yet again and she was all alone. She hated that.

She sank onto the couch and picked up a magazine, leafing through it. The thought nagged at her that she should have gone to Lizzie's opening, but she just couldn't. People might ask how she was doing. Or say how sorry they were about Ronnie. She just couldn't deal with that.

Anyway, what right did Lizzie have to ask that of her? She should know better. Know that it would be too hard.

But a hint of guilt slipped through her, which she promptly ignored.

The doorbell rang and she debated answering or not. With a sigh, she set down the magazine and crossed to the foyer, across the cold, marble floor, and tugged open the front door.

"Eric, what are you doing here?" She frowned and looked at a young woman standing next to him.

"I came to talk to you. Oh, and this is Chelle, my girlfriend. Chelle, Rachel."

"Nice to meet you, ma'am."

She stared at the two of them, then remembered her manners. "Would you like to come in?"

They stepped inside and she closed the door. "What did you want, Eric?"

"I… I came to see if I could convince you to

come to Mom's grand opening."

She shook her head. "No, I can't." Couldn't everyone just leave her alone?

"It's important to Mom. Very important. Like the biggest thing she's ever done and you are her best friend. She needs you there showing her support."

"Eric, I—"

Eric held up a hand. "No, I don't want to hear any excuses. I know. It's hard. And I am so, so sorry about Ronnie. But Mom has always been there for you. Always. She even saved your life. And... well, best friends are there for each other. Can't you be there for her today?"

She stared at Eric, wondering how the curly-haired toddler who got into all the things she told him not to touch when he came over had turned into this remarkable young man. A young man who spoke the hard truth. Well, he'd sure gotten *that* from his mother.

Silence echoed through the foyer.

"I can't..." She paused as Eric's features flashed in disappointment. "I can't go alone. Will you take me?"

"Of course." Eric nodded eagerly.

"Okay, just give me a few minutes to change.

Why don't you go on into the family room? I'll be back down soon."

She fled upstairs, her heart pounding. She could do this. Do it for Lizzie. And Eric was right. Lizzie was always there for her. Always. Even when she treated her horribly like she had for the last few weeks. Ignoring her calls and texts. She just hadn't wanted to face the truth of her life now.

But… maybe it was time.

She pulled out a favorite pale blue dress and slipped it on, noticing it was getting tight around her middle. She peeled it off and pulled on another, looser mint-colored dress. That was better. She dug in the closet for nice shoes and finished the outfit off with a gold aspen leaf necklace and simple diamond stud earrings. She took a long look in the mirror, seeing a stranger. When was the last time she'd dressed in anything more than casual capris and a t-shirt… if she even made it out of her pajamas? She had to admit, she would stay in PJs all day if not for her lunches with her mom.

She hurried down the stairs and into the family room. Eric rose when she entered. "Rachel, you look really nice."

"Thanks, Eric. I think I'm ready now."

"Mom is going to be so surprised. And happy. Very happy. Thanks for doing this."

"Thanks for coming over and making me see reason. Lizzie raised a very smart son."

Lizzie looked up in surprise to see Eric standing in the doorway to the shop. "Eric, what are you doing here? I thought you'd left."

"I brought a surprise." He stood there grinning that same grin he used when he used to pick flowers from her garden and bring them in for her. He moved aside.

Rachel stepped through the door. "Lizzie."

"Oh, Rachel. You came." She blinked back tears as her emotions overwhelmed her. She rushed over and hugged her friend tightly. "I'm so happy to see you here."

"Some incredibly brilliant young man convinced me that I wouldn't want to miss your grand opening. And he was right."

Lizzie turned to Eric. "You did this?"

He shrugged, still grinning. "Now Chelle and I are really leaving. You'll make sure Rachel gets home? We brought her."

"I will." She let go of Rachel, wrapped Eric

in a hug, and took Chelle's hand and squeezed it. "Thank you. So much."

They walked away down the street and she turned to Rachel. "This means so much to me."

"I should have been here helping you get the shop ready. Even before... before Ronnie's..."

She squeezed Rachel's hand.

"And I knew how important this is to you. That I should be here. I was just... scared to come out."

"Don't be scared. I'm right here with you."

"You always are." Rachel smiled with genuine appreciation. "And I should tell you more often how much I appreciate it."

And just like that, she had her best friend back. Best day ever.

That evening they all sat out on Martha's porch, celebrating the day. Rachel had even come home with them, insisting she wanted to join in the celebration. Gabe had picked up champagne and poured them each a glass.

"To Lizzie and her successful grand opening." He raised his glass.

They all toasted her—Rachel with some

sparkling water—and she settled back in her chair, basking in their praise and friendship.

Rachel sat with her mom in the glider, looking relaxed. She even laughed at one of Gabe's wisecracks. Maybe, just maybe, Rachel was going to pull through this.

"So you all ready to do that again tomorrow?" Gabe asked as he lounged against the railing across from her.

"I guess I am. It was busier than I thought."

"Lots of people in town for the Beach Days Festival," Martha said.

"I should come help you tomorrow. I bet you'll be busy again," Sara Jane offered.

"I couldn't ask you to do that."

"Of course, you could. And I offered. You didn't ask. Let me help you."

She hated taking help, but if it was that busy again, she could use help. Greet people. Show them around. Ring out purchases.

"So... you want a part-time job?" She surprised herself by even asking the question, but suddenly it seemed like a brilliant idea.

"I do believe I do." Sara Jane grinned. "Going to have to find something to keep myself busy, and I do love the shop. I can't help much with the design recommendations, but I can help in the shop."

"Mom, you're going to work?" Rachel's brow creased. "You haven't ever worked."

"High time I did."

"I was going to close my shop when I'm out doing consults, but maybe we'll figure out a schedule that works where I can do consults a couple afternoons or evenings a week. You could cover the store then."

"And I'll help on weekends when you'll probably be busier at the shop."

"Sounds like a great arrangement for both of you," Martha smiled as if satisfied with the lives of her friends.

"Eventually I want to get a full-time job, but this will be wonderful for now and help you get the shop up and running."

"It sounds like it will work for you both," Rachel said. "And then the shop is closed on Mondays, right?"

"It is." Lizzie nodded.

"So, I know you're busy…" Rachel paused and looked over at her. "But I was wondering. I mean… I think I want to go over to the house. My house. Just to check on things. Do you think you could go with me on Monday? If you're not too busy."

"Of course, I'll go with you. Does first thing in the morning work for you?"

"What time is first thing?" Rachel sent her a wry grin.

She laughed. "Okay, how about in the afternoon? I'll get up and get some work done, then we'll go over."

"That works." Rachel smiled.

"Then why don't you two come back here for dinner after you finish?" Martha offered.

"I'm sure not going to turn down one of your meals, Martha." Rachel stood. "I guess I should go now." She laughed. "Though I just remembered, I didn't drive."

"I'll drive you home." Gabe stood. "Come on."

The two of them left, and Lizzie looked over at Sara Jane who sat there with a hint of a smile on her face. "What are you thinking, Sara Jane?"

"I'm thinking that my Rachel is going to pull through this."

"I'm thinking the very same thing," Lizzie said.

34

Rachel paced back and forth at her parents' house. Well, her dad's house now. Her mother was never going to move back in, she knew that now. And really, she shouldn't. Not after what Daddy had done. He could deny it all he wanted, but she knew her mother was telling the truth. Her mother had never told a lie in her whole life. She was the most honest woman she knew.

Her mom had filed for a divorce and her father had been furious the day he found out, slamming around the house, insisting her mother would not get a dime.

Though, she was pretty sure her mother didn't care about that. She just wanted out.

How horrible that her mother had lived in such a loveless marriage for so many years.

And part of that was *her* fault. She was the reason her mother had stayed so long. So she wouldn't upset her daughter's life. Everyone was always trying to make things easier for her. And how many years had she just turned a blind eye to how her father treated her mom? Or at least did nothing about it. Occasionally she tried to buffer her mother from Daddy's bad moods. That was about all she'd done to help her mom.

She'd been so lucky to be married to Ronnie. Even if that was gone now. She slipped a hand down on her stomach, but the baby still didn't seem real to her. Or maybe she was refusing to let it seem real.

There was so much to this new life of hers that she'd just rather ignore. Hide from the pain. Whatever had convinced her to ask Lizzie to go over to the house with her today? Maybe she could just hire someone to go in and pack it all up. Should she sell the house? Move somewhere else? She'd already come to the conclusion that living here with her father forever was not an option. Not alone most of the time in this big old echoing house. Now it was time to try to figure out what she wanted to do. What did she want?

The doorbell rang and she hurried over to open the door.

"You okay?" Lizzie's brow furrowed.

"Yes." She sighed. "No. I'm regretting asking you to take me to the house."

"You don't have to go. If you need something I'll get it for you."

"No, let's just go. Get it over with."

Lizzie drove her to the house and pulled up in front. Rachel just sat there in the front seat, unmoving.

"Rach? You going to go in?" Lizzie asked, her eyes filled with concern.

Was she going in? It was easier to just sit out here. She could come up with a list of things for Lizzie to grab for her. But that was just avoiding the inevitable. "Yes, we've come this far." She pushed open the car door. "Let's go."

They headed up to the porch, then Rachel stopped. "I didn't bring my key."

Lizzie laughed softly. "That's okay. I have one." She opened the door.

Rachel stepped inside, holding her breath. Through the very doorway where the policemen had stood and told her Ronnie was gone. The very doorway Ronnie used to barge through after a long trip, calling out for her.

The house was deathly quiet and smelled stale and lifeless. She turned to Lizzie. "I… don't know where to start."

"How about I throw open some windows. Air things out. And I could make us some tea. Would you like that?"

She nodded as Lizzie walked over and tugged open a window. A warm breeze drifted in. Lizzie headed for the kitchen, and Rachel walked over into the family room. Lizzie must have straightened things, because she, herself, would have never left the room so picked up. No shoes scattered. Magazines in a neat pile.

No Ronnie.

She turned and fled to the kitchen and perched on a stool by the counter, unwilling to sit at the table where she'd had so many meals with Ronnie. She watched Lizzie make the tea. She should probably offer to help, but she barely had the energy to breathe.

"I cleaned out your fridge when I was here before. Threw out anything that might go bad."

"Thank you."

Lizzie reached up into the cabinet and took out two teacups and set them on the counter, seeming to sense that she didn't want to sit at the table. Lizzie poured the water and handed her a teabag. She sat and swirled the bag, watching the golden twirls darken in the water.

Lizzie sat on the other stool and sipped her tea, saying nothing.

Suddenly she couldn't bear the silence and jumped up to pace across the room. "I should go upstairs. Get some things I need." But could she stand to go into the bedroom she'd shared with Ronnie?

Lizzie nodded.

She set her tea down with a clatter. "Let's do it before I lose my nerve."

They headed up the stairs. Each step seemed to take an enormous amount of energy to climb. But they finally reached the upper floor. She walked to the doorway of the bedroom and put her hand on the doorframe for support.

The bed she shared with Ronnie with its pretty bedspread that Ronnie had just laughed at when she'd asked if it was too feminine for their room. He'd kissed her and said that anything she loved, he loved. She walked over to the bed and picked up the pillow from his side of the bed, clutching it close. Was she imagining it, or did it still hold the slight scent of his aftershave? She carefully set it back down and smoothed it into place.

She turned toward Lizzie. "Okay, let me get a few things I need." She pulled out clothes from the closet and handed them to Lizzie who placed them on the bed. She carefully avoided Ronnie's side of the closet… until she couldn't any longer. Tears began to fall as she pressed her face into his favorite t-shirt. The one that was a bit tattered but he refused to part with. She handed it to Lizzie to take with them, too.

She walked over to the rack of shelving in the closet on his side. Each shelf with neatly folded items. She ran her finger over a wooden box where he kept a few watches. Ronnie loved his watches, and if she ever ran out of ideas of what to buy him, she'd give him a new watch. She opened the box and peeked inside. There in the corner of the box was a wrapped box— obviously wrapped by Ronnie, with its mismatched seams, crooked tape, and lopsided ribbon. Tucked beneath it was a card. She sucked in her breath, barely daring to breathe. Scrolled across the card, in Ronnie's so familiar handwriting, it said Happy Birthday Sweetheart.

Tears fell, splashing on the envelope.

Lizzie came up behind her. "What's wrong?"

She turned around with the present in her hand, along with the card. "I found this present from Ronnie."

"Oh, Rachel." Lizzie's eyes filled with tears. "You know, at your Mom's party—wow, that seems so long ago—Ronnie told me he'd found you the perfect birthday present."

"Ronnie always bought presents way in advance. He always found the perfect gift."

They walked out into the bedroom and sat on the bed. She stared down at the card and present.

"You're going to open it, aren't you?"

She nodded, her heart squeezing in her chest. She opened the present first, just like she always did, and it always made Ronnie laugh. Tugging on the ribbon, then slowly opening the paper to unveil a small leather box. She opened the lid and the light glinted off a delicate golden locket. She opened it, half expecting to see a photo of Ronnie on one half and her on the other. But it was empty.

She pried open the envelope and slipped out the card, opening it to read the words he'd written.

. . .

Happy birthday, sweetheart. I saw this and knew you needed it. To remind you not to give up hope. I know someday you'll have our baby's picture in this locket.

I love you always and forever,

Ronnie

The sobs tore through her. The ones she'd held off for so long. She clung to Lizzie who sobbed right along with her, their tears mingling as they cried. When they were both finally spent, Lizzie got up and grabbed a box of tissues. "Here."

She wiped her face and picked up the locket. "Will you put it on me?" She held up her hair off her neck.

Lizzie nodded and fastened it behind her neck.

She gently pressed the locket between her thumb and finger. "How did he know?"

"Ronnie had a lot of faith. He knew you'd have this child."

"But I wanted to raise the baby with Ronnie."

"I know." Lizzie reached out and touched her shoulder. "I know."

Rachel dropped her hand to her belly and her eyes flew open wide. "Lizzie. I just felt the baby move."

"You did?" Lizzie sat back down beside her and rested her hand beside Rachel's.

"There. Did you feel it?"

"No, but it's early. You're probably feeling those first flutters. Aren't they magical?"

"It is. It's… a miracle." She stared down at her hand. "This baby… it's part of Ronnie. Part of Ronnie and me."

"It is."

"I've been so foolish. So wrapped up in my pain. I should have been so grateful that I have this child. To have this part of Ronnie."

Lizzie nodded. "Your pain was totally justified and normal. I think you're doing great with all that you've been dealt."

Rachel looked around the room. "You know… I think I might just move back in here. It would be a nice home to raise a child in, wouldn't it?"

"It would."

"It would be hard though. Without Ronnie. I see him everywhere."

"I'm sure he's looking down on you right

now. Seeing you. Watching over you. He'll be watching over your child, too."

She grabbed Lizzie's hands. "You know. Suddenly it's all starting to feel real. The baby. It's kind of… exciting."

"It sure is. There's nothing like having a child."

"Will you help me fix up a nursery?"

"Of course, I'd love to."

She stood. "I think I can do this." She could almost feel Ronnie right beside her, telling her she could, giving her strength.

"I know you can. You're going to be a great mom."

She laughed. "So, can I ask you one more favor? How about you help me put all this stuff back in the closet?"

Lizzie jumped up. "Can't think of anything I'd rather do. And didn't you say your dad was out of town?"

"He is."

"No offense to your father. Well, maybe some offense. I don't care if I ever see him again. But how about we go over to his house and grab your stuff to move it back here. You ready for that?"

Rachel paused, a load of clothes draped

over her arm, sweeping her gaze around the room. "You know what? I think I am. Let's go get my things." And she was ready. It would be hard, but this is where she belonged. In her home. With her and Ronnie's child.

35

Lizzie was exhausted by the time they got all of Rachel's things moved back into her home. It was nice to know that a hot meal was waiting for them at Martha's. She should tell Martha more often how much she appreciated her. She turned to Rachel as they drove through town. "I'm going to just pop into the florist's and pick out some flowers for Martha. For all she docs."

"And that, my friend, is why you are such a good person. Thinking of something like that. And it's a good idea." Rachel reached for her purse. "Here, let me give you some money."

She picked out a beautiful bouquet of light blue hydrangeas with delicate baby's breath poked in the arrangement. Martha had mentioned she used to have hydrangeas in her garden and missed them, so this would be a nice surprise for her.

When they arrived at the house and entered the kitchen, Martha was at the stove, of course. Doing what she loved.

"Martha, these are for you. Just a small thank you for all you do for us."

"Oh, Lizzie, they are lovely."

"I remembered you said you missed your hydrangeas."

"I do. And I'm going to plant some new ones when the timing is right. I just love them." Martha took the flowers and placed them in a pretty milk glass vase. "That looks beautiful."

Gabe walked up and whispered in her ear. "Thanks for doing that."

She smiled back at him, glad to see him here at the end of her long day. She loved how they were back to sitting on the porch after dinner and just chatting about their days. Rachel was her best friend since almost forever, but she wasn't sure that Gabe didn't know the Lizzie she was now, the person she'd become, better than Rachel.

Sara Jane set down a pan she took out of the oven, walked over to Rachel, and looked at her closely, then grinned. "You felt the baby move, didn't you?"

Both she and Rachel stared at Sara Jane in astonishment.

"How did you know?" Rachel asked.

"I guess it's just my mother-daughter connection. I just knew you did."

"I did. It was like a little flutter. So cool."

"And Rachel has other news," Lizzie prodded.

Sara Jane looked at Rachel expectantly.

"I'm moving back into my house. Or I should say I've moved back in. Lizzie helped me go get my things from Dad's house and bring them back home."

"Oh, Rachel, that's great news. You've always loved that house."

"I do love it. It was hard, though. I see Ronnie everywhere. But I guess that's not really such a bad thing."

"I'm so proud of you, Rachel." Sara Jane's eyes lit up with pride and happiness.

"I wanted to ask you something, though." Rachel frowned slightly. "Would you maybe move in with me when the baby comes? Or right before? Or even now?"

Sara Jane was silent for a moment, and

Lizzie couldn't read her expression. Was Sara Jane just going to become Rachel's caretaker again, just in a new house?

"You know what, Rachel? I think I'll let you move back in. Get all settled. I'd like to stay here at Martha's. I will move in with you right before the baby is due and stay a month or so. But then I want to get my own place. I've never lived in my own home. By myself. I'm actually kind of excited about it. I've already spoken to a Realtor to be on the lookout for the perfect little cottage. Maybe near the beach. I'm not sure how long it will take, but I can just picture it in my mind." Sara Jane turned to Martha. "If it's okay if I stay here as a boarder for a while longer."

"Of course it is. I love having you here."

"You want to live alone?" Rachel frowned as she stared at her mother. "Really?"

"I do. I want to pick out my own house. Decorate it just how I want it." Sara Jane turned to Lizzie. "And I'll want your help with that."

"You know I'll help you. It will be fun." Lizzie was relieved that Sara Jane was standing up for herself and going after what she wanted. It would have been so easy for her to slip back into the same role of taking care of Rachel's every want and need.

It was time for Rachel to stand on her own two feet, too. Nothing like having a child depending on you to make you grow up quickly.

"Okay, if it's what you want. And I do appreciate the help when the baby's born. I don't want you to feel like you need to be there all the time now either, checking on me. I think I'm doing better. And you don't have to worry about me eating because I'm ravenous all the time now." Rachel laughed, resting her hand on her belly.

"Then we should all eat," Martha motioned to the table.

They all sat and had a delicious meal with laughter and conversation swirling all around them. For Lizzie, it felt like she had a family again. A mismatched group of different generations, but somehow they all fit together.

Martha rose at the end of the meal. "Lizzie, why don't you and Rachel go sit out on the porch? You both look tired from your day."

"Oh, I want to help clean up. You did all the cooking."

"I'll help Mom." Gabe sent a warm, friendly smile her direction, and once again, she was so grateful they'd sorted things out.

"I'll help, too. You two go sit outside and

chat." Sara Jane stood and collected some dishes.

Gabe leaned close. "You two go have some nice girl talk. We'll catch up tomorrow."

She smiled, looking forward to spending time with him tomorrow. "Looks like we're outnumbered, Rach. Come on, let's go outside."

They went out and sat on the glider, watching as the sky darkened and stars began to flicker overhead.

"It looks kind of magical, doesn't it?" Rachel leaned her head over and rested it on her shoulder.

She leaned her head against Rachel's. "It is magical. I feel like everything is different now. I can't believe I own my own business."

"I know. And I'm so proud of you. I predict it will be a great success."

"I hope so." She did have a good feeling about it, though. She'd booked another handful of consultations this past weekend. "And you're going to be a mother."

"I am." Rachel slipped her hand down to her stomach. "It's hard to imagine."

"And you made the choice to move back to your house. I'm proud of you for making that decision."

Rachel sat up straight and turned to her. "But it's all going to be okay, isn't it?"

"It is. You're doing fine. You're going to *be* fine."

"And how about you and Gabe? Do I sense something going on between you two?"

"No, we're friends. But… he did kiss me."

"He did? You didn't tell me."

"You weren't speaking to me." She gave her friend a wry smile.

"I was a silly twit. I'm sorry." Rachel shook her head. "But back to that kiss."

"The timing was just all wrong. I'm not ready for anything like that. I just want to be friends. At least for now. And maybe forever." Gabe had been right. It was okay to ask for what she needed. To just be friends. "Anyway, he's really become a good friend, a good listener."

"Hey, he's not going to take over being your best friend, is he? Because that's my job."

She laughed. "You'll always be my bestie, I promise."

"You know, we're right here, right now, because you saved my life all those years ago. That chance moment when you were there just at the right time to save me. That chance moment made it so we became best friends all these years."

"It did."

"I'm not sure I've ever properly thanked you. Even after all this time. I'm so grateful you were there."

"It's funny how fate jumps in sometimes, isn't it?"

"If I had been you, I'd probably have let me drown. I was awful to you back then. I just ignored everyone who wasn't in my crowd of friends."

"You were pretty awful." Lizzie smothered a smile, trying to look serious.

Rachel laughed. "You didn't have to agree with me so quickly."

Lizzie stood and walked over to the railing, looking up at the sky. "So many stars."

Rachel came to stand beside her. "Oh, look, do you see that? A shooting star. Quick, make a wish."

"What did you wish for?" Lizzie asked.

"I wished for Ronnie to still be here. But that can't happen," Rachel said softly. "But I guess I want to get to the point you're at. Happy with my life. That is my wish."

"You're getting there, Rach. You're getting

there." She draped her arm around her friend's shoulder and pulled her close.

"What's your wish?" Rachel asked.

Lizzie thought for a moment as she stared at where the star had disappeared into the darkness. "I don't really have anything to wish for." She and Eric were back on good footing, and she really liked his girlfriend. She'd opened her own business and was proud of how far she'd come with that. She adored Martha and loved living here for now. She'd become friends with Gabe. And she and Rachel were back to being besties.

"Really? No wish?" Rachel nudged her.

"No wish for me. I have everything I've ever wanted and I'm totally content. I love my life right now, just how it is."

Dear Reader,

I hope you enjoyed Wind Chime Beach. Would you like to see more of Violet and the Blue Heron Cottages? Violet first bought the resort and restored it in the Moonbeam Bay series. Try The Parker Women, book one in the

Moonbeam Bay series. (The complete series is available now)

Or try the Blue Heron Cottages series. A heartwarming new series with Violet, the charming people of Moonbeam, and the guests who come to stay at Blue Heron Cottages. (Coming June 2022, preorder available now)

As always, thanks for reading my stories. I truly appreciate all my readers.

Kay

Return to the Island - Book Five

Bungalow by the Bay - Book Six

CHARMING INN ~ Return to Lighthouse Point

One Simple Wish - Book One

Two of a Kind - Book Two

Three Little Things - Book Three

Four Short Weeks - Book Four

Five Years or So - Book Five

Six Hours Away - Book Six

Charming Christmas - Book Seven

SWEET RIVER ~ THE SERIES

A Dream to Believe in - Book One

A Memory to Cherish - Book Two

A Song to Remember - Book Three

A Time to Forgive - Book Four

A Summer of Secrets - Book Five

A Moment in the Moonlight - Book Six

MOONBEAM BAY ~ THE SERIES

The Parker Women - Book One

The Parker Cafe - Book Two

A Heather Parker Original - Book Three

The Parker Family Secret - Book Four

Grace Parker's Peach Pie - Book Five

The Perks of Being a Parker - Book Six

BLUE HERON COTTAGES ~ THE SERIES

Coming June 2022

INDIGO BAY ~ Save by getting Kay's complete collection of stories previously published separately in the multi-author Indigo Bay series. The three stories are all interconnected.

Sweet Days by the Bay

Or buy them separately:

Sweet Sunrise - Book Three

Sweet Holiday Memories - A short holiday story

Sweet Starlight - Book Nine

ABOUT THE AUTHOR

Kay writes sweet, heartwarming stories that are a cross between women's fiction and contemporary romance. She is known for her charming small towns, quirky townsfolk, and enduring strong friendships between the women in her books.

Kay lives in the Midwest of the U.S. and can often be found out and about with her camera, taking a myriad of photographs which she likes to incorporate into her book covers. When not lost in her writing or photography, she can be found spending time with her ever-supportive husband, knitting, or playing with her puppies —two cavaliers and one naughty but adorable Australian shepherd. Kay and her husband also love to travel. When it comes to vacation time, she is torn between a nice trip to the beach or the mountains—but the mountains only get considered in the summer—she swears she's allergic to snow.

Learn more about Kay and her books at
kaycorrell.com

While you're there, sign up for her newsletter to
hear about new releases, sales, and giveaways.

WHERE TO FIND ME:
kaycorrell.com
authorcontact@kaycorrell.com

Join my Facebook Reader Group. We have lots
of fun and you'll hear about sales and new
releases first!
www.facebook.com/groups/KayCorrell/

I love to hear from my readers. Feel free to
contact me at authorcontact@kaycorrell.com

facebook.com/KayCorrellAuthor
instagram.com/kaycorrell
pinterest.com/kaycorrellauthor
amazon.com/author/kaycorrell
bookbub.com/authors/kay-correll

Made in the USA
Monee, IL
16 May 2022